DUCHESS

DUCHESS

Josephine Edgar

ST. MARTIN'S PRESS • NEW YORK

CHAPTER ONE

It had been a cold afternoon and Leeds lay under a pall of low grey clouds, creating a light more like November than late April. There were only fifteen minutes before the London Express left and Betsy Holder, waiting by the barrier with a small carpet bag containing all her possessions, was filled with anxiety.

Where was her friend, Viola?

Supposing she had changed her mind? It was not possible. It had been Viola's idea entirely that they should leave their local jobs and take positions in London. Betsy had waited nearly an hour. The carriages had been gently shunted along the platform. The mailbags had gone in. The guard with his flag and lantern had arrived along with the dining car attendants, and for the last fifteen minutes the passengers had begun to stream through the barrier. The engine, enormous, black and green and gold, emitting hoarse, steamy shouts like a harnessed dragon, had been coupled up. But Viola was not there.

What *would* she do if Viola did not come? She had given in her notice at Hardcastle's. Should she go to London alone? The thought terrified her. She would never have taken such a step on her own. Viola had received references for them from Mr Hardcastle. Viola had written to Dwyer & Netherby Ltd, Emporium for Ladieswear, Outfitters & Haberdashers to the Nobility and Gentry, of Oxford Street, London. In fact Samuel Hardcastle had also written personally to Arthur Netherby about them, thus securing Viola a position as second sales in the gloves, with Betsy as junior sales in the same department.

Betsy was very small, just five feet tall. Under her plain black straw hat, her straight hair of the nondescript colour known as 'mousy' was drawn back into a small tight bun. She wore a shabby navy blue costume, and a grey shawl about her narrow little shoulders to keep out the cold. Her usually pink face was white with anxiety, and her large gentle grey eyes behind her metal-ringed spectacles were clouded with anxious tears.

She watched the passengers streaming through the barrier. A tall young gentleman in an Inverness cape passed, smoking a cigar, followed by a manservant shepherding two trolleys of luggage, complete with gun cases, a polished racing saddle and a bag of golf clubs. The young gentleman was so handsome, in spite of the fact that his nose had, at some time, been broken, that it was difficult not to notice him. He strolled on without even turning his brilliant blue eyes to see if his possessions were following him, leaving his manservant to cope with everything. Betsy envied him. He looked so pleasant, unhurried, so indolently self-assured, as though he was quite sure the train would wait for him. Then she saw Viola.

Although she was only a working girl, Viola was like the handsome young gentleman who had just gone through the barrier: you had to notice her. She was tall, her new brown straw hat was topped with the defiant cluster of yellow buttercups, and her cloud of shiny, waving hair was a vibrant, burnished auburn. She was just twenty-one and very beautiful. Betsy adored her—her friend and protector. Viola apparently was scared of nothing, Betsy of everything. She had lived under Viola's wing ever since she had been apprenticed into the gloves at Hardcastle's when she was fourteen. She had gone to 'live-in' there straight from the orphanage. She was told she was lucky, training to be a 'shop-lady' instead of going into domestic service, especially at Hardcastle's, for Mr Hardcastle, though a sharp man, did not try to save money by half-starving his 'living-in' staff as did so many shop-keepers.

Betsy raised her arm to wave frantically to her friend, and then she saw whom she was with, and her eyes widened and her white cheeks reddened. Viola was with Mr Samuel Hardcastle.

The rumours about Viola and Samuel Hardcastle had flown round the shop, and Betsy had refuted them as indignantly as a little hen bird defending its young. Mr Hardcastle, they said, was sweet on Viola, and his wife had found out, and *that* was why Viola was leaving for London, and why he had been so generous with references and written personally to Mr Arthur Netherby.

He stood by Viola, talking to her very earnestly. Not a very tall man; very respectable in his frock coat and shining top hat. It seemed to Betsy that the hard face, which had always so terrified her when he came round the department, was contorted, as though at any moment he might break down and weep. Betsy was shocked. As she watched Viola put her hand on his shoulder, and with a warm smile bent down, for she was half a head taller, and kissed him full on the lips. When she raised her head, he touched his mouth with his gloved hand and then looked at it, as though he expected the kiss to be something tangible that he could see on his glove, like a butterfly. Suddenly he thrust his hand into his breast pocket, drew out a packet and pushed it into Viola's hand. Turning away, he plunged blindly through the crowds towards the entrance of the station.

As Viola turned, she saw Betsy, and walked towards her, smiling. A porter was wheeling her small trunk and valise. She did not hurry her long graceful stride, her slender hips swaying, like some tall and lovely flower bending in a summer breeze. 'Betsy!' she said. 'Where the heck have you been? We'll have to hurry. Let the man take your case.'

Betsy, swallowing her indignation, snatched up her carpet bag, unwilling to let it out of her hand, and followed in Viola's wake, puffing as she trotted along the platform.

The Reverend Matthew Lyttelton had reached the platform some ten minutes before the two girls, and had found a corner seat in the third-class carriage. The poverty of his birth, and the unexpected exclusiveness of his education had made his otherwise mild and gentle character a little snobbish. He had looked rather enviously into the first-class dining carriage with its rose-shaded lights and padded upholstery, where the last crates of wines and beers were being loaded and the uniformed waiters putting the final touches to the tables.

He had been to Low Ayrton, a bleak mining village north of Leeds, to visit his widowed mother. His father had once been the minister there. He was returning to London, to his curacy at St Botolph's in Tewkesbury Square. He put his bag in the net rack, his books on the seat, and at that moment a deep, drawling, upper-class voice said enthusiastically, 'Matty, old fellow, what a delight to see you! Are you off to London?'

Matthew's heart bounded and the colour flooded his thin, earnest face. He would have known that voice anywhere.

Lord Staffray was twenty-six and was by no means just a handsome man. In fact, if you analysed the charming face, the black-lashed, blue Irish eyes, the nose, slightly twisted from a hunting accident, the firm jaw, a little too long for symmetry, it was unusual rather than handsome. But his mouth was beautifully shaped, gay, tender, smiling under the clipped military moustache, and there was such an air of health, vitality and the joy of life about him that most people, men and women, found him irresistible. He stood over six feet and had the taut, strong, fine-waisted figure of a riding man. His clothes had the careless and restrained good taste of one who is used to having money.

He wore a tweed Inverness travelling overcoat, a hard brown hat beneath which his light brown hair curled crisply. After his first delight at seeing his friend again, Matthew was, as he had been from his first glimpse of this glorious personage at school, completely under his spell.

James Staffray, only son of the Earl of Louderdown, had been Matthew's one friend at school, and it was through his influence that he had obtained the curacy at St Botolph's where the Staffray family owned a large slice of London lying between the Euston Road and Oxford Street. A mixed parish of squares, streets and mews erected in the early part of the Queen's reign. Not aristocratic like Belgravia, nor plutocratic like Mayfair; not genteel like Kensington, nor like nearby Bloomsbury dropping in the social scale since the great London railway termini of Paddington, Euston, St Pancras and King's Cross—the gateways to the industrial north—had been opened.

The friendship between Matthew and Lord Staffray resembled that between Betsy Holder and Viola Corbett. Gratitude and hero-worship on one hand, patronage and good nature on the other. James Staffray, the school idol and athletic hero, had taken the bookish, delicate little boy under his wing, for Matthew was a natural muff and bully-bait. Otherwise, James said, 'The funny little cove would be eaten alive.'

They had not met since Matthew had taken his degree and been ordained, and James, much against his mother's wishes, had gone into the Guards. Balls, racing, hunting, country house parties, the rounds of fashionable London life, had been James' milieu. And, though Matthew's room in a small street off Tewkesbury Square and Lord Staffray's apartments in Half Moon Street were barely three quarters of a mile apart, they were socially so far removed that James might have been living in Greenland.

For a moment Matthew forgot the shabbiness of his darned linen, the Ulster that had once belonged to his father, and the worn nap of his clerical hat. He grasped the outstretched hand eagerly, engulfed in a warm glow of pleasure.

'Jimmy—how wonderful! You haven't changed a bit.'

'No more have you, old man.'

They were wringing each other's hands, back in the affection of schooldays, Matthew momentarily forgetting the great social gap between them. He remembered and drew back self-consciously.

'Jimmy . . . I suppose I should say my Lord . . .'

'You do, and I'll black your eye for you, you little muff,' said James laughing. 'D'you expect me to call you the Reverend every time I open my mouth?'

'Jimmy, then. How wonderful to see you! And what are you doing in Leeds?'

'I'm catching the London train the same as you. I've been up at Louderdown for one of Mama's spring house parties. She's been lining up a few local fillies for me to look over.'

'I know you're interested in horses,' said Matthew ingenuously, and James, who had been referring to the well-born local girls from whom his mother hoped he would select a bride, tried not to laugh, and did, and Matthew innocently laughed with him.

'Mothers!' said James darkly. 'They're always trying to marry you to some gel! And the minute a chap is interested, they start pulling her to pieces! Mama's gone back to London, a bit cross with me. I stayed for some rough shooting.'

It took Matthew all his time to support his mother on his stipend, and marriage for him was out of the question. But Lord Staffray was quite unaware of Matthew's agonizing comparisons with his splendid self. If his happy-go-lucky nature was insensitive to other people's situations, at least he did not humiliate them by noticing such things. If Matthew had been in rags, begging in the gutter, or rolling drunk, he would have been just as pleased to see him. It was this essential lovableness that was his greatest attraction.

His valet appeared at his elbow carrying a light travelling rug and a soft tweed cap for his master to wear on the train. He had been to purchase newspapers and to the dining car to reserve a table. Lord Staffray turned to him and said, 'See if you can get another seat in my compartment, Jevons, so that Mr Lyttelton can travel with me . . .'

'No, Jimmy. I'm travelling third. Thank you though.'

'Oh!' James had never travelled third or known anyone who did—or only servants and troopers. He did not like to offer to pay the difference in case Matthew might feel humiliated. 'Ah, well,' he said. 'I suppose that's because you're a parson—the needle's eye and all that rot. Don't they pay you enough? I'll speak to Papa about it.'

'Oh, no, really, Jimmy. I'm very happy at St Botolph's.'

'St Botolph's! That's it. Never could remember the name of the damned church. Of course. Well, anyway, Matty, at least have a bite to eat with me? Get along to the dining car at the first call. I'll expect you.'

'Thank you, I shall enjoy that,' said Matthew gratefully, warming with the idea of a good meal in the dining car instead of his mother's cold mutton sandwiches.

'Excuse me, sirs, would you please let us get in . . .'

They drew apart to let Viola and Betsy through, and both young men became instantly aware of Viola; Matthew because of a startled conviction that he knew her and James Staffray, that connoisseur of fine female flesh and style, because of her beauty. He was aware of a creamy complexion, luxuriant coppery hair beneath a small brown hat with a cluster of yellow flowers upon the brim; a swift, half-smiling glance from large, gold-green, seductively lashed eyes, and drew back deferentially, pulling off his hat. Her companion, a tiny, rather shabby, neat young woman, pink-cheeked, anxious-looking and quite insignificant, he took to be her maid before he realized that if she could afford a maid, she would not be travelling third.

Matthew searched his memory in vain. Not one of his London congregation. Her accent when she spoke was West Riding with a faint veneer of refinement. Not a lady, although, until she spoke, she could pass for one. Her companion seemed like a superior type of working girl, a shop or an office worker.

'Is there room in this carriage?' asked Viola. 'The train's due out, and I've no mind to be left in Leeds.'

Staffray took charge. 'I'm quite sure there is,' he said. He turned with the authority of wealth and position to the drab-looking family inside. 'I say there, would you move up a little and make room for these two ladies, if you please.' With blank resentment they obliged.

James turned to his valet. 'Jevons, see to the young lady's luggage. I'll get along to my seat. My man will see to your things for you, madam.'

He looked into the carriage where Viola had just seated herself, and for a long moment their eyes met. Both Matthew and Betsy could feel the current of their mutual attraction. They felt it like a live power, and glanced at each other, embarrassed, although there was nothing to take exception to. Lord Staffray was the model of a young gentleman, Viola was neither immodest nor inviting, and yet, if he had stepped into the carriage and kissed her before them all, his desire for her and her instant response could not have been more positive.

'See you later then, old chap,' said James. He bowed to Viola, and wandered off towards the first-class carriage, the train being held for him, not hurrying his progress in spite of the frantic warnings, and tossing a half-crown to a porter who held the door open for him just as the final whistle sounded and the great gold and green steam engine drew the London Express out of the station.

Jevons stacked Viola's luggage away into the rack and asked her if there was anything else he could do. His respectful manner covered the barest perceptible insolence. If his lordship fancied a young woman it was always advisable to be attentive to her from the start. Jevons was a smart Londoner, not one of the Louderdown family servants.

Viola unpinned her new hat, produced a brown paper bag from her handbag and carefully placed it inside, and with the utmost self-possession handed it over to Jevons.

'Would you put my hat up too, please,' she said as though she had been used to servants all her life.

Betsy watched, lips parted with astonishment. What a nerve that Viola had. Jevons' sly eyes glinted, but he merely said, 'Certainly madam,' took the hat with reverent care and placed it on the rack. 'That will be all, madam?'

'Thanks, that's grand,' said Viola.

Jevons bowed and went out into the corridor.

Betsy still clutched her carpet bag. If Jevons had noticed this he had made no move to assist her. To him she was merely a young person of a certain class. Viola he had catalogued mentally as a rip-snorter.

'May I put your bag on the rack?' asked Matthew politely.

Betsy went scarlet, shook her head, said: 'No, sir, it's all right, sir. I'm not bothered.'

'Oh, Betsy,' protested Viola, 'let the gentleman put it up for you. You're never going to nurse a carpet bag all the way to London!'

'I can do it myself.' Betsy rose, tried to reach the rack but she was far too tiny, and the lurch of the train would have toppled her if Matthew had not caught her about the waist, whereupon he nearly fell too. Finally he managed to get hold of the bag and place it on the rack, then both he and Betsy sat down, breathless and embarrassed. The stolid family of four had watched all this expressionlessly. Viola glanced at them, then at Matthew and Betsy, and broke into a ripple of laughter.

'Thank goodness that's settled,' she said. 'I thought you'd never let go of that bag, love. Folk will think you've got the Crown jewels in it.' She had taken a soft, fleecy cream-coloured shawl out of her hold-all, and wrapped it about her shoulders, nestling back as though the hard third-class seat were a comfortable armchair, looking at Betsy with mockingly affectionate eyes.

'*Well?*' she said. 'Say thank you to the reverend gentleman.'

'Oh, yes.' Betsy went scarlet again, turned to Matthew, stammered, 'Thank you very much, sir.'

'Please don't mention it,' said Matthew. He was not used to catching young women in his arms, and he was surprised at the multiple sensations. The tiny little waist and the lightness of her bones, like picking up a bird. He had actually felt her heart beating with fear. What a curious little creature. Frightened? Of *him?*

It made him feel unusually masculine and strong. No one was frightened of him. No one ever had been. He rather wished his Vicar, the Reverend Everard, or his wealthy sidesman, Mr Arthur Netherby of Dwyer & Netherby's in Oxford Street, who lived in Tewkesbury Square, would be just a little in awe of him. They reminded him of the boys who used to bully him at school. He wished the Vicar would not insist on his accepting all Mr Netherby's invitations, that Mr Netherby did not invite him so often, and that the plain Miss Netherby was not quite so keen to get married, nor her brother Herbert so earnestly over-anxious to become his friend. Herbert was the type James Staffray would have dubbed 'a daffodil' back in their schooldays. Matthew did not blame Miss Netherby

—anyone who had to live with her father would seize any chance of escaping. He was ashamed of these thoughts about his parishioners which he considered uncharitable but he could not help them.

Tewkesbury Square, so rich, so respectable, so middle-class, made him wish he had a living like his father had had in Long Ayrton, and thinking of Long Ayrton took his glance to Viola again. He was positive that he had seen her before. Viola was, apparently, dozing off to sleep. Her folded hands were long and narrow, with beautiful almond-shaped nails. Very clean, soft, and carefully manicured. Her brown suit was new and not very expensive. The toes of her buttoned boots shone with polish. She was as well-groomed as a lady of quality.

Her lashes lay like soft dark wings on the smooth white cheeks. Her thick cloud of hair was dressed in a simple knot on top of her head without any of the fashionable frizzings over the forehead. The collar of her pale yellow blouse was not high-boned to her ears but opened just at the base of her throat.

Matthew felt uneasy. He was not accustomed to scrutinizing young women as closely as this, particularly one of such seductive beauty. It was at this moment he realized that Betsy was looking at him with outraged indignation and that Viola was not asleep at all, but watching him beneath her long dark lashes, her soft red lips twitching with amusement.

Hastily he shook out a copy of *The Church Times*.

'Well,' said Viola sweetly, 'I reckon you'll know me if you see me again.'

Matthew glanced hastily at the other occupants of the carriage but faint snores reassured him. He put on his best clerical manner, superior and detached.

'I apologize, my good girl,' he said, and noticing the faint quizzical lifting of her finely arched brows, he immediately modified his tone. 'I apologize—er—madam. It's just that I seem to recognize you, and I can't place you at all. You do not by any chance worship at St Botolph's, Tewkesbury Square?'

Viola shook her head. She had recognized Matthew at once. She thought he hadn't changed much over the years, and he'd always been a nice, shy, quietly-spoken lad. She decided not to tease him.

'No. This is my first time in London. But it's not surprising you can't remember me, for it must be nine years since you left the school at Low Ayrton and went away to that fine boarding school your uncle sent you to.'

'You were at school with me at Low Ayrton?' Matthew said doubtfully. He did not care to be reminded of that low beginning. If his uncle had not come to the rescue after his father's death, he might have been a counter-jumper or a poorly-paid clerk in some West Riding mill office.

'Aye, but in a lower class. You were cleverer—and older. *My* mother used to scrub and wash for *your* mother. Monday washing day. Saturday morning scrub-through. Saturdays there was no school, so she brought me along to the vicarage.'

'Vi Corbett!'

The name flashed back into his mind with the memory of the copper-haired, lovely child, so tantalizing, so respectful to his parents, so mischievous behind their backs. So bleakly shabby, so spotlessly clean.

'You remember my name?' She laughed, delighted.

His confidence returned, knowing her mystery now and her social standing. The daughter of his mother's scrub woman. Mrs Corbett—the Mrs complimentary, for she had never married. A gaunt, horn-handed, silent woman with the remnants of a harsh beauty, only her height and her red hair reminiscent of this exquisite girl.

He had learned later that Lizzy Corbett had been seduced by an Italian acrobat from a travelling circus, and that his parents had stood by her, paying for her confinement and afterwards giving her work. Indeed his father had pared down their own expenses to keep a fund for this kind of helping hand, and this was one of the reasons why they had always been so poor. He supposed that the genes from the Italian had softened the harsh Corbett handsomeness to Viola's lithe attraction.

He decided on a kindly but distant approach. It would do no harm to talk with her a little, and it might reassure her small companion, who reminded him of a moorhen chick nervously darting in the shadow of a superb white swan. It was unlikely that they would meet again after the journey, although he could not be too careful. The Reverend Mr Everard, Vicar of St Botolph's, deplored what he called Matthew's socialist tendencies, which meant he tried to be just as nice to the poor as to the rich parishioners.

'And how is your mother?' he asked.

'She's dead these three years.'

'Oh, I am sorry. My mother did not tell me.'

'No reason why she should. I've not been back to Low Ayrton since they buried her.'

'And what have you been doing?' The minute he asked the question he regretted it, for if the little Betsy had the look of a poor but honest working girl of the popular and lachrymose songs of the time, Viola certainly had not. She could not be more than twenty-one. What did a poor single girl do to keep herself so well? An actress, a barmaid, or . . . he found the teasing little look in her eyes and knew she had guessed his thoughts.

'Nay, I'm still on the straight and narrow—or more or less, aren't I, Betsy?'

Betsy became loquacious in her defence. 'Take no notice of her, sir. She's a real tease. She worked at Samuel Hardcastle's shop in Brigate, same as I did. Only she was first sales and I was only a hand.'

Matthew knew the big shop, a high-class ladies outfitters. He also knew, very slightly, Mr and Mrs Hardcastle, who lived in a big stone house standing in some ten acres on the country road between Low Ayrton and Leeds. Mrs Hardcastle, an over-dressed, mean-mouthed woman had occasionally called on his mother when his father had been alive.

'Mother wanted me to be a lady,' said Viola, and although her lips smiled, her eyes did not. 'Aye, well. She didn't want me in a mill—nor on my knees all day, swilling stone steps like she did. She worked for the Hardcastles up at Moorfield House, and she talked Mr Hardcastle into taking me on as a "prentice in the shop."'

'You've left?'

'Aye. I wanted to better myself. I've got a crib in London. Second sales in the gloves. I persuaded Betsy to come too. Well, I couldn't leave her alone in Leeds . . . she might start leading a really fast life . . .'

'Viola! How can you say such things!'

And this time Matthew laughed with Viola and said very gently to Betsy, 'No one could possibly think such a thing about you, Miss . . . Miss er?'

'Holder,' said Viola promptly.

'Miss Holder. I have realized your friend is a great tease. May I ask where you are going to work?'

'At Dwyer & Netherby's in Oxford Street,' said Betsy quickly. 'Do you know it, sir?'

'Very well indeed,' said Matthew cautiously. 'Mr Netherby lives in Tewkesbury Square, off Oxford Street, and he is one of our parishioners at St Botolph's. He is the proprietor. He bought out Mr Dwyer years ago, and built the present store.'

'And what sort of chap is he?' Viola asked promptly.

Matthew hesitated before answering.

'He is very rich and an important man locally,' he said finally. 'He attends church regularly with his . . .' He swallowed uncomfortably. 'With his son and daughter. He—he is a widower, and has been very generous to the church.'

Viola gave him a long, slow look, and said, 'Hmmm? . . . You don't like him?'

'Please! I didn't say so.'

'No need. Never mind. We can always move if we don't like it.'

Matthew cleared his throat, coughed delicately, and ventured, 'May I ask if you have lodgings? Respectable lodgings? St Botolph's is near the London termini, and I am very distressed that many girls arrive in London with nowhere to live, and expose themselves to great danger and temptation. I have mentioned to the Reverend Everard that we should do something for them, St Botolph's being so near the termini, but he says that we serve quite a different class of society . . .' Matthew shook his head despondently. 'I always thought we should serve all classes. But I'm straying . . . Have you . . . ?'

He found both girls looking at him, Betsy's mild grey eyes beaming through her glasses, Viola silently smiling, and he was covered with confusion.

'He's *nice*, isn't he, Betsy?' said Viola, in her soft deep voice—just as though he were any boy she knew, not a clergyman and a young gentleman, and although he knew it was quite wrong, and that Mr Everard would not approve, it gave him a very happy feeling as though he had made two new friends. 'Thank you Mr Lyttelton, but we have arranged to live-in for the time being.'

'Oh,' Matthew hesitated, glanced about him, as though afraid of being overheard, then said in a low voice: 'Perhaps I shouldn't say it, but I have heard the food is not very good, nor—er—plentiful.'

'Thanks for the warning,' said Viola. 'If it isn't we'll look out for lodgings. Well, I don't know about you, but I'm going to have a nap,' with which she closed her eyes again and seemed to drop off. Matthew too was soon dozing. Only Betsy stayed awake, looking out at fields and villages, the new large world beyond Leeds, hoping they were doing the right thing, and wondering if London was as large and wicked as it was said to be.

But Viola was not asleep. She wondered who Matthew's handsome friend was. She had not asked, because there had been no mistaking that long, burning glance, and she knew she would meet him again. She thought of Sam Hardcastle, who had been so good to her, and the evening six weeks ago when he had told her she would have to leave because someone had informed his wife about their friendship.

'It would be no use telling Sarah there's nowt in it,' Sam had said despondently, 'though that's not rightly true. So far as I'm concerned there's everything in it. I couldn't think more of any lass. But she'd never believe it were—innocent like.'

It was true. He had no children of his own, and when she had been a little girl, her mother scrubbing the kitchens and long stone corridors of his house, he had given her sixpences, shown her the gardens, cut her grapes and peaches from his greenhouses in spite of his wife's sour protests and prurient hints that it was not a 'nice thing' to make such a fuss of a girl child. He had taken her on as an apprentice; he watched and guarded her for those first years and when she was eighteen he had fallen deeply in love with her. He was an ailing man, plagued with high blood pressure. But he had taken her out to the theatre, to dinner and, on her days off, to excursions to Scarborough or Harrogate. She had never felt she was cheating because he was so happy in her company. He was generous, giving her clothes and pretty trinkets, a little enamelled watch on a long chain. He had taught her a lot too, about the choosing of her clothes and the colours which flattered her rusty-gold hair.

'I know Netherby, of Dwyer & Netherby of Oxford Street,' he had said. 'We were apprentices together in London. I'll write to him for you . . .'

'And Betsy Holder,' she insisted. 'I can't leave her behind. She's a right soft little lass. They'll be at her like a rat pack if I'm not there.'

He had driven her to the station in a cab. In the buffet he had had a brandy, she a cup of tea. His hard square face had been so pale and his eyes were full of tears. She was distressed for all her apparent self-assurance. Only twenty-one, she had never seen a man cry before. Not a man old enough to be her father.

'If I hadn't been married, Vi, love,' he had said, 'would you have wed me, d'you think?'

To be Mrs Sam Hardcastle, and live in a big stone house on the moors with hothouses and stables, and ride in her own carriage? She looked at him with all the compassion of her conquering youth and was glad the temptation had never arisen. She had always known since childhood that she was beautiful, and she was learning the power of beauty. She had put her arms round Hardcastle's neck and kissed him, and to comfort him had said, 'Aye, I would have, Sam. I'll go a long way before I'll find a better and kinder man—and anyone as good to me as you have been.' Which was true enough. It was then that he had taken a long envelope from his pocket and thrust it into her hand.

'There's a bit of a present, lass, to start you off. If you're ever in a corner, or need a bit of help, you come to me, Vi. You can always write to me—personal—at the shop. I'm going now before I make a great fool of myself. Don't say good-bye.'

She was recalling how abruptly he had plunged away from her into the crowd when the corridor door shot open. Jevons, Staffray's valet, stood there. He bent and gently shook Matthew's shoulder.

'Mr Lyttelton, sir.'

'Yes, yes . . . ?' Matthew woke up, startled.

'Mr Lyttelton, they are just making the first dinner call. His lordship presents his compliments, and says if the young ladies would care to join him too he would be—ahem—honoured.'

Matthew was staggered. Jimmy did not even know the girls. Remembering James' reputation as a blood at school he opened his mouth to refuse for Viola, but realized she was not under his protection and he had no real right to do so. He looked at her helplessly. She looked at Betsy.

'Well, my Betsy, what shall we do? Eat our brawn sandwiches or have dinner with a lord?' Her long eyes widened mischievously, and she asked, 'I suppose he is a *real* lord? Not a circus one like Sanger?'

'Lord Staffray,' said Jevons coldly. 'The son of the Earl and Countess of Louderdown.'

'Well, Betsy?'

'I *couldn't!* I can't!' Betsy was in a real flutter of fear. 'Don't ask me to, Vi, I'd be scared.'

'I have already accepted,' said Matthew, 'but I assure you, Miss Holder, no harm shall come to you . . . you would be under my protection.'

'It isn't that, sir, thank you. I just don't *want* to go. I'd be dropping everything, and couldn't say a word, I'd much better just have my sandwiches here.'

'Miss Corbett?'

'I'd be happy to accept,' Viola said grandly. 'Would you pass my hat down from the rack, please?' Jevons did so. She took out a small hand mirror, tidied her hair, set the pretty hat on straight, and skewered it into place with an amber-headed pin. She picked up her gloves and handbag and rose, settling her skirts, twitching her brown velvet lapels straight.

Jevons led the way along the corridor, grinning to himself and thinking there were not many flies on this young piece. A filly who would give the master a run for his money, no doubt about that. Matthew followed Viola's long, swaying, graceful back, the yellow buttercups bobbing high on her head. He spoke in her ear.

'I met Lord James at Rugby. You won't talk about the Low Ayrton school, will you? I . . . well, at school I always said I had a tutor when I was small.'

She nodded understandingly.

'And I won't say anything about you . . .' he promised.

The gold-green eyes were grave and questioning. 'About my mother, you mean? Her scrubbing floors? And about the father I never had? Don't worry, Mr Lyttelton, I don't mind if you do.' Her smile softened consolingly. 'Young Matthew,' she said, 'you haven't altered. I'll tell you about me. I'm honest with honest folk, and the others can go hang themselves. And I know you're honest too.'

Matthew was covered with confusion—and was a little ashamed. Viola was full of such baffling contradictions.

Jevons was waiting ahead holding open the door to the dining car. They could see the rose-shaded lights, white napery, the silver and the uniformed waiters, and James rising from his table to greet them, his bright blue eyes fixed hungrily on Viola.

He stepped forward, shook hands formally, then took her arm to lead her to the table. Her eyes were just level with his mouth. It was a bonny, inviting mouth, made for kisses and laughter, and she had an impulse to lift up her head and kiss his lips. Meeting his eyes she knew he knew what she was thinking and her creamy skin glowed for an instant with rose. Confusion was a new experience. She was filled with a heady excitement. They were like two beautiful tropical birds, sparring and displaying themselves until the precise moment for mating arrived.

James was entranced with her. He thought her a real little ripper and not in the least affected, without any of the high-toned pretensions of the actresses and expensive tarts he amused himself with. She made the girls of his own class fade into innocuous puppets by comparison. As he and Matthew settled in their seats, Matthew beside Viola, himself opposite, he set out to exert all his charm.

The train was speeding through Hertfordshire towards the outer suburbs of London when Viola returned to the carriage, carrying a box of expensive chocolates and a large ripe peach, which she gave to Besty.

'Did you have a grand time?'

'We did. That Jimmy Staffray is a likely lad. I left the Rev with him, over their cigars. Eat your peach, Betsy, because we're getting near to London.'

When they arrived at King's Cross Station James sent Jevons to get a porter to take care of their luggage.

'We'll meet again soon?' he pleaded, taking Viola's hand.

She shook her head, smiling. 'You and I are different kinds of birds, my lord, and belong in different coops. It's been a grand evening, and thank you. But let's leave it at that. Would you ask your chap to call us a cab?'

Let him wait and wonder. She was not going to let any handsome young toff think she was easy, but she was surprised at the keenness of her own disappointment when he gracefully capitulated, and sent Jevons for a growler.

'Would you like Jevons to accompany you?' he asked. 'London is not a place for young ladies alone at night.'

She considered this. Betsy was standing, heavy-eyed, as though she might drop off to sleep there and then. Matthew held her arm solicitously, a large brandy with his coffee having relaxed him sufficiently to make this gesture. His mild face was flushed, and he was inclined to stutter.

'I w-will go with the ladies,' he announced with dignity. 'I live in the same direction. No harm will come to them through me.'

'Well said, Matty.' James handed them into the cab, their luggage was stacked in the boot, and with a jingle of harness they were off. Viola peeped through the small back window. James was standing, hat in hand, gazing after them.

As the growler drove away Jevons said, 'Shall I follow, my lord, and ascertain the young lady's address?'

'No need to trouble, Jevons.' Quite unreasonably he felt irritated by the accommodating valet. He knew where to find her, anyway, for Matthew had told him over his brandy, with many warnings and exhortations against renewing the acquaintance. Since Viola was only a working girl, it would be most unfair of James to pay her any attention. For the first time in his life James hesitated to pursue a pretty girl who attracted him. He drove home in a strange mood, not knowing whether it was Viola he wanted to protect—or himself. Instinct told him that there could be neither a light flirtation nor trivial affaire with this girl: if he went in, he would go in deep. When he arrived at his rooms there was a message to say he would be on duty at Windsor for the following month. A month out of town. Perhaps Viola's tempting, velvety beauty would have faded from his mind by the time he returned.

The growler clopped and jingled through the quiet streets of Bloomsbury. Matthew, now half asleep, wished he dared hold little Betsy's hand, and wondered what she would do if he tried to, and felt horribly guilty and confused because these were not the sort of thoughts a young clergyman should have. Sitting in the darkness of the cab his face darkened with shame. Betsy was such a timid, inexperienced little person, and the last thing any gentleman should think of was taking advantage of her, even in this most innocuous way.

The two girls both had their noses glued to the window. London. The great wicked metropolis about which they had heard and read so much. Sam Hardcastle had told Viola about his time there as a young apprentice, but stiff-necked in defence of Yorkshire, he was inclined to run it down.

'They've not much there we haven't got in Leeds,' he had said.

To Viola there seemed a great deal more of it—the streets seemed endless. It was a damp showery night, with a yellowish mist hanging about the open spaces. They passed rows of tall dark houses with iron railings guarding their deep basements; dank squares with huge plane trees, the branches just beginning to bud again.

A lot of small shops were still open and on almost every corner there was a public house, the doors of which swung wide as customers pushed in, disclosing bright interiors and the sound of noisy voices.

At intervals the street lamps, lit by gas, made a circle of yellow light on the wet paving stones. Pale, ragged children played in the streets, and women dressed in tawdry finery hung about with the patient, defiant stance of the streetwalker. They occasionally saw a policeman standing in a high helmet and shining black oilskin cape.

They were driving past better, cleaner and larger houses; Betsy caught a glimpse of a warm interior on which the curtains had not been drawn, where a family was seated round a table in the lamplight, a girl playing the piano, a young man standing beside her, singing a song she would never hear. It must be wonderful, she thought, to belong to a real family, which lived in its own house, to have a father and mother, and young men coming to call.

In one big square, Viola called, 'Oh, Bet—come and look,' and Betsy nearly fell over Matthew's feet to peer out, rubbing the moisture from the window. There was an awning over the pavement and carriages were drawing up. Gentlemen in evening dress alighted and ladies with flowers and ospreys and jewels, wrapped in warm opera cloaks.

Viola had an impression of a divided city. Islands where the rich lived, squares of great houses, surrounded by a sea of meaner dwellings where the lowly people who served them lodged.

It was not until the cab turned into the brightly lit thoroughfare of Oxford Street that London began to look like the city of her dreams. Big shops with plate glass windows filled with goods. Music halls with the names of the stars in electric lights across the façade. A great restaurant, glass-fronted entrance guarded by gold-laced doormen beyond which she caught a glimpse of red carpets, chandeliers, palms and parterres of flowers and people in evening clothes. Above the door written in electric lights she saw the name, Franconeri's. Her lips parted eagerly at this glimpse of the world she wanted so passionately. A world of gaiety, luxury, beautiful clothes and the company of men like James Staffray. She had already learned that the men who attracted you most were the dangerous ones. She knew too that, although her head was screwed on right, as Sam Hardcastle said, her Italian blood and fine young body were capable of a passionate response. She did not think for a moment she had seen the last of Lord Staffray.

On through the London streets—ragged boys, many bare-footed, swept the mud and horse-dung into piles at every crossing, and pedestrians, the women lifting their skirts distastefully from the mire, threw them an occasional coin.

Newsboys shouted as they raced along with their placards. *Uitlanders Petition the Queen, Kruger's Cruel Persecution, British Protests Ignored.* The girls did not listen. South Africa and its urgent affairs might have been on the moon as far as they were concerned. London was their whole and immediate interest. It sounded like a foreign language, this shrill nasal, flat Cockney, so different from the broad Northern sounds. But Viola's eager imagination responded to the great city as her mind and body had responded to the desire in James Staffray's handsome eyes.

There was a glimpse of fine wide plate glass windows; gilt letters, 'Dwyer & Netherby, Emporium for Ladieswear, Outfitters & Haberdashers to the Nobility & Gentry.'

'Is *that* where we'll work?' breathed Betsy. 'In that great place . . . ?'

But the growler went past into a long, ill-lit street behind the shop, and stopped at a tall, dark house.

'Right, miss. Twenty-seven,' said the driver.

Matthew helped them out, while the cabman put their luggage on the doorstep, and despite Viola's objections insisted on paying.

'My lodgings are only a short walk away,' he said when the cab had gone. 'I wish you happiness in your new work. I hope I'll see you at St Botolph's on Sundays—many of the staff here attend.'

'Oh, yes, I'll come,' Betsy said eagerly, and then hung back, ashamed of her outburst.

'Well, you've made one convert, Mr Lyttelton. Thank you very much for everything. We'll say good night, then,' said Viola, offering her hand. He raised his hat, shook her hand solemnly and then Betsy's and went on his way.

The two girls looked up at the large forbidding doorway, black-painted, with dirty brass and unwashed steps, and a feeble gleam of gaslight showing through the fanlight above the door.

'Well, here goes,' said Viola, and tugged on the bell pull.

After a pause, footsteps could be heard shuffling along the stone hallway inside, and the door was opened by a thin, slatternly girl, wearing a grubby apron and a cap from which long strands of wispy hair escaped.

'Yes, ma'am?' she said.

'Is this the assistants' hostel for Dwyer & Netherby?'

'Yes. Will you be the two new ones, then?'

'It looks like it.'

'Will you come in. I'll get someone to take your bags.' She peered curiously at the two contrasting figures. Viola, so tall and assured, Betsy peering nervously round her friend. 'It's too late for dinner. Saturdays we finish at seven.'

'Thanks, I've eaten. How about you, Bet? You've only had sandwiches.'

'I'm all right.'

'A cup of tea or cocoa?' suggested Viola.

'Tea would be grand.'

'Mrs 'Arding, the 'ousekeeper, don't allow no cups of anything after nine o'clock.'

Viola took a sixpence out of her bag, handed it to the girl and said, 'One cup of tea. And show us where we have to sleep.'

'All right, miss. I'll do me best. It's against the rules, but I'll do me best. Come this way.'

She took a candle from the hall-stand, lit it and led them up the tall, narrow stairs, the mahogany rail winding above them. A smell of dust and boiled cabbage pervaded the house. On the first landing, the servant girl, who told them her name was Sal Perkins, stopped and indicated a door with a dull glass panel behind which gleamed a feeble jet of gas. On the door painted in white were the letters W.C.

'There's one on each floor,' she said.

'What luxury,' said Viola gravely. 'And how many ladies sleep on each floor?'

'Fifteen. Five to a room. Some of the senior ladies, first sales, like, sleep out.'

'I'll bet,' said Viola. She thought of Sam Hardcastle's hostel in Leeds with the decent coal fires, good plain food, comfortable beds, and the piano in the rest room.

'Let's see our bedroom.'

It was one of two big rooms in the front of the house. There were five narrow iron bedsteads made up with unironed cotton sheets and grey army blankets. The floor was covered with linoleum. Five slim wardrobe cupboards and two wash-stands lined the walls, and beside each bed stood a yellow varnished commode on the top of which stood a candlestick and beneath there was a cupboard which contained a chamber pot. The curtains drawn across the windows were of a dull dark red rep. Sal Perkins lit a single gas jet, turning it carefully down to a small blue flame.

'Mrs 'Arding,' she warned, 'expects you to be very careful with the gas. The other ladies is out until ten thirty, it being Saturday.'

Viola sat on one of the beds. It was extremely hard. Betsy was nearly in tears. Compared with this, Hardcastle's in Leeds had been a palace.

'Better get that tea,' said Viola. When the girl went out, she said cheerfully, 'I see what Matthew Lyttelton meant when he said the food might not be very good. If it's as good as the sleeping accommodation, I reckon we'll starve to death, love.'

'Oh, Vi,' wailed Betsy, 'it's terrible. It's not even clean. I wish we hadn't come. I wish I was back at Hardcastle's.'

Viola rose, turned up the gas to a full flare, illuminating the room, in defiance of the as yet unknown Mrs Harding.

'Don't give up yet. When Sal comes up with your tea, give her this six-pence and tell her to fill our hot-water bottles. Mine's in my case, right on top. I'm going down to visit that extremely modern convenience on the landing.'

Viola picked up her bag and went downstairs. She opened the W.C. door, bolted it, and once again turned up the meagre gas jet to a full flare. Then she opened her bag and took out the envelope Sam Hardcastle had given her when they had parted and opened it. Bank notes—fivers. Twenty of them. A hundred pounds. Enough to keep her for a year—pro-tection against a rainy day. Sam had been a champion friend to her. She placed the money back into her bag and went up to the dormitory. Sal meantime had brought the tea for Betsy and was turning the gas down again.

'You'll get me skinned, miss, if Mrs 'Arding sees the gas burning like this.'

'Turn it up again,' commanded Viola. 'And if the housekeeper objects, you tell her to see me about it.'

Sal, open-mouthed, did as she was bid. The new saleslady had an au-thoritative air, which would not be gainsaid. And with it a smile that warmed the girl's starved heart.

'I'll get the hot-water bottles filled for you,' she said, and vanished down the stairs.

On the way she met some of the young members of the staff coming in from their Saturday night out, and said, 'The new one for the gloves has arrived. A proper young Duchess, she is.' The name stuck, and remained with Viola all the time she worked at Dwyer & Netherby's and followed her throughout her life.

When Sal returned with the filled hot-water bottles, Viola had her arms round Betsy.

'Cheer up, love,' she said. 'Now, here's that half-starved lass with the bottles. Get to bed, and we'll see what tomorrow brings.'

Later three shrill, over-dressed Cockney girls came into the room. They were sharp, and not unfriendly, but looked with surprise at Viola, sitting up in bed, wrapped in her creamy shawl, giving her long, waving silken hair a hundred brush strokes. She introduced herself unselfconsciously, and listened while they described Dwyer & Netherby's.

The shop was 'proper posh' they said, but the hostel awful. They described the housekeeper as a penny-pinching tyrant, and Mr Netherby as a wicked old hypocrite and a stickler for manners.

'Catch you laughing, or chatting to one of the fellas, and you're fined!'

They told Viola that Miss Heath was the first assistant and glove buyer, and when Viola questioned them about her, they laughed, sly-eyed, and said, 'You just wait and see. But don't you make eyes at old Netherby, or she'll poison you for sure. She's been after him since his missus died.'

'Fat chance she's got there,' said a thin, brash girl called Katy Martin. She sat down on the edge of her bed, rolling her lank hair into paper curlers. 'We've all 'eard what the Guvnor fancies on 'is days orf. You'll 'ave to watch out, Duchess, he'll be after a looker like you, and if he is, both Miss 'Eath and Little Herby will 'ave their knives out for you.'

Little Herby, it appeared, was Mr Netherby junior.

It was the first time anyone had called Viola, Duchess. It had a grand sound—she rather liked it. It suggested someone important, beautiful and very well dressed.

Viola was surprised by the servility of these Cockneys—bold enough here in the dormitory but timidly polite before authority. Another breed from the Yorkshire girls she had known, where even a poor mill girl would give you the rough side of her tongue if slighted.

By eleven o'clock the lights were out, and the girls settled to sleep. Betsy had said her prayers under the coarse sheets and tried not to cry. Viola lay awake. Unlike Betsy she had no doubts about coming to London, and when she fell asleep in the hard, narrow bed, it was James Staffray's face that drifted through her mind, and her long, lovely body stirred with delight as she remembered the look in his dark blue eyes watching her with tenderness and desire.

CHAPTER TWO

Viola woke next morning before the rising bell, which on Sundays went at seven o'clock instead of six as on working mornings. Behind the door was a large, framed, printed form of House Rules. To Viola, it seemed a formidable list of prohibitions and fines.

The shop opened for business at 8 am and closed at 8 pm Monday to Friday. On Saturdays it opened at 8 am and closed at 1 pm. Sunday was the only whole day in the week that the employees of Dwyer & Netherby had—supposedly—to themselves. 'Not much time for fun,' Viola thought. 'Though this road, you'd be too tired to have any.'

She continued reading the House Rules. Summary dismissal for any member of the staff who invited a member of the opposite sex past the hall-door, or, if it was reported to Mr Netherby that they had behaved with impropriety either on or off the premises. The staff were expected to attend divine service on Sundays, and there was a weekly bible class at St Botolph's Parish Hall under the supervision of Miss Emily Netherby. Attendance at this was expected but not compulsory.

Viola wrinkled her delicate nose and gave a faint hoot of derision, then, huddling her shawl around her, she drifted across to the window to look at London by daylight.

Overnight the wind had shifted to the south-west, sweeping away the clouds and the dank mist of the night before. Eastcastle Street looked bright and clean in the dawn, with street cleaners already at work, and a watering cart spraying roads and pavements.

A lamplighter went by with his tall rod, extinguishing the street lights one by one. A milk cart clattered behind a quiet horse, the milkman stopping at each area gate with a long drawn shout of 'Milk! Milk-oh-ho!' for the sleepy servant girls to trudge slowly up the steps with the cans to be filled from the tall brown urns.

A costermonger wheeled a barrowful of potted plants, ferns and cut flowers, brilliantly fresh and beautiful. He wore a red kerchief and cap with the peak pulled sideways over his ear, and every now and then he gave a sort of yelping bark, 'Luvly roses! Luvly vilets. All-a-fresh-and-blowing.'

A few shabby women passed. They looked strange to Viola, who was used to seeing working women wrapped head and shoulders in shawls, with clattering clogs to protect their feet from the swilling factory floors. In London the drabbest woman wore a hat, mostly of hard black straw, sometimes defiantly flowered or feathered. Distantly the bell of St Botolph's sounded from Tewkesbury Square for the early service. Sal Perkins came up the stairs ringing a handbell to signify that it was eight o'clock. The sleeping girls stirred. In the morning light they looked young and underfed, their frowsy hair in curlers, the smudge of last night's rouge on their thin cheeks, their finery of the night before replaced by cheap, flannelette nightdresses.

With her pure apple-blossom skin Betsy looked so childishly innocent beside them that Viola had a guilty pang—perhaps she should never have brought her to London. The little snub-nosed face was touching without the steel spectacles, the straight hair fastened in two sprouting little braids.

At the clang of the rising bell Betsy sat straight up in bed, staring about her short-sightedly, pale with terror. She fumbled for her glasses, hooked them over her ears, and with relief recognized Viola's tall figure, the morning sunlight making a fiery nimbus of her red-gold hair.

Viola sat on the bed and took her hand.

'It's all right, love,' she said gently. 'I'm here. It's Sunday. No need to rush.'

Betsy looked round with a shudder. 'For a minute I thought I was back in the orphanage.'

'Well,' said Viola ironically, 'we might just as well be. You ought to read the House Rules. Sam Hardcastle's place was a grand hotel compared with this. But it does say we can buy a can of hot water to wash in for tuppence. So let's be devils and do that, eh?'

She pulled the bell rope, which brought the other girls struggling awake, staring in astonishment, as though no one had ever done such a thing before.

Sal Perkins appeared, startled. 'Did you want something, miss?'

Viola twitched the grey-looking threadbare towels from the rack. 'Good morning, love,' she said cheerfully. 'Will you bring us some hot water— and some proper towels. I see we are charged for them. If your housekeeper thinks we're paying for these rags, she can think again.'

With a terror-stricken glance Sal went out, and presently returned weighed down with two brass jugs of hot water, and told Viola that Mrs Harding would be coming up about the towels. Viola shrugged and took a good towel out of her case. When Mrs Harding, a black-clad, harsh-faced lady, born to be a prison wardress, appeared, breathing with heavy fury that anyone should ask for anything new, or indeed dare ask at all, Viola was standing, naked and beautiful, white skinned and firm, her breasts pink-tipped, her raised arm-pits fluffed with red-gold down, washing herself all over, everyone else staring at her open-mouthed.

'Miss Corbett!' cried Mrs Harding in affronted horror. 'What are you thinking of? Cover yourself immediately!'

Viola smiled and continued with her toilet. Drying meticulously, rubbing herself with cologne, slipping her lace-edged chemise over her head.

'And what is this about the towels?' demanded Mrs Harding in a suffocated voice.

'Didn't the girl tell you? If we have to pay for towels we want good ones. Those are worn out. If I don't get them, I'll complain.'

'Complain? Who to?'

Viola put on her corsets, hooking up the front. Her waist measured twenty-two inches. She smoothed her chemise over her hips, and pulled on a pair of long drawers, frilled with lace below the knees. She tied the drawstrings, and sat down on the bed to put on her stockings. She did everything very slowly, with a deliberate and provocative grace.

'To the Master, of course. The Guv'nor you say down here.'

'You'd complain—to Mr *Netherby*? For a new girl, you're certainly above yourself. You won't last long here!'

Viola's nonchalance unnerved her. Miss Heath, the senior assistant and glove buyer, had told her Mr Netherby had engaged a raw girl from Yorkshire. She had not expected anyone like this.

Viola smoothed her stockings, setting the seams straight. She looked up. The long-lashed eyes were dangerously cold.

'If *I* have to complain,' she said, 'it'll be to the boss. Who else?'

Mrs Harding lost her nerve, stammering furiously, and retreated. A few minutes afterwards Sal Perkins, wide-eyed with admiration, came up with two new, clean towels.

''Ere you are, Duchess,' she said. 'You beat cockfighting.'

The three other girls, now washing and dressing, laughed incredulously.

'You certainly took the wind out of her sails.'

'You watch it, Duchess. That old cat'll get back at you.'

'She's in with Miss Heath now telling 'er all about it,' said Sal Perkins.

'That means straight to Little Herby after church this morning!' said Katy Martin, unrolling her paper curlers. She looked enviously at Viola's wealth of red-gold waves. 'Curly hair! Some people 'ave all the luck. Though I don't fancy ginger.'

'Does Miss Heath go to church with the Netherbys?'

'Yes, most Sundays. Morning service, and to dinner mid-day—luncheon they call it.' She put a finger beneath her nose and tipped it up to indicate the degree of swank. 'She's a friend of the family. Alwus on about it.'

Viola fastened her blouse cuffs, her head on one side, and critically regarded her own charming reflection in the meagre, fly-spotted mirror. She smiled at herself, satisfied, and said, 'I think we'll go to church this morning, Betsy love. We want to do the right thing on our first morning, don't we?'

Betsy nodded, startled. It was the first time Viola had ever suggested such a thing, although she herself was a regular church-goer. She hurried to wash and dress, putting on her best blouse for Sunday. Viola sometimes worried her. She was, after all, only a working girl like herself; a shop assistant, even if she was second sales and getting 26 shillings a week. Would she always find a Sam Hardcastle to protect her? Betsy thought she would say a little private prayer for Viola: that she would not be too arrogant or dare too far!

St Botolph's Parish Church stood on the northern side of Tewkesbury Square, a fine neo-classical façade with Ionic pillars. It faced a long, rectangular garden enclosed in iron railings, which was private to the surrounding houses, with lawns, arbours, shrubbery walks and plane trees grown tall and majestic since their planting some forty years ago.

The square consisted of five-storey houses, handsome and symmetrical. The basement areas were guarded by wrought-iron railings. Imposing front doors were topped by high fanlights, flanked with stucco pillars. Neo-Grecian pediments hid the attic storey where the servants slept.

Katy Martin gave Viola and Betsy a brief history of the Netherby family on their way to church.

'Owns ever so much property beside the store. That's where he lives.'

The two girls looked up at the big house and noted the scrubbed steps and polished brass. From each window hung starched Nottingham lace curtains, through which they could see a large aspidistra plant in an elaborately convoluted pot.

'He must have plenty of brass,' was Viola's comment.

'Brass?'

'Money,' explained Betsy.

'Stinkin' rich,' said Katy, grinning. 'He's got plenty of that all right, the psalm-singing old hypocrite. He'll give a girl the sack for staying out a bit with her gen'leman fren' and hand her a religious tract and pinch her bottom at the same time.'

Viola burst out laughing, a laugh, so gay and spontaneous, that it penetrated the silence of the front parlour of Number 40.

Mr Netherby was waiting with his son, Herbert, and Miss Heath, the buyer of his glove department, for Miss Emily Netherby to join them. Both men wore frock coats, and their top hats rested with their prayer books on the table. Miss Heath, a close friend of the late Mrs Netherby, was a sallow-complexioned lady of uncertain age, and wore black plumes on her hat like a funeral horse. She was filling in the time with her weekly report on staff behaviour at the Emporium. Nothing missed her watchful eyes.

'And,' she was saying, 'the new assistant in the gloves who is to start as my second on Monday, has arrived. From what Mrs Harding has reported to me, we seem, if I may so dare, to have made a mistake.'

'Ha?' Mr Netherby picked up his Morocco-bound bible. 'You surprise me. Mr Hardcastle of Leeds gave her a first-class reference.'

'No doubt Mr Hardcastle had his reasons,' said Miss Heath darkly, 'but I have never *seen* Mrs Harding so upset. The new girl arrived last night, and although she is only a common provincial girl she has done nothing but complain about the state of the linen, the food, and the general condition of the hostel.'

'Ha,' said Mr Netherby again. The hostel saved him wages, for every extra service the girls had to pay, and every small misdemeanour could be fined. He knew Mrs Harding made a bit for herself by saving on food, linen and general expenses, but it was worth his while to overlook this.

'What is wrong with the linen and the food?' he demanded.

'Nothing, nothing at all,' Miss Heath assured him. 'It is quite good enough for her sort. It appears to me she is impudent.'

'I will not employ trouble-makers,' said Mr Netherby firmly. 'I am, I hope, a fair employer, Miss Heath?'

'Oh, you are. Indeed you are, sir,' breathed Miss Heath. 'You are known for your fairness and generosity.'

Herbert Netherby, who worked as a shopwalker for his father at a minimum salary, sniffed.

'Well, I shall be seeing this young woman on Monday. She will be told that she subscribes to the rules or leaves.'

'From what Mrs Harding says it seems to be that she is a bold and immodest young person.'

'Indeed?' said Mr Netherby, his voice rising like a biblical prophet. 'That I will not tolerate.'

It was at that moment he heard, from the pavement outside, a woman's laugh. A light, gay, rippling laugh, and automatically lifted the starched white lace curtain, and saw Viola.

He vaguely recognized Katy Martin as one of his more lowly employees. The little creature in the black straw hat and spectacles, he did not know—but the third girl was a woman the like of whom he had never seen, or only distantly in the theatre or park. One of those visionary beauties, maddeningly beyond the reach of ordinary men. A tall, slender, beautifully proportioned girl, with a swaying, seductive walk, a mass of red-gold hair beneath her neat brown hat topped with a brave cluster of yellow flowers. She was laughing, throwing back her head, showing perfect white teeth, wide full lips, and as her companion spoke she glanced up at his window. Mr Netherby dropped the lace curtain hurriedly.

'That's one of our gels,' he said in a stifled voice. 'The thin one, a junior in your department, Miss H. Who's the one with her? D'you know her?'

Miss Heath went to the window and peeped cautiously between the aspidistra leaves.

'I have not met this new young woman, Miss Corbett, from Leeds, or her friend by the name of Holder. But it could be them.'

'Ah,' said Mr Netherby slowly, watching through the curtains as the bright hair and swaying, long-waisted back continued along the square.

'Well,' he said, tugging fiercely on the silk lapels of his frock coat, 'I'll have a word with that young lady on Monday morning.'

Monday seemed light years away. Impatience possessed him.

'What on earth is keeping Emily?' he asked irritably.

Mr Netherby was a stoutish man of over fifty, his bald head was somewhat recompensed by his magnificent side-whiskers and moustache, dyed jet black and shining with macassar oil. His shoes shone. His linen was expensive and immaculate. His tailor the best that money could buy. His fat, pink hands were manicured and clean. His personal clerk reported that he washed them in lavender-scented water twenty times a day.

Miss Heath thought him a splendid figure of a man. Once she had nursed hopes of replacing the late Mrs Netherby, but his two children had an hysterical fear of him marrying again, and the vaguest suspicion would have immediately ended their friendship. In the shop Miss Heath was a martinet, but at Tewkesbury Square she was a mildly ingratiating toady, anxious to please the whole family.

Mr Netherby took his gold hunter from his waistcoat pocket where it was secured with an 18-carat chain, weighted with seals, and looked at it irritably.

'Where is Emily? The first bell had already gone.'

'Shall I hurry her, sir?'

'No. I'll send one of the girls.' But before he could pull on the embroidered bell-rope Emily appeared, flurried and self-conscious before her father's disparaging eyes. She was nearly thirty, with no style, her whey-faced looks reminding him of his late wife, lank-haired, sallow, over-genteel. His wife had disliked and despised him with the subdued ferocity of a woman who knows that she has been married for her money, the money which had enabled an ambitious young draper to build up a fortune. Arthur had been her only suitor and her parents had insisted upon the match. The intimacy of marriage had revolted her, and she had cultivated a chronic, complaining invalidism in self-protection. She had clung to her two children, teaching them to look upon their father as a coarse parvenu. When Arthur had put Herbert into the business instead of university she had been distraught. Her people had been gentlefolk, not trade, and throughout her married life she had never let anyone forget it.

'Well,' said Mr Netherby, with heavy irony, 'after all this time, I was expecting you to rival the Princess of Wales.'

He picked up his silk hat and put it on, and led the way out, pulling on his pale grey gloves of French leather with the care of one who has sold and fitted gloves all his life. Herbert, Emily and Miss Heath walked a few paces behind, like the family of an oriental pasha.

Matthew Lyttelton, assisting at the service, was conscious of the bright buttercups of Viola's hat immediately she entered the church. And he was equally conscious of Betsy's small figure bobbling beside her. The first five rows of pews were private, bearing the names of the holders on printed cards. Viola and Betsy took their places about half-way down the aisle towards the side door, among the lesser members of the congregation, the petty tradesmen, upper servants, and boarding house roomers who lived in the smaller streets surrounding the imposing square. Because he was at heart a very good young man, Matthew was genuinely pleased that they had come, although he wished Viola would not favour him with her slow, sweet smile. During the psalm, however, he found himself looking at Betsy instead of Viola, and he found something touching and appealing in the small, rather shabby little figure, and the way her round pink-cheeked face glowed as she sang earnestly.

Trying not to yawn at the long and boring sermon, Viola became aware of Mr Netherby's attention. Mischievously she kept her eyes lowered until, reassured that he was unobserved, Arthur indulged in a long, lecherous stare at the lovely young face, when she raised her eyes with such teasing awareness that he paled, and looked furtively about him. But Miss Heath was nodding, letting her ugly long jaw drop, and Emily was making sheep's eyes at that fool Lyttelton, the curate. Herbert was avidly studying the choir boys. He glanced cautiously at Viola, but her eyes were once again lowered over the hymn book, and he wondered if he had imagined her teasing look.

After the service Mr Netherby hung about, watching the door, but

Viola and her companions did not appear. Emily Netherby drooped disappointedly, because Matthew Lyttelton had once again avoided the regular invitation to take Sunday lunch with them. Herbert shot his cuffs, fidgeted with his pince-nez impatiently.

Viola and Betsy left by the side door, and spoke to Matthew while Katy Martin went to meet her young man—whom she called her gentleman friend—in the park. They arranged to meet Matthew for a coffee and a bun at a Bloomsbury teashop.

In the vestry Matthew took off his surplice and cassock, feeling like a boy let out of school. He knew that both the Reverend Mr Everard and Mr Netherby would be shocked if they knew he was meeting a couple of 'shop girls', but it was delightful to avoid that rich but gloomy luncheon party at Tewkesbury Square, and Miss Netherby's moistly reproachful eyes.

It was Monday. At six o'clock the assistants of Dwyer & Netherby's rose, washed and dressed and descended to the bleak, cabbage-smelling dining-room, a room with a glass roof built out over what had once been the garden of the house. Three long tables covered with white American cloth filled the main space, there was an iron stove, which gave the minimum of heat and the maximum of fumes during the winter. In the winter the rain drummed dismally on the glass roof. In the summer the girls wilted beneath the heat. It was a combined dining and recreation room, the only place where they could sit during their few free hours. Mrs Harding had her own parlour where the heads of departments and the first sales were allowed to eat and sit.

Breakfast consisted of thin porridge with no milk, weak tea, slices of bread and margarine, and plum and apple jam, runny from being watered down in the kitchen, so, Mrs Harding explained, that it would spread better.

At eight o'clock another bell sounded and the ladies went across the road to the back entrance of the main shop, where they checked in under the eye of the staff manager, before proceeding to their departments to take down the dust sheets, dust and polish counters and display stands.

Dwyer & Netherby Ltd consisted of four large houses in Oxford Street knocked into one continuous shop, linked by imposing arches. The glove department was on the ground floor. The shop was carpeted in moss green, the ceilings and connecting archways were painted cream, the cornices heavily gilded, the fittings and showcases were all mahogany and plate glass, and at each counter stood two bentwood chairs for the customers to sit down. The assistants never sat down. From eight am to eight pm, apart from an hour for lunch and half-an-hour for tea, they stood until their legs ached, and their feet burned.

All cash payments were sent to the general counting house on the entresol floor by a system of overhead wires on which were attached small wooden, screw-fastened tubs. The invoice and money were placed in the tubs and projected by a spring. Any change and the invoice were returned in the same way, a system which confused Betsy the first week: she was always sending the money without the bill.

At 8.30 am precisely Mr Netherby's door on the entresol opened. He stood for a brief minute, looking down at the glove and handkerchief departments below him, and then slowly walked down the wide circular staircase, flanked with potted palms, and made his round of inspection, followed by Herbert, nervous and self-conscious, who, though he despised his father, tried, with no success, to emulate his menacing dignity.

Mr Netherby's coldly observant eyes missed nothing. His hands, and Herbert's, were clasped beneath the tails of their frock coats.

Viola had her back to the counter, arranging boxes. Through the mirror behind the counter she saw Mr Netherby approaching. She recognized the expression. It was one she usually aroused in men of his age, type and position. The sort of man who thought a good-looking girl working for a low wage was fair game. She had a momentary qualm—she could sense trouble ahead with Mr Netherby. She continued to concentrate on her work, despite Miss Heath's hissed, 'Miss Corbett! Leave that!' and with an ingratiating change of tone, 'Good morning. Mr Netherby. Mr Herbert.'

'Good morning to you, Miss Heath,' Arthur said. He twirled his perfectly groomed moustache, eyeing that slender, indifferent back, that tantalizing white nape of neck with the small red curls. If Viola was due for an inquisition or reproval no sign of it showed in his beaming face. 'So *this* is our new young lady?'

Viola swung round, her head tilted a little, and smiled her frank, lovely smile. Arthur Netherby ran a hand round his high starched collar, and a slight perspiration broke out on his domed bald forehead.

He made an unprecedented gesture—he extended his hand in welcome. Miss Heath paled.

'Father,' stammered Herbert, on a note of protest. His father, the owner of the store, offering his hand to a *new junior assistant!* It was unheard of! Everyone in sight was watching furtively, pretending to be about their work of dusting and display. By midday, gossip about the Guv'nor's new fancy would be all over the store and the embarrassing hints and innuendoes would begin again. He knew it so well. Every time a pretty girl came into the store. His father might be a fine businessman but he was a fool about women.

'Well, sir, well?' demanded Arthur ferociously, dropping Viola's hand at the unexpected interception.

'Don't you think—' Herbert pointed vaguely towards the display—'I wondered if, perhaps, pink, is *quite* . . . *quite* the thing for gloves . . . ?'

'Pink?' roared Arthur, and Herbert's pince-nez tinkled down on to his waistcoat button at the end of a black cord. 'Why *not* pink? It *is* spring. A nice touch.' He looked, not at the daisies but directly at Viola, and held out his hand again, saying, 'Very pretty. Very pretty indeed. I hope you will be happy with us, Miss—er—Corbett?'

Viola gave him her hand briefly—she had no choice—and withdrew it quickly, but not before she had felt a significant pressure on her palm. Her colour did not heighten nor her eyes waver. She was used to such situations.

'Thank you, sir,' she said gravely, and it was Mr Netherby who looked confused.

He turned furiously on Herbert. 'Well, come along, sir, come along. What are you dawdling for?' Herbert, who was doing everything in his power to get away, tried to think of something to say. But his father was striding off into the next department. Turning, Herbert saw the new assistant press her hand to her mouth to repress a smile, and that everyone in the department, except Miss Heath, was doing the same.

At about 11.30 in the morning a hansom cab trotted round the corner of Lower Belgrave Street and drew up outside one of the handsome terraced mansions of Belgrave Square. Lord Staffray, resplendent in the scarlet jacket and bearskin of his regiment, carrying in his white-gloved hand a charming gilt basket in which red roses, lily-of-the-valley and Parma violets were arranged amongst a small cloud of maidenhair fern, alighted, and threw the cabby his fare. He ran up the steps and, ignoring the knocker, beat a sharp tattoo on the front door with his swagger cane.

Everyone in the house heard it, including his mother who was lying on a chaise longue in her boudoir, and everyone's face lit up, from the butler to the little scullery maid in the basement. They said to each other, 'There's Lord Jim come to see his mother. Bless his heart!'

The butler threw the door wide open, his distant and austere face breaking into uncharacteristic smiles of welcome.

'Your lordship. My lady will be so pleased to see you before she leaves on Monday.'

'Hallo, Bradman.'

James took off the tall bearskin and handed it to Bradman with his cane and spotless white kid gloves. Bradman was an old servant who had been in the family since before James was born. Before taking his gift of flowers upstairs James hesitated. 'Bradman.' His blue eyes clouded with anxiety. He worshipped his mother. 'How is her ladyship? It's nothing serious, is it?'

'No more than usual, my lord. Her ladyship felt that the season might be too much for her.'

'You're travelling with her, Bradman?'

'Yes, m'lord. And Castle.'

'I shan't worry then. I know you'll look after her.' He touched the man's shoulder gratefully. If James Staffray had one great quality it was what a poet of his time called 'the common touch'. Servants worshipped him, his troopers would die for him. An exacting employer and a strict disciplinarian in his army career, he could express tender concern and gratitude towards his inferiors. Lord Staffray was a real gentleman, they said. He has a feeling heart, not like some, who would order you about and treat you like dirt. James disliked sullen, discontented folk, so he merely tried to make everyone about him happy. 'Where is the Countess going?'

'To Lake Maggiore, my lord. Then to Florence and Rome, and when it becomes hot we shall travel to Marienbad. Her ladyship is in her boudoir, my lord.'

The splendid house had been bought by his grandfather when his parents had first married, as a London home for the fashionable young couple, but now it was only occupied for a few months of the year.

The paving of the large hall, the wide shallow staircase, and the Corinthian pillars carrying the arch of the ceiling, were all made from Travertino marble, cream, brown and red, especially imported from Italy. The balustrade of the stairs was in wrought-iron. In the curved well of the staircase stood a large *jardinière* where ferns and orchids, sent down from the hothouses of Louderdown, were stepped in a mass of colour and perfume. Family portraits, interspersed by some valuable paintings, hung on the walls. On the hall-stand stood a silver salver stacked with visiting cards.

Everyone called, but the Countess seldom returned a call. The days when his father would leave Louderdown to do the London season were long past, and his mother hated the fashionable London round as much as she hated shooting and hunting parties. When he had finished at Sandhurst and joined his regiment James had fled from the mausoleum, as he called it, to take bachelor rooms in Half Moon Street.

James hoped his mother would not start lecturing him about getting married. So far he had not met one woman in his own set whom he had the slightest desire to marry. He had met plenty of pretty girls whose company he had enjoyed, but his mother, naturally, did not know about them.

With his hand raised to rap on his mother's boudoir door, he remembered the girl in the train. The girl called Viola Corbett, the girl with the mass of red hair, the slow-lifting white lids over dark gold-green eyes, and the quick, ready laugh. Was it a month ago? Never in his whole life had he met a woman who had attracted him so much. The temptation to get in touch with Matt Lyttelton to find her again had tormented him, but he sensed danger in that brief mutual attraction.

He drew in a long breath of regret, for in spite of his virile strength, his assurance and sophistication, he was still only a very young man. He knocked, and his mother called for him to come in.

The Countess of Louderdown was resting on a heap of satin and lace-edged cushions, a fine lacy Shetland shawl about her shoulders. She was wearing a loose tea-gown of pale satin, heavily trimmed with flounces and frills of cream coloured lace. Her pretty delicate face rose from a froth of lace, the thinness of the beautiful hands was accentuated by the cascades of lace about her wrists. Her fine white hair was dressed high and her face was most skilfully and delicately painted, so that she looked like a Dresden china marquise, exquisite and fragile. The Louderdowns were lucky that their son and heir had inherited both their finer points, the Earl's magnificent physique and his wife's magnificent colouring, the brilliant blue eyes, the tempting, curling mouth, the thick, clustering light brown hair which the summer sun would bleach to gold.

'Mama.' James went across to his mother, and lifting her slightly towards him, he kissed her gently on the cheek, then tucked her feather-light body up against the back of the satin chaise longue again. The pretty room with its satin striped wallpaper and gilded cornices, decorated in delicate lilac and rose colours, had silver framed photographs standing everywhere, mostly of James throughout his childhood and adolescence.

He put the basket of flowers in her lap, and she touched it with joy.

'My darling. How lovely!' Lady Louderdown placed her hand on his broad shoulder with the gold laced epaulettes and captain's stars, and said, 'Why are you in uniform, James? I was hoping you'd stay to lunch. I have one or two charming people coming—that nice girl of Mountjoy's . . . Now, don't pull a face!'

'I can't, Mama,' he said, glad to have a genuine reason for avoiding the suitable débutante she had invited. 'I know Miss Mountjoy is delightful, but there's a Drawing Room and I'm on duty. I'll have a hock and seltzer with you here, and a sandwich. No, don't get up—I'll ring.'

He rang the bell, and Bradman came in and took the order. For the next ten minutes preparations for the luncheon party stopped while the cook carefully made a plateful of sandwiches for James alone with pâté with truffles, cold salmon and breast of duckling. Bradman brought them on a tray which he set on a small table, opened a bottle of chilled hock and poured the drink.

'Anything else, m'lady?'

'Tell Castle to come up to dress me for lunch in half an hour. That will be all.'

'Yes, m'lady.' The door closed silently behind him, and James said anxiously, 'What's this about being ill? D'you really feel unwell, dearest? What does Sir Bainbridge say?'

'Oh, doctors! It is just my miserable nerves. But he says I must have a rest. So I'm slipping off to Florence.'

'Wouldn't it be better to go to Monte or Biarritz?'

'Oh, darling, no! They are always full of all the people one expressly wants to avoid. No, I have taken rooms in Florence. I so wanted to open up the house properly, and ask a lot of nice young people for you to meet this year.'

'Mama, I'm not a girl. You haven't got to marry me off.'

'But you *must* get married, James. You are twenty-six.' He made a grimace of mock despair, and she went on more sternly, 'You must settle down soon. I don't know what you want in a woman . . . I worry sometimes that you have tastes like your father. I have heard that you spend riotous times with quite unpresentable young women, actresses and such and yet, when you meet someone like Elizabeth Mountjoy, you run away!' He pretended to look ashamed, so she gave him a little slap, and then leaned forward to kiss him.

'Mama, I'll find a wife in my own good time. So far as Elizabeth is concerned, everything is wrong with her.'

'I thought I might have a small ball here. Nothing great. About a hundred people—some of your friends from the regiment, and some really nice girls . . .'

'Mama!' he said in exasperation. 'The trouble with me is, the girls I like you would not want me to marry.'

The laughter left her face, her fine blue eyes became icy with suspicion. 'Someone special?'

He hesitated. Should he be honest and tell her about the shop girl with the red-gold hair and the buttercups in her bonnet? He knew it would be madness. She would not go to Florence. She would worry herself into nervous collapse. He shook his head, and lied. 'No one special.'

'James, is there any more talk of war in South Africa?' The big eyes looked at him fearfully, and she seemed to shrivel and age.

'No more,' he assured her hastily, although the regiment like many others was down at Aldershot, fitting out. Only his company was in London at the moment for guard duties, and at any moment they could get the word to join the battalion. 'Don't look like that, little Mama. I'm sure those Boers won't go to war. They have too much sense to take on the British Army. They're only untrained farmers.'

'James . . . *promise* me . . . *promise* me that you *won't* get into any naughty fixes? With someone—well, some girl, we could not *possibly* countenance . . . not while I am abroad. You will be good while I am away, won't you?'

'I am always good, Mama darling. Now I must get over to the Palace.'

'Is it the Queen receiving?'

'No, she's not well enough. She's still at Osborne. It will be Princess B. or His Nibs. What time is your train? I'll come to Victoria to see you off.'

'Ten-thirty on Monday. You haven't promised. Say I promise you, Mama, I will not chase after worthless girls, and I will try to find someone you and Papa and Louderdown will be proud of and welcome as my wife.'

For answer he stood up, picked her up and kissed her, so that when he set her down again she was laughing like a girl . . .

'I can't remember all that. But I do promise, take it as said. Good-bye, precious. Ten-thirty at the boat train. I'll be there.'

He ran downstairs, twitching his scarlet tunic straight, his epaulettes and gold braid gleaming like his closely brushed hair. He knew there was a dreadful seriousness behind her foolishness. To be of a great family, to be rich, to have vast estates, and only have one child, and that child an officer in Her Majesty's Army. He always felt guilty because he had insisted on going to Sandhurst from school and knew even his father would not have permitted it had there not been a great army tradition in the family. But the Earls of Louderdown and their sons who had fought and survived or fought and died at Blenheim, at Waterloo and out on the Empire frontiers, had been sons among many sons. The Louderdowns had always had large families until the present time. He was all his mother and father and Louderdown had. If he was ordered to Africa and killed they would be heartbroken, and Louderdown would go to some obscure cousin of his father. But James had never wanted to be anything but a soldier, so reluctantly they had given way.

'Get me a cab, Bradman,' he called.

'I took the liberty, m'lord, of telling them to harness up the carriage for you. It does the horses good to have a turn, and her ladyship isn't going out today. I expect, m'lord, you'll be having the use of it while we are in foreign parts. As usual.'

'Thank you, Bradman. Nothing like arriving in style.'

He pulled on his gloves, picked up his bearskin, while Bradman ran a proprietory eye over his broad shoulders for any hair or face powder from her ladyship's embrace.

The elegant light landau with its smart bay cob stood at the door when he ran down the steps. He looked up and saw his mother waving from the first floor drawing room window, and he waved back. From this distance she looked frail and as sweet as a young girl, and his heart ached with protective tenderness for her. Well, he could not do anything about the country going to war or his regiment abroad, but he could keep his promise about girls and that meant, of course, no effort to find Viola Corbett. Because he knew for certain that if he deliberately sought her, it would mean something far deeper than what his mother called a 'nasty fix'. It would mean something deep, and wild, and joyous and abandoned—something that would go on for years. Perhaps for ever. He sighed despondently as he drove towards the Palace.

It was the middle of June. The weather was fine, the London season had started. The young ladies working at Netherby's were on their feet all day serving customers, and too tired to do anything but tumble into bed after they had put away the goods, covered the models and displays with dust sheets, marched back across the road and eaten their late supper.

Viola and Betsy had been in London for two months. The food and the general cleanliness of the hostel had improved after Viola's complaints. This had not improved Viola's popularity with the housekeeper.

Herbert Netherby was becoming increasingly anxious, because his father could not hide his infatuation for the new assistant. He told his sister about it as he escorted her to her bible class. She had noticed that the new assistant did not attend. Every attractive woman their father met was a threat to them. Weak and misguided men were known to marry young wives *and* to leave their money to them over the heads of their rightful heirs.

'There have been other occasions, Emily, which I have not troubled you about, but this is different. He is making himself ridiculous. Everyone on the staff is talking and laughing about it.' When agitated he invariably plucked nervously at his stock, his gloves, or took off his pince-nez and replaced them. 'He simply cannot pass her in the shop without stopping to speak to her. If Miss Heath or Mrs Harding make a complaint he ignores it.'

'I expect she is playing him up.'

'Then she is being *ever* so clever about it,' Herbert said pettishly. 'She *pretends* not to notice him. As though she could help it!'

Emily and Herbert Netherby were frightened. The idea of a step-mother younger than themselves appalled them. Their father had never been generous with them, Herbert was paid the same salary as the other floor-walkers, and Emily subsisted on a meagre dress-allowance and weekly pocket money. They remained dutiful and obedient because of their comfortable, luxurious home and the fortune they would, one day, inherit. For these benefits they suffered Arthur's sarcasm and sadistic bullying. When they thought of his obsession for the alluring newcomer they almost wished he had married Miss Heath. She would be preferable to a young and beautiful stranger.

It was closing time on Friday, the height of the season and they had been frantically busy. But now the last customer had left, the last overhead container whirred along the wires to the cashiers. Betsy and Viola, their legs aching, put away their stock and dust-covered the displays.

Miss Heath nodded coldly as she went up to collect the wages. The thing she found most irritating about Viola was that she could not fault her work. She made up for this by picking on Betsy who was apt to lose her head if criticized before a customer, relying on Viola's swift protection, smoothly intervening, soothing the customer, checking Betsy's bills and seeing her stock was in order.

Mr Netherby was in the counting house—he was always there when the wages were being paid out. He picked up Miss Heath's wage packets and handed them to her personally. He seemed full of good nature.

'You see, you were wrong about Miss Corbett,' he said benignly. 'She is every bit as good as her reference. She has made more commission than anyone in your department this month, including yourself.'

Miss Heath went huffily back to her department to find everything in order, and the three girls and the apprentice waiting for their money. She took her own pay packet first and handed over the other four, wishing them good night.

Viola opened her packet, checking her commission with thoroughness. Inside the money she found a folded note. Falling behind the other girls as they went towards the back entrance, she read it quickly. It was from Arthur Netherby.

> *'Dear Miss Corbett, I would be delighted and honoured if you would dine with me, tomorrow, Saturday night. If you are free, and would like to do this, just leave this envelope on the counter, and I shall see it on my way out. If it is not there I shall be very disap-*

*pointed. But if you decide in my favour, will you meet me at 8.30, in
the foyer of Franconeri's Restaurant. I will see you have no difficulties over the late night pass and key. Your sincere admirer, A.N.'*

In the weeks she had been in London, Viola had been waiting for James Staffray, certain that he would seek her out. He had not. Yet she knew from Matthew's occasional references that he was back in London. On her free Saturdays and Sundays she had gone out with some of the boys who worked in Netherby's, insisting on paying her own way because they earned very little more than she did. They walked in the park and took tea and buns in ABCs or, greatly daring, went up in the galleries of the music halls. Matthew had accompanied Viola and Betsy to the Zoological Gardens, Madame Tussaud's and the Science Museum. It was all very well for Betsy to go pink with fear at the Chamber of Horrors and cling to Matthew's arm so that he, too, went pink in embarrassed delight, but these pleasures were not what Viola had expected from London.

She wanted the great world. She wanted to go into one of the fine restaurants and dance to their orchestras; she wanted to go to the theatres, ride in carriages, wear lovely clothes, eat delicious food. At the music hall she peered down from the gallery at the ladies and gentlemen in evening clothes, thronging into the stalls. She peeped through the plate glass of the smart restaurants, longing to be inside where everyone looked so rich, well-dressed and leisured. In the park on Sundays she searched among the riders, and the open carriages where the ladies looked like flowers in a basket with their big feathered hats, and little silk parasols. She looked for London life as she had dreamed it, and she looked for James Staffray.

Viola knew he was far above her, a rich young aristocrat. She knew that to imagine anything further than a pleasant flirtation was absurd. And yet, as they had talked together in the dining car coming from Leeds, she had been as certain that he desired her, and would seek her out, as she had ever been of anything in her life.

But two months had passed, and she was bored, and the spring nights seemed to beckon with adventure. She did not want to walk in the park or see the Elgin Marbles. And perhaps, if she went to a restaurant like Franconeri's she might see James again.

Standing just concealed within the archway into the next department, Arthur Netherby saw her read his note, and put it away. She went towards the back of the shop with the other girls, laughing and talking, and his disappointment was so great that he put out a hand against a showcase to steady himself.

Anger possessed him. It was all he could do not to call after them and curse her. The bitch! Who did she think she was? Did she imagine just because she had a good figure and pretty face that she could play fast and loose with Arthur Netherby? He would throw her out without a reference, and that stupid girl friend of hers!

Then he saw her speak to her companions, come back as though she had forgotten something, and with a reckless little gesture, toss the envelope on to the empty counter. He heard the staff door close. There was no one there but himself and the night watchman. He picked up the envelope and put it in his breast pocket, and went back to his office to compose himself, for he was shaking with relief.

CHAPTER THREE

Count Eugene Erhmann arrived by the early evening train from Paris and, accompanied by his manservant, took a cab to his London flat, which was situated in one of the new apartment buildings in Victoria Street.

Eugene rarely occupied the flat for more than a week at a time, as he lived mostly in Vienna. His flat was considered very up-to-date with electric lighting and a large, elaborate lift like a huge bird cage hissing conveniently up and down at the touch of a button. There was also a hall-porter, a certain amount of service and steam heating, quite in the American and Continental style, but foreign to England where anyone who was anyone had, from time immemorial, lived in a house.

Eugene also had that modern innovation, a telephone, installed, and as soon as he arrived, he lifted the receiver, turned the hand-wheel, and got in touch with his broker.

Eugene had investments in South Africa, both in gold and diamonds, and he was buying heavily on the market. As the threat of war between England and the Boers grew, with the likelihood of trade being interrupted, he was certain that the more stocks one held, the better one's position would be when hostilities ceased. History had taught him that hostilities invariably did this sooner or later, and one must be prepared for the rising market that would follow.

His stockbroker, a serious businessman but also a gay man-about-town, was a fellow after Eugene's heart, and he was delighted to hear from him. They had a long conversation and made an appointment for the following Monday, and then Grant Eckersley said, 'Are you free tonight, Gene? I have a little party at Franconeri's. You know the Gaiety is shut down while they rehearse the new show? Some friends and I are taking four of the girls to dinner; the poor little pets get so miffed rehearsing all day, and no fun. Won't you join us?'

'I will not be *de trop?*'

'My dear fellow, of course not. We shall be delighted. Eight-thirty then? I'll look forward to seeing you.'

Eugene went into the comfortable sitting-room. His man brought his dressing gown and slippers, a Scotch and soda, which he considered one of the more civilized British tastes, and all the evening papers.

'I'll be dining out, Vatel. Run me a bath in about an hour. You can take the evening off.'

'Merci, m'sieu.'

Eugene settled with his exceptional powers of concentration to read the disquieting news from South Africa, and to analyse the world stock markets in conjunction with it. The Erhmann family was an old aristocratic one. They had a small ancient *schloss* on the Danube and a fine eighteenth-century mansion in Vienna, now converted into large and luxurious apartments, both of which Eugene, the last of the family, owned.

He should have been an army officer of high degree attached to the Imperial Court, but his father had married the only daughter of a Jewish banker and Eugene had inherited the fine blond looks of the Ehrmanns and the financial wizardry of his mother's family. To his father's astonished dismay, he went into finance.

He was nearly forty years old, a bachelor, tall, fair-skinned, grey-eyed, with the profile of a bored, aristocratic eagle. Money was the main purpose of his life; not in possessing it, which he did, nor in spending it, and no one knew better how to do that, but in manipulating it. The stock markets of the world were to him an enormous game of baccarat, at which he was a superb player, and which never bored him. Boredom was his enemy. It waited, like a grey ghost, to catch him unawares.

He spoke several languages. His taste and sophistication were by-words in European capitals: it was said he had the ear of the Emperor and the confidence of millionaires. He had known a great many women, all beautiful, and some talented, but had never married. Jealous rumour made him a Tsarist agent or international spy. Actually Eugene was merely a very clever man, caught in a life which had given him every gift but love.

He had thought of dining at his London club and having an early night. But he liked theatre people; they were hard-working, charming and amusing, so he was quite pleased to bathe, allow Vatel to shave him, to put on his evening clothes, complete with scarlet-lined cape, opera hat and ivory cane, and, just after eight, ask the hall-porter to summon a cab for him to drive to Franconeri's Restaurant in Oxford Street.

It was a beautiful summer evening—not too hot. The sort of evening when great cities, under the clear, transparent sunset light, take on the appearance of Old Masters. Grey stone and worn red brick, huge London plane trees heavy with leaves, the gleam of a scarlet uniform, a gilded tower, the shimmer of the wide grey river bearing the black barges with their rusty sails; the sudden magical opening up of familiar vistas as the cab bowled along past Parliament and the Abbey, along Whitehall, past

Inigo Jones' great Banqueting Hall and the window on the room from which Charles Stuart walked to his execution.

A well-read, well-informed man, Eugene liked the big old cities of Europe, their foundations sunk in history, where the new slotted effortlessly into the ancient past.

Sitting behind the apron of the open cab, he lit a cigar, and as he was driven through Trafalgar Square and up the gradual, book-lined slope of Charing Cross Road, he looked, to the average Londoner, the perfect picture of a 'great swell'. The comfortable, well-off, well bred, cosmopolitan man-about-town.

The season was in full swing, and carriages, open because of the heat, were taking people to theatres, restaurants, receptions and the opera. The men were all in formal evening clothes, for at that period the dinner-jacket, or 'le smoking' as the French so quaintly called it, was never worn when ladies were present. The ladies were beautiful in their chiffons, satins and feathers, their shoulders bare except for jewels, their arms hidden by long kid gloves, the bosoms of their gowns garnished with clusters of hot-house flowers.

Eugene was early and his party had not yet arrived. Franconeri himself greeted him delightedly, and assured him that the table had been booked on the ground floor, not too near the orchestra.

'A good position, I hope—tonight we are entertaining pretty ladies who like to be admired.'

'The Signor Count would like to sit at the table?'

'No. I'll have a hock and seltzer at the bar, and perhaps you'd get me the latest newspaper.'

'Si, si, at once.'

The bar of Franconeri's restaurant opened immediately out of the large circular vestibule from which a double flight of stairs with gilded banisters mounted to a circular gallery leading to the private rooms on the first floor. The vestibule was paved with white marble, the stairs carpeted in crimson. From the glass dome above, hung an enormous gilt and cut-glass electric chandelier. Below it, in the vestibule, was an ice-packed stand upon which were displayed a wealth of tempting and expensive delicacies. Huge scarlet lobsters, pale turquoise eggs, peaches, asparagus, strawberries and globe artichokes like huge green flowers.

Standing at the bar Eugene Erhmann read the flaring headlines. President Steyn had placed large orders with Germany for Mausers and cartridges to arm the rapidly forming Transvaal army. He had investments in Krupp, so he would not lose money whatever happened. Both sides now wanted war, and he felt certain that it had gone beyond negotiation.

He put the paper down on the bar, to watch the vestibule for the arrival of his party, and saw Viola come through the main entrance, and stand, hesitatingly, looking around her. Instantly his attention was caught.

Afterwards he could not say exactly what it was about her that attracted him, apart from her magnificent and undeniable beauty. She was not, as were all the women dining at Franconeri's that night, in full evening dress. The peridot green muslin had elbow sleeves and a modest décolletage. He guessed that it had cost about £2 in a West End store. If she had chosen it to dramatize her creamy skin and wonderful hair she could not have made a better choice. Her one piece of jewellery was a gold chain with a small enamelled watch, and in her hair and at the cleft of her lovely high breasts were small pink roses. Accustomed to women who could spend a fortune on one evening's *toilette* he was enchanted. The child had dressed herself within a £5 note, and had not made a single error.

It was, perhaps, her manner that fascinated him most of all. It was quite obviously her first time at a public place as expensive as Franconeri's. She did not seem overawed, or embarrassed at being alone in a place where all the women were escorted. She appeared to have two qualities which carried her on wings. Her belief in her own splendid beauty and a kind of crazy innocence, the sort of naive belief that is only held by the very young, very desired, and very healthy, that no harm can possibly befall them. He saw her look at the magnificent display of food, at the rose-shaded lights in the restaurant, beyond which the orchestra could now be heard playing a popular waltz. She seemed to him like a lovely young cat animal, a lioness, cautiously emerging from the sheltering jungle.

He waited a second or two, but no one came forward to claim her, and he then deliberately approached her, saying with quiet courtesy, 'Can I help you, *gnädige fräulein?*'

The heavy-lidded, long-lashed eyes lifted, bright with interest. She looked him over, and decided he was trustworthy. He felt, ridiculously, for a man of his age and position, that he was honoured.

'I have to meet a friend here,' she said. 'He's late it seems.' Her voice was pleasant, low-pitched, her accent, as a foreigner, he could not place. He only knew it was not the flat London whine. Her smile was sudden, wide, self-mocking, confiding. 'To tell the truth, sir, I've never been to this sort of place before. What should I do?'

'The best thing,' he said, smiling, 'is to ask Franconeri if your host has made a reservation. *Padrone, prego . . .*'

'Signor le Count?'

'What is the name of your friend, *mademoiselle?*'

'Netherby. Mr Arthur Netherby.'

'Has Mr Netherby made a reservation?'

'*Si, signor.* For eight o'clock, a private room. Number four on the gallery.'

The count felt shocked. For all his experience he had not for a moment thought she would be dining in one of the discreet and luxurious upstairs rooms.

'You see—' he turned to her—'your host has booked a private dining-room. The *maître d'hôtel* will show you the way.'

Viola's delicate dark brows drew together, puzzled.

'Private? What does that mean?' she asked.

At that moment, Arthur Netherby, flushed with anxiety at being late, large and ovoid within the great expanse of white shirt front, came hurrying through the door. Immediately following him came Eugene's party of four young men-about-town, and what seemed an absolute bower of beautifully dressed professional beauties, capturing everyone's attention as they were accustomed to take the footlights at The Gaiety.

Eugene was drawn into a hubbub of introductions and enthusiastic greetings, and Netherby, not realizing he had been speaking to Viola, seized her arm with a greedy and proprietory air, and hurried her towards the stairs.

'This way, m'dear. Sorry I'm late. Unavoidable . . . such a crush of traffic. I got out of the cab in the end and walked. The waiter should have shown you up. I thought a nice little dinner to ourselves, no interruptions . . .'

Eugene watched her being led away, saw her little resentful frown as she looked down over the banisters towards the restaurant, full of people and music, where she would so obviously rather be. Viola glanced over his party, with a touch of envy for the gay chattering girls, and met Eugene's eyes. She gave a little smile and an appealing shrug. She was no lamb being led to the slaughter, just an unsophisticated provincial girl wondering why on earth anyone should prefer to dine in a private room instead of in the busy, glamorous and interesting restaurant.

'If you will excuse me,' Eugene said to his party, and went to where Franconeri and his *major-domo* consulted their reservation book.

'Is it Number four that has the piano—where I gave the musical party to Madame Piastrelli last year?'

'No, signor, that was Number five, in the next room. The rooms connect if you remember, and you engaged them both.'

'A most successful evening.' Eugene put a sovereign on the reservation book. 'Don't book Number five tonight.'

'But are you not dining with Mr Eckersley?'

'Yes. But I wish Number five to be kept empty. Which waiter will be serving Mr Netherby?'

Franconeri and the *major-domo* exchanged a glance and Franconeri spread his expressive Italian hands in protest. Eugene shook his head.

'No scenes, my friend, I promise. More likely a scene if you don't tell me. The young lady, with Mr Netherby, does not, I think, quite understand her position.'

The two Italians exchanged another glance, and Franconeri nodded. The *major-domo* called over a young waiter.

'Jacomi is serving in Number four.'

'Ah, Jacomi. A word.' Eugene drew the young man aside, placing a sovereign in his hand. 'If the young lady dining in Number four upstairs shows any sign of distress, or anger, or wishes to leave, would you let me know? No fuss. Just come to me in the restaurant and say I am wanted. And, Jacomi—' he produced another small gold coin—'unlock the door between Numbers four and five. No need to tell anyone.'

'*Si, si signor.*' Jacomi gave a broad and understanding smile, but the cool grey eyes gave no encouragement for confidences. The waiter pocketed the two gold coins and made his way upstairs, carrying an ice bucket containing two bottles of champagne. On the way to Number four diningroom he stopped in the heavily-carpeted, gold-papered corridor, slipped into Number 5 and silently slid back the lock.

Earlier in the evening, while Viola was upstairs dressing, Betsy had been sitting at the long bleak table, covered with American cloth, in the diningroom of Dwyer & Netherby's hostel, eating her evening meal.

As it was Saturday all the other girls had gone out; Saturday night was the night for the park, promenading from Marble Arch to Hyde Park Corner in their best clothes, arm in arm, making eyes at the groups of young shop assistants or city clerks who hung about, fondly hoping to be mistaken for society men.

Viola had created a sensation in her new green gown which she had bought only that morning from the dress department. As she had no opera cloak she put her fine wool lace shawl over her head, lightly, like a mantilla, with the moss rose in her hair just showing. Betsy thought she looked glorious. She did not mind her going out without her, but she guessed where she was going, and this filled her with anxiety, for she had been taught that unprincipled rich men preyed on innocent working girls, and she did not think that Mr Netherby was a nice man at heart.

'You look champion, Vi,' she said. 'You look a real Duchess, like the girls call you. You—you will be good, won't you?'

Viola laughed and hugged her. In her opinion Arthur Netherby was no sexual temptation, although she guessed he might be hard to handle. But in a public restaurant there was nothing he could do that she could not counter. She was longing to have a dinner, like dear old Sam Hardcastle used to buy her at the fine country hotels within reach of Leeds.

'Aren't you going out, love?'

'No. The girls asked me, but I didn't want to go.'

'You don't like mashers? Their sort of fellow?' Viola said shrewdly, and then, unexpectedly: 'Why don't you go to church? There's an evening service, isn't there?'

Betsy remembered there was evensong at St Botolph's.

Viola kissed her. 'Well, do as you like, love, but don't keep awake for me. I shan't be too late, I promise.'

When Viola had gone Betsy went back into the dining-room, which was empty except for two middle-aged women, alteration hands, who sat together near the empty stove as though they could still feel its winter heat.

Betsy, unlike most girls, had never even entertained the idea that some man, at some future time, might want to marry her. Why should anyone feel like that about her? She was both poor and plain, too prudish and reserved to like the rough, working-class boys or the skinny, smart-alec young counter-jumpers the other girls went out with, the 'fellas' with their greased-down quiffs, their immature moustaches, their high, hard, celluloid collars, their heavily doggish airs, their nudging winking 'hot' jokes, scared her to death.

As she looked at the two faded women she was filled with a poignant dread, wondering what the future held for her. She was not very good at selling. Perhaps she would end up like these two in their brave, shabby finery, sitting in the deserted dining-room with nowhere else to go.

Betsy thought wistfully of Matthew Lyttelton. Sometimes on Saturday or Sunday afternoon she and Viola would walk in the park and it was surprising how often they ran into him, and he would join them.

Betsy was not quite sure why he accompanied them, a gentleman like him, because it was obvious that he did not quite approve of Viola, who often shocked him. Her enthusiasm, for instance, for the suffragettes who held their meetings at Hyde Park Corner.

'Oh, Miss Corbett,' he would say, 'I cannot believe you would really support these viragos. You are saying it just to tease us. A woman should be modest and gentle, and support her husband in every way. That is what being a help-meet means in the truly Christian sense.'

Viola would laugh, and say there were two worlds, one for men and one for women, and the men had the best of it every time. But Betsy agreed with him, and envied the modest gentle girl who might one day be lucky enough to be his wife.

She looked up at the dining-hall clock and realized she could be at St Botolph's just in time for the service.

Matthew was taking the service, and the church was half-empty, because the chief attendance was for Mr Everard's eloquent and accusing sermons, bringing hell-fire and the glory of the golden gate equally near. She slipped into a pew right at the back of the church, knelt down and said a little prayer.

When Matthew, warbling away in his light uncertain tenor, saw the little black hat bob into place far down the aisle. He hesitated slightly and in embarrassment coloured to the thin brown hair on his forehead. Completely forgetting where he was, he broke into a delighted smile.

Betsy felt herself shaking. Cautiously she peered about her, but there were no other worshippers nearby. There was no doubt, no doubt at all, that the welcoming smile was for her alone. She could hardly believe it.

After the service she drifted down Tewkesbury Square in the evening light. Through the trees, Mr Netherby's house reflected it in panes of bright gold. Everything seemed extraordinarily clear and beautiful and she felt so happy, not for any reason in particular, because life was just the same. She simply felt blessed.

Matthew hurriedly took off his cassock and surplice and picked up his jacket and shovel hat. The choir boys were chasing about, scrapping and fooling, while the organist and choir master tried to hurry them out. Matthew nipped out by the side door, and looked along the square. He saw Betsy's small, black-hatted figure walking slowly along in the rosy sunset light and experienced a strange trembling sensation.

He knew he should not go after her, and that to do so in Tewkesbury Square itself would be fraught with danger; any of his parishioners might see him. For the curate of St Botolph's to be seen walking with a shop girl was nearly as immoral as to be seen with a prostitute. A gentleman could only have dishonest intentions towards one of such an inferior station.

It was one thing meeting Viola and Betsy, apparently by chance, in the crowded park—they were, after all, members of his congregation and it was his duty to be courteous to them. But in Tewkesbury Square he could easily be seen by the jealous Miss Netherby or her preening, patronizing brother, both of whom would consider it their duty to report the matter to the Vicar or even to Mrs Everard, a lady of paralysing virtue, who regarded all young curates as upstarts and sluggards. Whenever Matthew prayed, he prayed for forgiveness, for his lack of charity towards this small group of people who had such power over his behaviour in or out of church. Sometimes he thought of giving up the whole thing and becoming a tutor but his mother depended on him and his stipend at St Botolph's was comparatively generous.

But the summer evening was enchanting; the small, pensive figure of Betsy Holder was walking away, very slowly down the north side of the square—the side furthest from No. 40, and screened from those inquisitive windows by the shrubs and plane trees of the centre gardens.

Suddenly Matthew forgot he was a curate and a gentleman. He pulled down his shovel hat, and sprinted after Betsy like any lad after a girl, and when he was near enough, called her name.

She turned round, surprised, and stood waiting while he caught up with her, wrenched off his hat, and stood breathlessly peering down into the smooth, rosy, short-sighted little face.

'Miss Holder,' he said. 'Betsy, are you thinking of taking an evening walk?'

Betsy swallowed, found her voice, whispered that she was, but that she had to be in by ten o'clock. Matthew consulted the large clock, set rather incongruously into the classic pediment of St Botolph's.

'It is but eight-thirty,' he said, and offered his arm. 'It's not right that you should walk alone. If you will permit me to accompany you?'

Betsy, stunned with joy, put her hand in its darned cotton glove on the shabby black broadcloth of his sleeve. In silence, but extraordinarily happy, they made their way towards Regent's Park.

Viola went with Mr Netherby into the private room and stood looking disconsolately about her. It was attractive enough. A circular room, painted in cream and gold, a large double-door on one side, and on the other three sides, sets of heavily draped curtains. The table was laid for two, and there was a charming épergne of red roses for a centrepiece. The wall mirrors were painted with views of Italian lakes, Venice and the Coliseum in Rome, and a large, highly coloured painting of a luscious Venus being disrobed by a satyr dominated one wall.

Mr Netherby took Viola's shawl and laid it with his cane, top hat and opera cloak on a settee, and drew a chair for her at the table. Jacomi knocked, and came in with the champagne and two large gilded menu cards. Mr Netherby put on his gold pince-nez and began to choose their menu without consulting her. It never crossed his mind that a girl in her position would know anything about food.

'Oysters to start with, I think? A dozen for me,—' he beamed at Viola— 'and for the little lady, half a dozen? Just the thing—oysters to begin our little *diner à deux*. You know what they say about oysters, my dear?'

Viola did, but she looked at him blankly. She had long since learned that if a man was either coarse or suggestive, it was safer to pretend not to understand.

'No oysters, thank you,' she said. 'They make me sick.'

'Oh, come now . . .'

'I don't like them.'

'You've tried them, then?'

'Yes.'

'You've tried a lot of naughty things, I'll be bound,' said Mr Netherby, heavily playful.

Viola suddenly turned away and began to move round the room with her slow, swaying walk; the walk that, when he watched her from the first floor balcony outside his offices, drove him insane.

He *was* going to be tiresome, she was thinking. She had not anticipated a private room. It was not the sort of thing they had in Leeds, at least not in grand places that cost a lot of money. Up there if you spent money on a night out you wanted to be seen and to see everything.

The draped skirt of her gown swished like an angry tail. She went to the first heavy curtain and twitched it back. It was a large window looking out on to the lights and traffic of Oxford Street. She went along to the next heavy parterre; that too was a window—outside was a dark ventilating shaft from which came heavy kitchen smells. Without hurrying she went to the third curtain and found it concealed an alcove with a mirrored ceiling containing a large silk-covered divan strewn with embroidered cushions.

She turned back to Netherby, furious with herself for being so naive. It was exactly what she might have expected from him.

Her eyes met the waiter's and she gave the faintest, appealing little shrug.

Netherby said with irritable haste, 'Bring the oysters and a tray of hors d'oeuvres, pour the champagne and leave us. We will decide what we want to follow and ring for you.'

Jacomi poured the wine and served them; when he held the tray for Viola to take her glass, he gave her a swift, understanding look and his dark eyes seemed full of mischief. As soon as the door closed behind him Netherby was by Viola's side.

'Now, come to the table.' She allowed herself to be led to a chair, and he put the menu before her. 'Isn't this cosy, my dear? Let us choose what to eat so that we need not be disturbed. Here's to your health.' He drank, put down his glass, and Viola felt his moustache tickle the back of her neck, and his lips move over her shoulder. She did not move. He lifted his glass, refilled it and drank again.

'And to our first evening together. The first of many, I hope, for I can do a great deal for you, my dear, as you can guess.'

'I would rather have been in the restaurant,' said Viola. 'It's more fun. You can't even hear the music here.'

'I'm afraid that would be impossible,' he answered testily. 'I am extremely well known in the West End. It would be most indiscreet if I were to be seen dining with a junior member of my staff.'

'I can see that it might,' said Viola reasonably. She could also see he had been drinking before he met her. He put down his glass, his thick clean hands on her shoulders and made a dive towards her lips. Adroitly she swayed away, and rose, sliding from under his hands, moving around the table. It reminded her of a melodrama she had once seen at the theatre in Leeds, where the villain, in full evening dress, had pursued the heroine round a circular table until an irreverent boy in the gallery had shouted bets on the lady and sent the whole house into laughter. The involuntary smile that touched her lips momentarily deceived Netherby.

She was, he decided, young and skittish. Out to give him a run for his money. Well, he liked it that way, for a while.

He drew two chairs close together, and stood leaning on them, smiling with what he imagined was tender invitation.

'Now come and sit down, and don't be a naughty little girl. I don't like naughty, teasing little girls. I shan't eat you—not yet. Don't play the little innocent with me, Duchess. I've been watching you ever since you came to work for me, and you know it, don't you? You little devil!'

Viola stood quite still, looking at him across the crystal and silver and the red roses on the dining table. Her face was calmly beautiful and inscrutable. No one could have guessed the panic that was beginning to rise within her. He took another gulp of champagne. It could not be possible that the girl would refuse to stay? He reached across the table for her hand, spilling the roses, knocking over the glasses, but the white, slender fingers slipped out of his reach.

The blood rose darkly to his forehead. If she had raged, or cried, or pleaded with him, he might have felt magnanimous, but her calm silence infuriated him.

'Mr Netherby,' said Viola, 'it seems to me that we've both made a mistake. I wanted a real night out, with music, and grand folk to watch and some life going on. It looks as though you had quite a different idea. I'm sorry. I am, really. I'd better go.'

'You will not! You bloody well will not leave!' His voice rose furiously as he blundered unsteadily round the table towards her. 'They may call you Duchess at work but I'll not tolerate your high-and-mighty ways. If you value your job you'll sit down and have your dinner, or in the morning you'll be out without a reference from me. Pretending you had no idea what I wanted . . . You're no country cousin. You knew quite well.'

'Yes,' Viola said frankly, 'that's true. But I thought I'd have the right to say no, and I thought if I did you'd be a decent enough sport to let me go.' She picked up her shawl and gloves decisively. 'You didn't think I could be had for the price of a dinner, did you, Mr Netherby? It looks like I've behaved cheaply. If I have, I'm sorry.'

He went over to the door and turned the key.

'You won't leave this room!' he shouted.

Viola could still see the absurd stage scene in her mind. The situation was ridiculous and undignified, and yet there was something menacing about him and for the first time she was frightened. Panic and absurdity fought within her. She put her hands to her mouth, and broke out into uncontrollable laughter. Netherby heard the note of hysteria and saw the fear in her eyes and the anger in his heavy face lit with triumph.

Helplessly she played for time, trying to make him laugh with her. 'It's like a melodrama. The villain still pursued her!' She stretched out her arms theatrically. 'Oh, sir, spare me, I pray you. Think of me aged mother, and me poor fatherless child . . .'

Not a gleam of humour touched his blood-darkened face.

'You are laughing at me,' he said thickly. 'You damned little cheat. I'll teach you that I can't be laughed at.'

Then she was really frightened. The full coarse face had gone pale, and his hands were shaking. She had thought he was just an overbearing, conceited, rich, middle-aged fool . . . but the tormented look told her more than that. It was not just a sordid, foolish escapade that she could get out of with a bit of blarney and a laugh. She meant something to him. In his crude, cruel, blustering way he was trying to conceal it, just as she was trying to conceal her fear. Yet she felt fear was what he wanted from her, just as he wanted it from everyone, his children, his staff. But she could see her teasing was unbearable to him. Suddenly she was not just afraid, she was deeply sorry for him.

'Mr Netherby—I'm sorry, I shouldn't have laughed. I didn't mean to be rude. Please let me go now.'

'You could have it with old Sam Hardcastle, but not with me, eh? We'll see . . .' He lunged over, seized her wrist, and pulled her down into a chair.

Jacomi knocked on the door, and Netherby, beside himself, yelled, 'Leave it outside, you fool . . . I'll ring when I want you.'

Jacomi put the oysters and the hors d'oeuvres down on a dumb waiter which stood outside the door, went downstairs into the restaurant and across to where Eugene Erhmann sat with Grant Eckersley's party.

'The gentleman upstairs is shouting, sir,' he whispered, 'and seems very angry. I think the young lady wants to leave.'

'Thank you,' said Eugene, and rose, smiling urbanely about him. 'Will you excuse me for a moment? As our party is unbalanced I got in touch with a young friend of mine and asked her to join us—if she could get away. She has arrived and I will bring her in.'

He went out into the vestibule and ran lightly up the stairs, slipped into Number 5 dining room—the one with the piano. Voices were raised angrily in the other room, and he heard a sharp noise, like a blow with a open palm. He opened the piano lid and with considerable panache played a few chords. There was immediate silence. He opened the communicating doors wide and stood regarding the scene.

Viola's pretty green dress had been torn from her shoulder and breast and there were angry marks on the white skin . . . the petals of her moss roses were scattered on the carpet. She stood there, humiliated, frozen-faced, trying to pull her dress into place. Netherby stared at Eugene—his face was crimson and his breath came in long, painful gasps. He leaned on the table, trying to control the wave of murderous temper that had swept over him. He looked extremely ill.

Eugene pulled out a chair, and said with the utmost courtesy, 'My dear sir. You look unwell—do sit down.'

Netherby swung his head towards Viola like a tormented bull.

'Who is this? Who's this bastard? Another of your fancy men?'

Eugene addressed himself to Viola. 'I was told you wished to leave?'

Viola nodded. She put her shawl over her torn dress, and said gravely to Netherby, 'I *am* sorry, sir. I made a mistake. It was stupid of me. I really am sorry.'

Eugene picked up her bag and gloves from the carpet, and offered his arm; she gave him a small, tremulous smile of gratitude, and they went from the room together. He felt the long slim hand on his sleeve shaking, and when her lashes lifted, the pupils of her eyes were so enlarged they were almost black.

'Be calm, try to be calm,' he said quietly. 'It is all behind you now. A man without imagination tends to be offensive!'

Viola found her voice. 'I'm not angry with him,' she said shakily. 'I'm mad at myself. How could I have been such a fool as to go out with him!'

'Why did you?'

'Because I was bored.'

'Ach, boredom—*that* I know. But at your age?'

'I've been two months in London. I wanted to see a bit of life. I wanted to wear a pretty dress, and have a nice meal in a smart restaurant. I've seen the Zoo and the Tower and the British Museum.' He smiled behind a concealing hand. 'When you've grown up in a provincial town you dream about London. I was sick of seeing it from the pavements and the wrong side of the counter. I wanted a bit of it for myself. So when he asked me to have dinner with him, I thought I'd take the chance.' Her eyes flashed, full of self-disgust. 'Well, I've learned my lesson. Thank you for coming to my rescue, Signor le Count.'

She had remembered what Franconeri had called him.

'What would you like to do now, *gnädige fräulein?*'

'Well, I suppose I'd better go to the Ladies' Room and see if I can get my dress mended, and then get a cab . . . oh . . .' she began to laugh with real amusement. 'I shall look a great ninny getting back so early, after asking permission to be late, and buying a new dress and making a great exit. All the girls where I work will think my beau let me down . . .' She met his questioning eyes, indicating the room they had left with an eloquent little jerk of her head. 'He is the Guv'nor. My employer. He owns the big shop where I work.'

'Ah,' said Eugene understandingly. 'That explains his chagrin. Employers don't like being disobeyed even in matters outside business. But I have a better idea. I am with a party downstairs, the girls are all about your age—they are young actresses. May I presume so far as to ask you to join us?'

Her eyes opened wide.

'Down in the restaurant? Where the music is? Can you dance there?'

'You can dance. And you shall have supper, and some fun, and see a little of the London you dreamed about, and afterwards I shall see you safely home.'

She looked at him a little doubtfully, holding her dress together over her beautiful bare shoulder. 'Why are you asking me?'

He thought this over, amused at himself, his light-coloured East European eyes speculative on the lovely, upturned face.

'Because, somehow, I like you very much. You are very beautiful, but you know that, and I've met many beautiful women. It's something . . . *je ne sais quoi* . . . I don't know. A little defiance? A little bravery? A lot of honesty?'

She still gazed at him with big, enquiring eyes.

'Yes, honesty. Most girls would have blamed this—Netherby—entirely. But you didn't, did you? You had the dignified honesty to blame yourself as well.'

'I think that's a nice thing to say,' said Viola. 'It makes me feel better about the whole daft business.'

'May I know your name?'

'Viola Corbett.'

'And you are English?'

'Aye—from Yorkshire. I sound it too. But my father was Italian.'

'Ah, that explains a great deal. I too come from mixed bloods—we are the most interesting people, are we not?' She laughed. He went on: 'You will dine with me—and my friends. Yes?'

'I'd like to.'

'Viola? It is pretty, but too sweet for you.'

'The lasses in the shop call me Duchess.'

'Ah!' The silvery eyes lit up. '*C'est parfait!* And so you are. Go and get your frock mended, my Duchess, and we will drink Tokay together and waltz the night away.'

While she was having her dress mended by the attendant in the ladies' retiring room, a girl came in carrying a tray full of flowers.

'The gentleman said you were to choose whatever you wished,' she said, 'to replace the ones that were spoiled.'

Alight with excitement Viola took the faded moss rose from her hair, and chose gardenias. She fastened one in her hair, two to cover her shoulder where the seam was being drawn together.

'*Bella!*' said the attendant appreciatively, when she had finished the repair, and pinned the gardenias in place. '*Molto bella!*'

'Lovely,' agreed the flower girl. 'The gentleman is waiting.'

Viola smiled, gave them some silver, and ran downstairs to where Eugene was waiting for her.

Arthur Netherby sat alone with the wreckage of his evening, cursing until the rage died down in his heart, leaving only frustration and despair. As his breath came more easily he covered his face with his hands to hide the tears that ran down his cheeks. He had behaved like a brute and a fool. He had treated her as he would have treated any little drab. She would never forgive him.

He rose shakily, looked in the mirror at his red eyes, picked up his hat and cane, gloves and opera cloak, and with a feeble attempt at bravado, straightened the carnation in his buttonhole. She was not the only woman in the world. There were places not ten minutes from here, where there were a dozen fine girls to accommodate him.

He left the money for the wine and the food that had been served without calling the waiter.

As he reached the top of the stairs he saw Viola, fresh flowers in her hair and at her bosom, radiant with pleasure, running down to meet Erhmann who was waiting in the vestibule below, saw the smiling, courteous way in which the Austrian offered his arm, and led her into the restaurant, to join his party.

Netherby gave a stifled, inward groan, and went down the stairs and out into the street, not glancing towards Franconeri or any of the waiters, nor at the flower girl or doorman, convinced that the brief scandal had been bruited through the staff, and they were all laughing at him. He would never dine at Franconeri's again.

Automatically he turned his steps towards St Giles, and a certain house. Its gilded and mirrored pleasures seemed sordid and unappetizing when he thought of Viola, but he could think of nothing else to do.

At ten o'clock on Monday morning Lord Staffray arrived punctually at Victoria Station to see his mother off on her journey to Italy.

The Countess, beautifully dressed for summer travelling in a caped coat of pale grey moiré, and a grey-veiled violet-trimmed toque which brought out the lights in her still beautiful blue eyes, came drifting down the platform. She was preceded by her usual entourage. Her maid, Castle, carrying her jewel case, a light rug, her silk pillow stuffed with fragrant herbs, a small bag of toilet and medical necessities, smelling salts, sal volatile and eau de Cologne. Bradman, in a covert coat and tweed cap, carrying her ladyship's travel documents and bills of credit, fussed along to find the two first-class compartments reserved, one for the Countess and one for himself and the maid. There was a footman from Berkeley Square with a luncheon basket, books, magazines, a hot-water bag and foot-warmer, in case her ladyship found the carriage cold. And there were two porters wheeling trolleys piled high with monogrammed dress trunks and hat boxes.

Lady Louderdown's eyes lit up as she caught sight of her son waiting for her. In his well-cut grey morning suit, a red rose in his buttonhole, and carrying gifts, some new and exclusive scent in the most charming cut glass spray, a box of bon-bons, and a spray of flowers, James was enough to delight any mother's heart. If Lady Louderdown only had one son, at least he was a very splendid one. They embraced and James went to sit in his mother's compartment with her until departure time. They sat, talking, his hand in hers, until the guard came, touching his hat to say it was time for James to descend if he was not travelling.

'Now, you'll write, Mama. And take care of yourself. And enjoy your holiday.'

'I will try,' said the Countess, but she was already feeling a great deal better at the thought of leaving all her tiresome responsibilities and going to her beloved Italy and her distinguished and cultured friends. 'And you write too . . .'

'I will, darling.'

'I hope there won't be a horrid war . . .'

'Don't worry about that, Mama.'

'And remember your other promises?'

'Yes, of course, indeed, Mama.'

'I hate saying good-bye to you.'

'It won't be for long, Mama. I might even take a trip to see you, if we're not called up. *After* Goodwood, of course . . .'

The whistles shrilled. They kissed again and James hurriedly alighted from the train and stood on the platform, waving his hat until the train vanished.

With the train now out of sight, James replaced his topper and strolled off down the platform with a decided sense of relief. He loved his mother dearly, but he knew, with rueful good humour, that she kept him on apron strings—apron strings as diaphanous as gossamer, but distinctly there. He squared his broad shoulders, signalled a cab and set off for the Park.

It was a lovely day, the flower beds in full bloom and a fashionable drift of people strolling, sitting, driving or riding, the hats and parasols of the ladies like bouquets of brilliant blossoms, the light breeze fluttering their long trailing skirts.

James moved along the Row, greeting friends and acquaintances, lifting his shining topper to the ladies, exchanging horse and regiment gossip with fellow officers. He was prepared to chat and flirt the pre-luncheon hour away with the happy idleness of which he was such a master. Some rich society people had pangs of conscience about what they called their useless lives. Not James. Young, handsome, popular, he enjoyed every minute of his.

Though posted in London, he was off duty. He could not quite make up his mind what to do during the afternoon, for there was no race meeting adjacent to London that week. He could pay calls, visit a few drawing-rooms where there would be pretty women and he could look over the season's crop of débutantes at close quarters, or flirt with their much more attractive and sophisticated mamas. He could play squash rackets at the club or go to the gymnasium and practise with the foils.

He was leaning on the railings watching one of his troopers exercise his own charger, Brighteyes, putting her through her paces on the tan of Rotten Row, when a high voice called him. He turned to see a charmingly dressed woman, in her early thirties, beckoning him to where she sat with some friends, their hired chairs surrounded by a group of attentive gentlemen.

Mrs Cuthbert Drew was the wife of a major in his regiment. He walked towards her.

'James.' She held out her hand accusingly. 'You have forgotten your debt!'

'Debt, Mrs Drew?'

'Remember, when we were riding on the Heath, on Gold Cup morning, you bet me a pair of gloves that I could not beat you on Melchior, and I did.'

He had given her a start and raced her across the Heath. She was a fine horsewoman and had beaten him by a head. He had completely forgotten.

He gently took her hand, smiling and apologetic.

'Will you forgive me? I had not forgotten—but I have been on duty, and besides, I did not know what colour, what size, or what kind.'

'Kid, five-and-a-half, wrist length, lavender, three wrist buttons.'

James wrote this information down in his betting book.

'*Very* exact. And where shall I find these particular objects?'

She laughed, and rising, took his arm, and they strolled towards Hyde Park Gate, followed by her friends.

'You needn't bother, James. I was but teasing.'

'No, really. I must pay my debts.'

'Oh, well—Dwyer & Netherby's in Oxford Street. It is where I always get them.'

He had been thinking that she was a nice woman and a good sport, and that Major Drew was an old stick. Together they might amuse themselves very pleasantly through the rest of the season. The regiment could be going to the Cape at any time and he would like to have some fun before he went and this pretty, bored married woman would be an excellent companion. But his breath caught in his throat at the name of the haberdashers in Oxford Street as the memory of the girl he had tried to push from his mind came back like a remembered dream. It was where she worked. He saw her again in the rose-shaded lights of the restaurant car, that cloud of auburn hair, those tempting lips, the slow lift of the weighted white eyelids.

'It's fate,' he said, absurdly, aloud.

'What is?' asked Mrs Drew. 'What is fate?'

'It is fate that has brought us together,' he teased glibly. 'I shall get your gloves today and bring them to you. When?'

'Can you dine tonight? I have some amusing people coming. You would even up the table as my husband is away.'

'At what time?'

'Come early—about seven o'clock. We dine at eight—we shall have a little time alone before the others arrive.'

'At seven, I shall be there.'

When he left Mrs Drew, James decided to lunch at White's alone, and debated whether to go back to his rooms and send his man for the gloves. But at two o'clock he was peering through the plate-glass door which led directly into the glove department of Dwyer & Netherby's.

Viola was serving a customer. He felt ridiculously happy, as though he was not breathing, or his feet were not touching the ground. It was like being drunk or mad, that he could just *look* at this girl and forget everything else. He opened the door, and walked across the green carpet towards her. It seemed a long, long way. He was conscious of the stuffy heat and the drapery smells, bombazine, satins, perfume. He could not take his eyes from her.

She was all in black, with a little white frill, like that in an Elizabethan portrait, edging her high-boned collar. She gave the customer her change, and turned towards him, and her face lit up, as he knew it would. No coquetry, no pretensions of indifference. Just that clear look, the lips parting, the marvellous eyes lighting with delight.

For a moment he could not speak.

A yellow-faced woman with dyed black hair came forward, ingratiatingly, and asked if she could help him. James said firmly but courteously, 'Miss Corbett will serve me, thank you.' He whipped off his hat, and turned to Viola. 'Lavender kid gloves, size five-and-a-half, wrist length, three pearl buttons.'

She turned to find the drawer. James froze Miss Heath with an autocratic air. Betsy, busy serving, saw him, and nearly dropped a tray of gloves. 'Oh dear, oh dear, what next?' she thought, scurrying towards her customer like a scared rabbit.

Viola put down the drawer, took a pair of gloves out of tissue paper, slipped one over her long slim hand and held it for his inspection.

'Perfect,' he said. 'Six pairs. When will you meet me?'

'Next Saturday,' said Viola.

'Ah, no. That's *ages!* Tonight? *Please* tonight?'

'I work until eight. I have to be in at ten.'

'Only two hours! That's hell. But yes. I'll send the carriage.'

'No,' she protested. 'Do you want the whole shop talking?'

'At Marble Arch then? At ten minutes past eight?'

She wrapped and boxed the gloves, took his money and snapped it into the change tub which she sent sailing across to the counting house.

'You've been a long time coming, my lord,' she whispered. 'I was getting tired of waiting.'

He did not lie to her.

'I have tried not to come. I felt it would not do.'

'For you—or for me?'

'For both of us.'

'What made you change your mind?'

'A pretty, silly woman with whom I had a bet. Her stake was new gloves and she told me to come here for them.'

'I'm glad she won her bet then, my lord.'

They spoke in low voices, outwardly circumspect. Yet every glance and word was heavy with unspoken meaning. Their eyes were incandescent with mutual longing. As once before Betsy looked away, shocked and disturbed.

The wooden tub came hissing back along the wires. All round the shop the other girls were looking covertly across at Viola and the tall, handsome, fashionably dressed young man.

She unscrewed the lid of the tub.

'Your change, my lord.'

'Thank you.'

As she gave him the coins their fingers touched for a fleeting second, then they smiled and parted. Outside in the sunshine James walked like a sleepwalker, unaware of his direction, until he found himself in Bond Street outside a flower shop. He stood for a moment, gazing dazedly at his own reflection against the banks of roses, carnations and lilies, and suddenly, as though coming awake, plunged into the shop.

He chose a beautiful bouquet and had it sent, with the gloves, to Mrs Drew with his apologies that, after all, he would be unable to dine that night.

Count Eugene Erhmann sat at his desk in his study in the flat in Victoria Street. He had bathed and changed after a long day in the city, had slipped on his dressing-gown and was attending to some letters. It was Monday—a working day, so that Viola could not get away before eight o'clock, and she had to be back by ten. She dare not, she said mischievously, ask for leave of absence from Mr Netherby after Saturday night's fiasco. But there would be time for supper at one of the little French restaurants in Soho, famous for their cuisine, and he had promised to get her back on time. He had told Vatel to book a table and order special flowers and had chosen the wine to be put on ice for them. One thing about his Duchess—she appreciated good things.

Yesterday, Sunday, had been fine. He had called for her early, arriving in a hired carriage to the astonishment and excitement of all the staff, whose noses were pressed against the windows of the hostel in Eastcastle Street, to watch Viola run out in her white summer muslin, and a hat of white crinoline straw with some blue cornflowers in it.

She had been waiting for him in the hall.

'Here comes my friend, the Count,' she had said, laughing, as she picked up her parasol. All the girls were now convinced that Viola had a wealthy lover.

Erhmann had taken Viola by train to Maidenhead, where they had lunched at Skindles and he had hired an electric launch to take her on the river. The friends of the supper party at Franconeri's had joined them after lunch, and Erhmann had watched her enjoy herself, unaffectedly taking her place as the centre of attention among the smart, gay, theatre girls and rich young men. She was, he thought, like a creature at last in its own element. She seemed to him born for luxury and laughter.

Tomorrow he had to return to Paris, and from Paris to Africa. It was many years since any woman had caught his imagination like this. He wondered, if he asked her to come with him, whether she would. She was greedy and avid for life and adventure, but he knew she was unpredictable. He thought of his home city, of the life he could give her, and the luxuries with which he could surround her. Emeralds—she should wear emeralds with those long, heavily-lashed, gold-green eyes. Sables—she should wear Russian sables, the natural ones with the faint foxy tint to complement her rust-red hair.

On the table before him was a jeweller's box containing a small brooch of very pure emeralds, amethysts and diamonds which he had bought for her that afternoon in the city. He had bought it, not to tempt her with, but as a gift, because she had given him so much pleasure during the few hours he had known her. She had brought back his youth again.

He heard a ring at the doorbell and presently Vatel came in with the blue envelope of an express letter. The boy was waiting. Erhmann slit it open, reading the big, bold, flowing hand. A direct letter, slightly ill-spelt, straight to the point.

> 'Dear Count, I am really very sorry but I can't come tonite. Someone has come who is important to me and I've been waiting to see since being in London. Thank you for the luvly time you gave me, and for helping me on Saturday. I have herd nothing from A.N. so do not expect trouble from that direcshun. I hope you have a good journey home to Austria tomorrow. You have been so kind and I shall not forget you. I am really sorry about tonite but it cannot be helped. Yours sincerely, Duchess.'

'Is there an answer, Herr Count?'

'No.'

With a bitter little smile he made to tear the letter, but as the valet reached the door, he stopped him. 'Wait, Vatel. Yes. Give the boy a shilling and tell him to wait.'

He wrote a brief note which he enclosed with the jeweller's box in a heavy, white envelope and addressed it to Viola at Eastcastle Street. He sealed it, pressing the crest with the crusader's half-moon down into the wax, and rang for the valet.

'Tell the boy to take this to Miss Corbett at Eastcastle Street, Vatel, and cancel the supper table. I'll dine at the club.'

Ehrmann folded up Viola's letter, and put it carefully away in his note-case. He caught sight of his reflection in a large gilt-framed mirror and gave a wry smile of self-mockery. To lose his heart? At his age? To an uneducated girl?

'Damn her siren's eyes,' he said good-naturedly, as he changed his dressing-gown for an evening jacket. 'I thought I was too old for that kind of tomfoolery!'

At Marble Arch, at 8.15, Viola stood waiting on the pavement. She had had no time to change from her black working dress, and wore no hat, just her cream lace shawl, mantilla-wise, over her hair. She had taken a cab from Eastcastle Street. She had hardly alighted when Lady Louderdown's beautiful little closed carriage came spanking to a standstill, the door opened and James lifted her up beside him.

Unexpectedly she was afraid. The fringed blinds were drawn against the summer twilight. The close darkness smelled of polished leather and parma violets. She could only hear the sound of the horse's hoofs as they drove on through the park, and the pounding of her own wild heart. She would remember it all her life. She lay still in his arms, waiting for their first kiss, both of them hesitating on the brink of an engulfing passion that they knew could not be denied.

She felt James tremble, as she was trembling, and suddenly had no more fears. She raised her mouth to his and heard him speak her name against her lips.

CHAPTER FOUR

Lady Louderdown's equipage stood on the carriage road by the Alexandra Gate in Hyde Park. Carson had descended and loosened the snaffles of the two shining bays so that they could stretch and shake their heads. He stood patiently, stroking the smooth noses. Usually when he drove the carriage and pair, the young footman sat up on the box beside him, to jump down and lower the step to assist her ladyship to descend. But he had given the lad the evening off. Young servants were apt to gossip, and it was better he should be on his own when driving for Lord Staffray. You never knew what that young fellow-me-lad might be up to, especially now, on the brink of going to war. Carson, like Bradman and Mrs Castle, was a family servant of long-standing, unlike James's smart and cynical valet, Jevons.

But now the horses were tired, and Carson himself wanted his supper. He yawned and peered across the open grass towards the Serpentine. Presently he saw them walking slowly towards him under the tall plane trees, their arms entwined, young lovers, lost to the world, drowning in each other's eyes.

Carson shook his head doubtfully. This one was a real beauty and no mistake—*and* no tart if he knew it. It was obvious that his lordship was smitten.

Viola tilted her head against James and her thick, shining hair fell across his shoulder. He smoothed it back from her forehead, and kissed the white skin where the hair made a shining, springing line. She raised her lips to his again, with a yearning murmur. The white cravat at her dress neck was askew, where he had parted it to kiss her throat and breast, so that she had put her fingers against his lips, and said, 'No, you mustn't.'

'Why, oh why, Viola?'

'Because it sends me off . . . you only have to touch me.'

It was that way with him too. He was wild with desire for her, and yet restrained, and very tender. Every kiss a preliminary, as though they were both afraid of the pleasure they knew their bodies would share. James was a skilled, appreciative and experienced lover of women, but with Viola he held himself back. He did not want anything rash, greedy or slight. He wanted her for ever.

She touched the mobile lips beneath the clipped fair moustache, loving him. 'Crumpled handsome,' she said, 'that's what you are, my lord . . . crumpled handsome. How did you get that twisted nose?'

'I fell off a horse when I was twelve.'

She shivered. 'You might have been killed, and I might not have met you.'

'Ah, Viola, but I didn't. I'm here—and I love you. Say you love me.'

'I love you.' A church clock towards Knightsbridge way chimed one stroke, and Viola looked at her little enamel watch. Twilight was falling, and the yellow street lamps glimmered through the park.

'It is half past nine. I must get back. They lock the door at ten o'clock sharp, and I shan't get in.'

'If you can't—will you come to me?'

She said, 'I'll come to you anyway. When you're ready.'

'When will that be?'

'We'll both know, won't we, my lord?'

They had stopped, face to face—a great elm hid them from the waiting coachman. He put his hands on her shoulders, strong and gentle, let them slip over her breasts, so that the firm, sweet globes were cupped in his palms, the nipples proud beneath the tight black bodice.

'There's been no one else yet,' she said. 'Kisses . . . flirtings. But no one else really, not like we'll be.'

'Viola, Viola . . . when shall I see you again?'

'Whenever you wish. Any evening—but only for two hours. On Saturday the shop closes at one as its half-day. On Sunday, I'm free all day.'

'I'm on duty . . . all this week. It will not be until Saturday, my darling . . . Saturday I'll send the carriage for you at one o'clock.'

'At the same place?'

'At the same place. We'll make plans, Viola. You can't stay at that damned shop. We'll make plans for the rest of our lives together.'

They went swiftly across the grass towards the carriage, both tall, fine and handsome, moving proudly side by side.

'Like a blooming god and goddess,' said Carson, long afterwards, when the scandal of their love became public property.

He tightened up the snaffle bits and opened the carriage door. James put his hands on Viola's waist and lifted her inside.

'Where to, my lord?'

'Eastcastle Street. I'll tell you when you stop.'

He stepped into the carriage. Carson shut the door and James pulled down the blind.

Carson turned the horses into Park Lane, then towards Oxford Street, clucking ruminatively at their ears.

This one *was* different. Not at all his lordship's usual style. This one might talk like a mill girl, but she had the looks and manner of a queen. This was something serious.

Carson's honest face fell. *Serious!* He hoped not. With her ladyship away, and the Earl up at Louderdown, getting ready for the first shooting party on the 12th. He hoped his young Lordship knew what he was up to! Serious? Jesus, if her ladyship knew! And with Mr Bradman and Mrs Castle away in foreign parts with her ladyship there was no one into whose ear a warning word might be dropped.

Upstairs in the dormitory Betsy waited at the window, her hopes rising every time a carriage came along Eastcastle Street. At every footstep she peered anxiously through the glass. Surely, *this time* it would be Viola.

At 9.45 she went down into the hall, the small blue glimmer of the gas-jet making her shadow enormous as she went quietly down the stairs. On the hall-stand beside the row of candles and the unlit oil-lamp, she saw a heavy white envelope. It was addressed to Viola in large, Gothic writing, and had been sent round by hand. She picked it up and put it into her pocket.

Cautiously she turned the handle of the front door and ventured out on to the step. It was hot—a real summer night. Above the roof tops a new moon cut a silver crescent in the sky. One or two of the girls, who had been out for a walk in the evening air came in, arms linked, glancing at her curiously.

Miss Heath came in with a fussy rustle of skirts, and a venomous glance from under her bonnet. She went straight into Mrs Harding's room, and Betsy could hear their voices raised in indignant dialogue.

She was sure they were talking about Viola. As she was praying for Viola to arrive, they were hoping she could be late, and sure enough, at five minutes to the hour, Mrs Harding appeared in the hall. She advanced to the door.

'May I ask what you are doing out on the step at this time of night, Miss Holder? It is not at all the thing for our young ladies to hang about on the step after dark,' Mrs Harding said coldly. She went to a row of hooks above the hall-stand where the keys hung, and took down one for the front door. 'Will you please come in, so that I can lock up.'

'It is not yet ten o'clock, Mrs Harding, and Viola is not in. I'm that worried, Mrs Harding . . . something may have happened to her.'

'Something certainly will if she goes on flouting every rule in the firm,' said Mrs Harding. 'Permit me to lock up.'

Betsy, very small and white, took a step forward. She pointed to the hall clock.

'It is not yet ten,' she repeated stubbornly.

Miss Heath came out of the housekeeper's room.

'Come in at once, Holder, and let Mrs Harding lock up. I will not have impudence from junior hands.'

'It is not ten o'clock, ma'am, and Vi's not in yet. I know she'll come . . . please don't lock her out. Where would she go?'

'Corbett knows the rules, and ten is the time for all our workers to be in. If she is fool enough to be late she knows what to expect . . .'

Mrs Harding made to shut the door, and Betsy grasped the inner and outer handles, clinging to them. Mrs Harding lost her temper, let go of the door and tried to drag Betsy away. The noise attracted a few of the girls, and they came crowding out of the dining-room, their eyes bright and excited, murmuring among themselves.

A carriage came at a fast trot along the road outside and drew up just beyond the front door. The door was heard opening and closing, there was the crack of the whip, and the carriage drove away towards Oxford Street. Viola, her lovely hair loose about her shoulders, her cream shawl draped about her head, came slowly in. Her eyes looked enormous, dark, shadowy. She looked slowly about her like a sleepwalker, then consciousness returned, and her glance raked the small crowd, her lips curled with a faintly mocking enquiry.

'I was about to lock the door,' Mrs Harding said furiously. 'You know the rules as well as anyone.'

'I do, surely. We close at ten.' Viola made a pretty show of turning up the gas jet, and looking at her watch. 'I make it just ten. There—I thought so.' St Botolph's clock struck the hour. 'So I'm just in time.' She beckoned to Sal Perkins, the slatternly little maid who, with the cook and houseman, had crept out from the kitchen premises to watch the fun. 'Light a couple of candles, Sal. I'm going straight up.'

'Yes, Miss.' Sal hurried forward, lit the candles, and Viola gave Betsy hers, took her hand and began to mount the stairs, turning her head, smiling at the gaping crowd of girls and the infuriated women in the hall below. 'Good night to you all.'

Mrs Harding turned and flounced into her parlour, red-faced with indignation, followed by Miss Heath. The girls, even those who had maligned Viola behind her back, burst into a raucous clamour of laughter, delighted to see authority put down. Viola and Betsy went into the dormitory together.

Viola lit the gas, turned it high, Betsy sat on the bed and looked up at her and was afraid for her. She seemed to glow with new beauty. She moved with a languid and sensuous grace, her eyes were deep and dark, weighted with unspoken memories. Her soft lips seemed bruised with recent kisses. Betsy burst into tears.

Instantly Viola was by her side.

'What is it? What is it, my little love? Has anyone been nasty to you?' The strong, smooth arms enfolded her. 'Tell me, and I'll skelp them.'

'Where have you been, Vi? They wanted to shut you out, those two. They've got it in for you. And all the girls—they know who that was . . . that chap who came in for the gloves, and they're all talking, saying dreadful things about you . . .'

Viola took out her handkerchief, removed Betsy's glasses, wiped her eyes, cleaned the glasses, and put them back on the small upturned nose, now shiny and red from crying.

'Let them talk, talk can't hurt anyone.'

'Vi—tonight, you didn't . . . you haven't . . . ?' The question stuck in her throat, the words unformed. Viola touched her face as though she were a child, and smiled. 'No.' Betsy sighed with relief, and Viola added softly, 'Not yet.'

'What do you mean? Not yet? You mean you're—*going to*?'

'Yes. With him!' Viola was suddenly fierce. She sprang up and started to pace up and down the long room. 'With him *first*. Whatever my life is going to be . . . he's going to be the *first*.'

'You mean you're in love with him?'

'We're in love with each other.'

'But Viola—you can't. He'll never marry you. How can he? He's a great gentleman. What would his family say?'

' "For the rest of our lives," he said,' Viola smiled. 'For the rest of our lives.' She turned a blazing glance on Betsy. 'Don't you think I'd rather have James anyhow, married or not, than any fool who can make a respectable woman of me?' She suddenly pulled off her shawl and threw it down, and began to undo the hooks of her dress, her cheeks flushed, her heavy eyes feverish. 'It's stifling in here.' She slid out of the dress and stood in her white chemise bodice and full taffeta skirt. Her tumbled hair fell about her shoulders. 'What did I come down to London for, Betsy? To be a shop assistant, and live in this god-forsaken hole? I came as all girls come, aye, even the rich society ones, to find me a man—and I've found one, and in the whole world there's not a bonnier or braver fellow.'

She seemed taller, stronger, wilder.

'You're never going off wi' him, Viola Corbett?' said Betsy, aghast.

'If he wants me, yes. To the end of the world.'

There was silence. Viola went to the window and thrust it open. The new moon had gone, London was an arc of yellow light under the deep blue summer sky. Somewhere, out there, was James. She counted the days —four days and a half—before she would be with him again. It seemed like four and a half years.

Betsy unpinned her little plaited bun, silently let down her hair, and began to take off her dress. In her pocket was the envelope packet that had come for Viola.

'Here!' she said dully. 'This came for you this evening.'

Viola took it, opened it, read the letter inside. The strong foreign-looking script with pointed letters.

'*My dear Duchess,*

I am more disappointed than I can say. For one evening and half a day you brought back my youth. Tomorrow I must leave early for Paris, and then to Marseilles for Africa. For a few hours I had the unwarranted illusion that you might accompany me. Alas for dreams. I wish you and he—the Someone who is important to you—much joy. He is an exceedingly lucky man. If ever I can be of service to you, please do not hesitate to get in touch with me. I enclose my addresses in London. Meanwhile I also enclose a small gift—which I had already bought for you, hoping to give it to you tonight. A small tribute to a most beautiful girl, who will become one day soon a fascinating woman.

Your devoted admirer,
Eugene Erhmann.'

'It's from my friend, the Count,' said Viola.

She opened the box. The small brooch, the centre a viola in amethysts with leaves of emeralds and stalks of green enamel caught in a bow of diamonds, was set into a square frame of diamonds.

'Oh,' exclaimed Viola, 'how lovely! How *grand!* Look.'

Betsy looked. 'It's pretty. Are you going to take it?'

'Am I not!' said Viola. 'I love it.' She went to the mirror and set it against her hair, then her throat, then her white bosom. 'I love things of quality . . .' Suddenly she threw back her head, and laughed. 'Happen that's why I love my lord James . . .'

Katy Martin came in, flushed and grinning.

'You've set them all by their heels downstairs, Duchess. Half are for you and half against you.' She began to undress. 'A lot of jealous cats really.'

Viola returned the brooch to its case, and put it, with Erhmann's letter, into her handbag, undressed and got into bed. She lay back, her hands beneath her head, listening to Katy's chatter as she undressed and rolled her hair into curling rags. Betsy was very quiet.

When the lights went out Viola thought of Erhmann, his beautiful manners, the cool amused interest, remembered how courteously he had kissed her hand as though she were a real duchess. Paris, Marseilles, Africa? If James had not come, would she have gone? It would have been a temptation. But James had come, and now nothing else mattered in the whole world.

Mr Netherby had behaved very strangely. He had not accompanied his son and daughter to church, nor had he appeared at the ritual Sunday luncheon. On Monday he had not appeared in the store at all, and had sent Herbert to take his usual inspection. Herbert had strutted like a cock-sparrow, the unusual authority going to his head. But today, Tuesday, Mr Netherby was back again. Miss Heath, seizing her opportunity, went up to his office on the mezzanine floor, and asked his clerk if she could see him.

'He's not seeing anyone this morning.'

'Tell him it is about the new assistant, Miss Corbett.'

The clerk shrugged, went into the inner office, and came out at once, jerking his head. 'He says he'll see you,' he said.

Miss Heath went in, and stopped, shocked at her employer's appearance. His usually ruddy face had a leaden pallor and his prominent eyes were red-rimmed. His appearance was as immaculate as ever, but there was something about him, something deflated and broken, and when he spoke, he did not meet her eyes with his usual imperious glare.

'Are you not well, sir?'

'Of course I'm well,' he answered tetchily.

'When you didn't come in yesterday, I thought perhaps—'

'I suppose my fool of a son has been chattering nonsense. I am perfectly well. Now—' he tapped on the mahogany desk with an ivory letter-knife,— 'now what is this about—Miss Corbett?'

Miss Heath plunged into her story. There was no doubt the new assistant in the glove department was giving the firm a bad name. She told of Viola's outing on Saturday night, returning in the early hours in a hired carriage, with a gentleman in evening dress. Then she had gone out on Sunday, the same gentleman calling for her in a carriage and bringing her back at ten o'clock.

Mr Netherby listened impassively, not looking at her, still tapping the shiny surface of the desk. She felt he had not even heard.

'I know how you feel about good behaviour both in and out of the store, sir. She is, and has always been, a disruptive element ever since she came, criticizing the amenities of the hostel, and being very impertinent. She sets the girls against us. They think, if she can do those things, so can they. I cannot see how we can be expected to control the junior staff with due authority if she is kept on.'

For the first time Mr Netherby raised his eyes, and Miss Heath was startled. They were the eyes of a man in agony. He must really be ill.

'You have no reason to complain of her work?'

'Well, no,' Miss Heath said reluctantly, 'but that's not all, sir. I think—I am sure—she made an assignation with another man—a customer, this afternoon. Over the counter—*in the shop!*'

A slow dull red suffused Mr Netherby's heavy face. Such behaviour rated instant dismissal.

'The young man was well known to several people in the store, sir. His mother is one of our most valued customers. The Countess of Louderdown. The young man was Lord Staffray. You will agree, I know, sir, that only one thing can be assumed when a young man of his position stoops to . . . to pay attentions to a shop girl.'

Netherby rose, turned away, covering his face with his hand. *Not* the foreign fellow! Young Staffray. A rich, handsome youngster who could get any girl he wanted. What a fool he had been, imagining because she was young and poor and worked for him, that he was the only man who had noticed her. A girl like that could set the whole of London on its heels.

That damned Heath woman was rabbiting on with her stupid jealous complaints and he had hardly heard. He turned to her, and said heavily, 'That will do, Miss H. I will speak to Miss Corbett. Will you kindly send her up to me.'

'Now?'

'At once.'

When the door had closed behind Miss Heath, Arthur Netherby went across to the large gilt-framed mirror on the wall and peered doubtfully at his reflection, touching the thinning hair, turning his heavily jowled and veined face from side to side.

There was a light tap on the door, and in response to his call Viola came in, and stood waiting quietly.

The morning light pouring through the windows gilded the glorious profusion of her hair and made the green eyes glint like emeralds. She was wearing a small brooch at her throat, and his practised eyes recognized its value. He had never seen her wear it before, and immediately he was wracked with jealousy, wondering who had given it to her, and what favours she had granted for so valuable a trinket. But he dare not ask. He must not frighten her away again. His loins were melting with longing; he rubbed his fingers across his full lips to hide their trembling.

He sat down at his desk, and indicated the chair opposite.

'Please sit down, my dear.'

Viola's delicate brows went up. So it was not to be an ignominious dismissal, such as Miss Heath had anticipated.

'Thank you, sir,' she said. 'I would rather stand.'

He looked up then, and like Miss Heath she was startled by the unconcealed suffering in his eyes.

'I implore you, Viola,' he said, 'sit down. You have nothing to fear from me now, I promise you.'

She swayed forward, sat down opposite him, very erect and straightbacked, her lovely face very still but wary.

'They're right to call you Duchess,' he said, 'you move like one.' She made a little movement, as though she would rise, and he put out a hand in desperate appeal. 'No, don't go.'

'Miss Heath said you wanted to speak to me, sir. I understood I had displeased you in some way.'

'No. No. I would have sent for you anyway.' He brought out a large, spotless cambric handkerchief, dabbed his forehead. 'I have to ask you to forgive my behaviour on Saturday. It was—inexcusable! I can only say that I had taken too much to drink . . . and I lost my head.' He leaned across the desk. 'In all my life I've never met a girl like you. I would not have had it happen for a fortune. Will you forgive me?'

'Nay, Mr Netherby,' she said simply, 'there's no need to take on so. We all make fools of ourselves, sometimes. As I said, we both made a mistake. And what's the odds? I had a grand time after all, dancing until they closed. It's all past and forgotten. I'm sorry too. Will that be all, sir?'

She stood up and held out her hand frankly. He took it and came round the desk, holding it tightly. She was surprised at his strength.

'No. No. I must say something more. Viola, I know that a girl like you will have many men wanting you, rich men, and young and handsome, perhaps of good family. But what will they offer you? A good time? Their protection? But it cannot last. I can offer you a great deal more. I can offer you a future, a life of security and great comfort . . .'

Her lovely eyes lifted with a startled look.

'Mr Netherby, please—don't say any more!'

'Viola, I am asking you to marry me!'

She had managed to release her hand, backing away to the door. She was full of profound pity for him. She could not regard him with the mischievous indifference she had on Saturday night. She had changed; since then she had been held in James's arms, given him her lips, known the sweet agony of desire, and though she could not bear Mr Netherby to touch her, she knew that in his own awful way he was sincere.

'I'm sorry, Mr Netherby, I couldn't think of it. You don't really mean it. You'll think better of it too . . .'

'Viola . . .' To her horror and astonishment he fell on his knees before her. An overweight, middle-aged man at her feet, literally sobbing with longing. It was pathetic. It was ridiculous. She was ashamed for him.

'I make no terms. Just come to me. I will do anything, give you anything if you will let me have you . . . touch you . . .' The clean fat hands were pressing through the stuff of her skirts, feeling the long slim legs, clinging round her ankles. She could feel his hot face through her clothes, and struggled once again to free herself.

'Mr Netherby, get up . . . it's not right. Have you forgotten where we are? Someone might come . . . it would go through the shop in a minute, and the staff would be laughing . . . Mr Netherby, *please!*'

With all her strength she pushed him away, and left him kneeling in the middle of the room, his hands covering his face. She waited anxiously, wanting to give him a chance to recover before his clerk saw him again. In a few moments he put a hand on his desk, pulled himself erect, and stood wiping his face. Presently, not without a despairing dignity, he said, 'The very sight of you seems to make me behave like a damned fool. But I don't withdraw. I mean every word. I want you to be my wife.'

'No, sir.' Viola was embarrassed and confused. 'Thank you, sir. I appreciate what you are offering me, but I cannot. You're upset. You'll think differently soon.'

'You think I am too old? Then will you see me sometimes? Will you let me take you to the theatre? Or to dinner? I promise no more private rooms. No scenes. Will you visit my home as my guest, and meet my family? Give me a chance to show you what I can offer you.'

'No, sir. Thank you. I am sorry.'

'There is someone else?' he said fearfully.

He saw the slow droop of her eyelids, weighted with a sweet, secret memory and he knew why men killed from jealousy. The soft, voluptuous, yielding look, the curve of her lips—a woman remembering her lover's kisses.

'Yes,' she said, very gravely and simply. 'Yes, there is someone else. But —you must believe me, on Saturday, when I said I'd go to dinner with you —I did not know. May I go now, Mr Netherby?'

He made a little gesture of dismissal, he could not speak, and she went quickly and quietly from the room.

During the following week the news darkened, the headlines spoke of imminent war. The mood of the country swung into an extreme display of popular patriotism. Music halls drummed out their jingoistic songs. Cartoons portrayed Kruger like an ageing ape in a top hat. Headlines stated

'WE HAVE HAD ENOUGH. BRITAIN MUST ACT.' Everyone was infected. The young men at Netherby's argued feverishly in their free hours, talked about duty to their country and of volunteering for the army. Only Viola, counting the hours, dreaming, longing for Saturday, did not read the news, did not think about it, did not heed.

It was true James was a soldier, but he was not a soldier who went to war. He was a fine, large as life toy-soldier in a beautiful uniform, who guarded the Royal family, who had to attend court balls and levées and march in spectacular parades.

She dipped into the money Sam Hardcastle had given her to buy a new dress, spending more money on it than she had ever done in her life. It was a creamy chiffon strewn with faint coppery flowers over a foundation of pale ochre taffeta. She bought a hat trimmed with a flutter of pale bronze ostrich fronds. If she was not a real lady at least she would look like one for James. He was going to be proud of her.

For the first time in her life she was in love, and she was living for the moment when she would see James again. Next Saturday, when the gong went for the closing of the store, it would be like a door opening into a new world. She could not eat, she could not sleep. She burned with longing.

Betsy was very frightened for her friend. But whatever she said fell on deaf ears—Viola merely looked at her with those entranced eyes, and smiled. If death had awaited her she would still have gone to James.

On Saturday, because of the heat, the door into the hall had been left open, and when Viola appeared, every head in the dining-room turned, every mouth stopped chewing. Beautiful, elegant, ladylike in her cream flowered chiffon, her hat of cream and bronze ostrich fronds crowning her piled-up auburn hair, she stopped, at the dining-room door, fastening her long gloves, then leaned on the handle of her fringed parasol, her eyes glancing round the room with amusement. Then she came slowly forward and paused by Betsy's side, stooped and kissed her.

There was complete silence. Everyone's eyes were fixed upon her. No one said a word.

'Good-bye, love. Don't wait up for me.' She sought in her small handbag of moiré silk, and finding a shilling, gave it to the gaping Sally Perkins. 'Get me a cab, Sal, and hurry. I'm late.'

Sal scuffled out to do her bidding, and Viola followed. They heard the front door close behind her and there was an outburst of outraged chatter.

'I reckon she's off with you-know-who,' said Katy Martin, who had recognized James in the shop. 'Orf on the randy-dandy. 'as she arsked for a late-night pass, Betsy? I'll bet she won't come 'ome ternight.'

'It's my opinion the Guv's stuck on 'er too,' said another girl excitedly.

'Little Herby got into a right paddy when 'is Dad wouldn't sack 'er—after she'd been cheeky to 'im. She's a lad, that Duchess! He's sacked girls for even looking at a chap in his precious shop.'

'Of course he's stuck on her. 'aven't you seen his gooseberry eyes when he thinks nobody's looking.'

There was a peal of laughter. Betsy rose and went up to the dormitory, face flushed, ears tingling, ashamed for her friend.

Katy had come up later to change prior to going out, and found her lying on the bed in tears.

'Oh, come on, Bets,' she said kindly. 'Don't take on. It's not your business.'

'She's—she's my friend.' Betsy sobbed inconsolably. 'She's always been grand to me. She's always been a—h-hard-working—g-good girl—she's n-not like they say . . .' Her tear-stained little face came up defiantly. 'And if she's gone to do anything she shouldn't then it's for love. She's crazy in love with that young Staffray, and he's the wrong one for leading her on. He's a great gentleman. He ought to know better.'

Katy Martin's sharp little Cockney face softened.

'You're a daisy,' she said gently. 'Don't you worry. You're her friend, ducks, but you ain't her keeper. Come out with me and forget it.'

But Betsy shook her head.

She stayed in through the beautiful afternoon. She thought about Matthew Lyttelton, and how far above her he was, and cried again. At four o'clock she ventured down for a cup of tea. No one else was there— the big room was empty, hot under the glass roof, with some flies buzzing over the white oilcloth on the tables, and some heavy-footed pigeons walking and cooing on the glass roof.

It was not until Betsy heard the clock at St Botolph's strike that she remembered with a start that she had arranged to meet Matthew that evening. She lived for their meetings, and it showed how upset she was to forget about him, even for a minute. She washed her face, put on her hat and hurried out into the summer dusk.

Matthew was waiting for her at the usual corner, and when she approached he did not, as usual, come forward and take her hand but stood, stiffly, looking about him, evading her eyes.

'Good evening, Matthew,' she said.

He coloured, then hurriedly took her arm, and they walked in silence into the park.

'Is something wrong?' she ventured.

He stopped, dropping her arm. 'Everything. I'm so ashamed. I feel awful . . . less than a man.'

She felt an emptiness encompass her.

'You can't see me any more,' she said quietly.

'How did you know?'

'I thought it might happen.'

They began to walk again, but this time her hands were folded tightly and she kept a gap between them.

'It's Mr Everard,' he burst out. 'The Vicar. The Netherbys—Mr Herbert and Miss Emily—have seen us meeting, or else someone has told them about it. Mr Everard—and Mrs Everard—she was worse than he was—told me about it today. After morning service. They said if I continued to see you they would dismiss me.'

She blinked behind her glasses. She was not going to cry. She had cried enough. It was only to be expected. She wished he did not look so pale, wretched and ashamed. She wished she could find the words to comfort him but it was as if all sense and feeling had left her.

'It's—so unfair,' he cried desperately. 'It's not their business. If I do my work properly, and look after the parishioners, and believe truly in God. To try and make it—dirty! Why, Betsy, I would not harm you—not for anything in this world.'

In spite of her efforts a tear slid down her cheek.

'I know that. I know that, Matthew,' she managed to bring out.

'If I had some money. Just enough to keep Mother, I would leave, I would walk out. But I'm a pauper, Betsy. My mother depends on my stipend. I write—and sell—one or two articles, but it's only a little money. One couldn't live on that!'

They had as though by common consent started the long walk down Marylebone towards Tewkesbury Square. He looked down at the small girl in the plain print dress and round straw hat. His little peg-top doll. He saw how white and woebegone she looked, a pathetic small thing. He wanted to shelter and protect her from the whole world. The Everards had been as outraged as though he had broken every commandment.

'For a clergyman and gentleman to go out with a common shop girl can only mean *one* thing. I am horrified, Lyttelton, that you, of all men, should do this. Not only will you compromise the foolish girl's honour, for of course any question of marriage is out of the question, but that you should sully the reputation of St Botolph's.

'You have been received in Tewkesbury Square. At one time I thought Miss Emily Netherby quite favoured you. That you should choose such low companionship is unspeakable. It is an insult to her and to us!'

He had protested. He had assured them of his and Betsy's innocence. It was useless.

At the corner of the square he stopped, and grasped Betsy's thin shoulders. 'Let's take no notice. Let's meet secretly. Why should we give each other up?'

'You've your mother, and I need my job,' she said with the first sign of bitterness she had shown. 'We haven't any choice. I'll not come to St Botolph's any more.'

'Betsy, they can't drive you away from church.'

'There are other churches,' she said flatly. 'That way we won't meet. Good-bye, Matthew.'

They stood staring at each other in mutual despair, and then parted, and went their separate ways.

When Betsy got back to the hostel it was empty—almost every other girl was out enjoying herself. It seemed darker and grubbier than ever. She sat in a chair by the window, looking out on to the street, praying that Viola would return soon.

It must have been half an hour later when Sal Perkins came into the room with a note for her. It was from Viola. With trembling hands Betsy opened it.

> 'Dear little friend, I'm not coming back to Netherby's. Don't you fret about it. My lord has to go to S.A. soon so I am going to spend all my time with him until he goes. Stay in your job and when he has gone . . .' there was a big, damp blob on the paper . . . 'it's awful to write that, but he will go, and I'll have to come down to earth again. Then I'll come to you—I promise I shan't forget or desert you. I am sending in my notice. Will you pack up my things, and I will send his lordship's man to call for them. You remember him on the train from Leeds? Don't be sad. I may be wicked but I'm too happy to care. All my love to you, Viola.'

First Matthew. And now Viola was gone as well. She was alone, utterly alone, in the huge menacing city. It seemed to press down upon her. She felt herself shrinking into such insignificance that she began to wonder if she existed at all. Nothing had any meaning. Nothing.

At two o'clock Viola was waiting at Marble Arch and promptly on time Lady Louderdown's carriage appeared.

As Carson climbed down from the box, he said, 'His lordship's compliments, miss, but he's been detained at Headquarters. He sent a message to say would you mind waiting for him in his rooms. He hopes to be there soon.'

He handed her into the carriage. They trotted sedately down Park Lane past the great stone, bronze-railed mansions of the millionaires, down Curzon Street's charming curve of 18th-century brick houses, into the narrow canyon of Half Moon Street, with the trees and grazing sheep of Green Park framed like a landscape at the end of it. The carriage stopped at a tall, narrow house with a long row of names on a mahogany board just inside the entrance hall. Jevons, obsequious and attentive, was waiting there to guide her to the first floor. On a brass plate on a mahogany door she read the words, 'Captain, Lord Staffray'. Jevons unlocked the door, leading her through a tiny hall into a large, sunny, chintzy room with family and regimental photographs, rows of silver cups awarded for riding and polo, hunting and social magazines, the smell of cigars and a well-stocked sideboard.

'Make yourself at home, miss,' Jevons said jauntily. While not insolent, there was a touch of familiarity in his voice. 'Cup of tea? Glass of champagne?'

'No thanks. I'll just wait.'

'Well, his lordship shouldn't be long, specially as he knows a pretty girl like you's a-waiting for him.' He met the sharp, wary glance of the green eyes, and bowed himself apologetically out of the room.

Viola wandered about the room, looking at the photographs. There was a beautiful woman in a court dress and feathers, with James's dark-lashed Irish eyes. A tall, soldierly man in dress uniform, very handsome, with broad shoulders and James's crisp hair—James's nose must have looked like that before he broke it. There were various groups. A school group, James splendidly nonchalant in front, Matthew Lyttelton peering shyly from behind his shoulder.

There were social pictures. James in racing colours for a point-to-point, shooting parties with James, the tall soldierly man and the beautiful lady, and the Prince and Princess of Wales sitting stiffly in the front, black Labradors at their feet. There was also a painting of a great house among trees and spreading fields.

She became uneasy. It was like looking into little windows at a landscape she had never known. All these people who made up James's life, all the people from the other side of the counter. The ones that bought and did not serve. A rich, leisured world.

It was an hour before James came and he was in uniform. He looked so big in the scarlet jacket and gold epaulets, so soldierly with the sword by his side.

And there was a difference about him. A preoccupation, and when he looked at her she felt chilled, not rejected, but as though, somehow, he was already bidding her good-bye. She was frightened. He couldn't *not* want her. She had been so sure.

'What is it?' she cried. 'James, what has happened?'

He came across to her and grasped her shoulders tightly. She realized the new and beautiful dress and hat were wasted, he had not noticed them, but he was looking at her, seeing her in some strange, new, vivid way.

'The regiment is being mustered,' he said. 'I'll be leaving for Aldershot in a short while. We should be sailing for the Cape at the end of next month. Duchess, suddenly we have no time.'

She went white, she felt the blood drain from her. Her hands closed over her mouth as though to repress a scream. He thought she would faint, and caught her against him. She put her arms around him.

'How long have we got together?'

'Perhaps six weeks. I have two weeks' leave, and then I will go to Aldershot. I must go to see my father at Louderdown. My mother is in Italy and I do not want her to know until I have left England. We have no definite date for sailing as yet.'

'Why don't you want your mother to know?'

'She would weep. She would be afraid. She would go running round to every ambassador and cabinet minister she knows trying to pull strings to keep me here.'

'She loves you very much?'

'Yes—and I love her, but this is men's business. There is going to be war, and nothing can change that.'

'You would be ashamed not to go?'

'It would be unthinkable not to go with the regiment.'

'Ah . . .' She let out a long, quivering sigh. She would not cry, or be afraid, not while he was here. 'When will you go to see your father?'

'At the end of my leave—before I go to Aldershot.'

'So we have two weeks together?'

'Yes.'

'More. I could come to Aldershot. I can get rooms there, or stay in an hotel—you could come to me sometimes?'

He raised his head and looked into her eyes, overthrown, humbled. She was not asking anything from him. She was giving him herself, asking nothing in return.

'Viola . . . Duchess . . . I swear to you that if I return . . .'

'Ah-h . . .' Again the long, soft, quivering sigh. 'That *if*, love, that's the devil in it!' Her hands touched his mouth, closed over his hair. She kissed first one eyelid, then the other. Her hands moved down over his shoulders, closed round his back, as though she would press herself into him then and there, driving him wild with desire. 'That's the snag. If you could say to me—*when* I come back, that'd be quite a different kettle of fish. But you can't.' The tears swam beneath her eyelids but did not fall; her glance, her touch, seemed to be drawing him, the very essence of him, into her memory. As though she was registering, with every touch and glance, and sigh. This is James, my love . . . this dear and bonny crooked face, these blue eyes, this fine body . . . so young and strong, warm and virile, and for a short while—a month, maybe—it can be mine—and then, perhaps never again. 'We've got to be together,' she cried, 'until you go. Every minute, until you go. Not one minute must we waste. We'll not be miseries. We'll pretend we've got forever, my lord.'

His face lit with delight.

'What shall we do?' he asked. 'This is our first day—and our first night— our beginning. What would you like to do? Anything you want. Shall I take you out to dinner and the theatre? To the opera, the Gaiety, the Empire, or a play? What would you like . . . ?' He stopped, sat down on a nearby chair, pulled her on to his knee and removing her hat he ran his fingers into her mass of soft bronze hair, so that the pins fell out, and it tumbled down about her shoulders, almost to her waist. 'There's something—isn't there?—that you'd like to do—very much. I can see it. What is it?'

'You'll think I'm silly.'

'What does it matter? We'll be silly together. Tell me.' He raised her chin, so that she had to meet his eyes.

'I'd like to see your home, James. I'd like to see where you live—not here. This is just a place to be on your own. I mean your *real* home.'

'Louderdown?' he said, surprised.

'I'd like to see that too. But the house in London. It's funny to explain. You've been brought up in these two big houses, and you know who your folk were way back. For generations. I've lived in digs since I was born. A room with my mother, and the landlady treated her like dirt because she wasn't wed. I never knew my father. All I've got of him is a photo and a letter saying he was coming back, but the cholera was bad in Naples and he was in quarantine.' Her eyes were as serious as a questioning child's.

He held her closer, his child, his luscious woman, his bride. His Duchess. His love.

'I'll get out of this damned uniform into civvies,' he said. 'I'll order the carriage, and I'll take you round to see Staffray House. And afterwards we'll go out to dine.'

She sat very erect, every hair in place, as they drove up to the house in Belgrave Square. Once there, James took her hand and led her up the steps to the front door.

He rang the bell. 'My mother's abroad, as you know.'

'That's why I suggested it,' she said mischievously.

'I expect most of the staff have gone to Louderdown while she is away, and the house is empty.'

After a while they heard footsteps and a footman, not in uniform, opened the door.

'Why, my lord,' he exclaimed, 'I wasn't expecting you, her ladyship being away!'

'It's quite all right, Simpson—it is Simpson, isn't it?'

'Yes, my lord.'

'Miss Corbett wanted to see the house, so I'm going to show her round. Are you staying here alone?'

'There's the cook, my lord, and one of the maids, but they've both gone home for the weekend. I said they could, no one being here.'

'That's all right.' James led Viola into the great marble paved hall with the yellow and red Travertino pillars, the curving staircase with the wrought-iron and gilded banisters tortuously entwining the Louderdown staff and sunray crest. The *jardinière* was empty of ferns and orchids and no visiting cards were on the silver salver. A large portrait gazed down at them—his mother by Sargent with himself, at three years old, angelically fair and blue-eyed, in a white satin suit, leaning against her knee.

Viola, speechless, slowly turned round, gazing at everything, fingers to her lips, impressed by so much grandeur.

'It's like a museum,' she said.

'I'm afraid all the rooms are dust-sheeted, my lord,' the man said apologetically.

'That's all right. We'll manage.'

'Can I get you anything, m'lord?'

'No, thank you, Simpson. We'll ring if we need anything.'

'Very good, my lord.'

He vanished through the large, baize-lined door at the back of the hall.

Viola looked up at the little boy in the Sargent portrait, then at James, her mouth curling with laughter. 'What a little angel . . .' She touched his lips with hers, mocking. 'Things have changed a bit since then, my Jimmy, haven't they?'

They went through the morning and dining rooms, up the stairs into the huge first-floor drawing room, which could be opened by folding doors into a large L-shaped hall, big enough for a ball. They went into the winter garden at the back, filled with tropical plants, singing birds, and plume-tailed goldfish in a small pond where a fountain tinkled. They went into his mother's boudoir and bedroom, so feminine, so pretty, filled with pictures and mementoes of James. Into his father's austere bedroom furnished with the 18th-century mahogany, a shaving-stand, a commode, a small red-curtained four-poster. On the walls were yellowing army photographs of his father in India as a young man, and some excellent paintings of racehorses.

'He never comes here,' he explained. 'If he has to come to town, he sleeps at his club.'

'Not with your mother?'

He shook his head. 'Not for years.'

Viola shivered. 'It wouldn't suit me,' and she twisted her fingers into his.

They stopped at a door in the front of the house, and as he opened it James said, laughing, 'This is Her Royal Highness's Room. No, I mean, her Imperial Majesty's.'

'What—the Queen's? Old Vicky?'

'No. The Empress of Austria—she was assassinated last year. She loved to come to England for the hunting at one time, and one year she stayed at Louderdown. My father bought and schooled a special thoroughbred for her visit. She stayed one night in London on her way to Louderdown, and this room was specially decorated and furnished for the occasion. No one has ever used it since. Wait, I'll open the curtains . . .'

Viola stood in the doorway. The room had a faintly dusty, unused smell. She heard the curtains being drawn, the shutters folded back and then the late afternoon light flooded into the room.

'There's no electric light,' he said. 'Mother wouldn't have it put in. She wanted it just as the beautiful Elizabeth used it and there was no electricity then.'

'Was she very beautiful?'

'So I am told. She patted my head, but I don't remember. I was a baby.'

The room, faded and tarnished a little, was papered, hung and decorated in pale turquoise and gold brocade, like the inside of a jewel box. Walls, curtains, bed hangings. The 18th-century French furniture was fragile and gilded. The one painting over the hearth was a Boucher, delicate and sensual.

James indicated the rosy Venus and the plump pink-winged cherubs. 'I understand the Empress was not very impressed, although my mother brought it down from Louderdown especially. She preferred my father's paintings of his thoroughbreds.'

The great bed dominated the room, a gilded swan holding the draped brocade curtains, the bed end was curved cream gilt shell.

Viola went slowly forward, twitched back the dust cover. Beneath was a brocade bedspread. She pulled that back, exposing the bare mattress and down-filled pillows. She turned, her eyes wild with excitement. She crossed the door with her slow, swaying, seductive gait, closed it, locked it, walked back to the bed. Before James's astounded and entranced eyes she took off her hat, sent it whirling, pale bronze feather fronds twirling like a Catherine wheel, to the other side of the great bedroom. She pulled the pins out of her hair and let its magnificent length ripple down about her shoulders, sat on the edge of the bed, took off her shoes, threw them aside, then stretched out her arms to him.

'Viola!' He was shocked, tormented, then, suddenly caught into her mad reckless mood, he went across, took her in his arms, laid her back on the unmade bed, began expertly to unhook the high lace collar and the skin-fitting, boned bodice, while she lay back looking at him, smiling, mocking, abandoned.

'I may never be a duchess,' she whispered, 'or a countess, or a lady—perhaps not even just a plain Mrs—but this is the first time for me. So, James my lord, if it's going to be, then it's going to be on the Empress's bed.'

There, in the brocade jewel-box of a room, these two splendid and mutually obsessed creatures made love through the late summer afternoon. There James ravished her through the initiation of pain into a superb fulfilment. There was neither fear nor shyness nor embarrassment between them; they taught each other, claimed each other, calling forth heights of joy which neither of them was ever to forget or experience again.

CHAPTER FIVE

During the days that followed James and Viola lived intensely, locked in their own private world. Recklessly he insisted that they stay on at Staffray House until the time came for him to leave London, and when Viola protested that his mother would be outraged, he said his mother was in Italy and would not know.

'People will tell her.'

'Who?'

'Servants, people in the square.'

'And if they do? It will soon be forgotten. She will be angry, but she will forgive me, as she always does all my scrapes.'

Viola, lying deep in the bed with his smiling face against her breast, could very well believe it. She too would forgive him anything.

They had a cook, a housemaid, a footman and the ubiquitous Jevons to serve them in the house and Carson to drive them out anywhere they wished. Viola could guess what these servants were saying, but it did not worry her: she was lost in her own illusion that these few weeks were an eternity of happiness. At some future time they would both look back upon their conduct with bewildered amazement. Perhaps with deep regret. But not yet. For them there was neither past nor future, only the wonderful, passionate, extravagant present.

Viola thrived in the atmosphere of luxury, blooming like a rose in June, a tawny, silken rose. She gave her orders with charm and authority, as though she had lived in a big house all her life, delighting James and the servants—all of them, that is, but Jevons, who watched her with veiled insolence in his hard, predatory eyes.

The season was nearly over so far as the fashionable world was concerned, and the houses round the square were emptying. Word went round the mess that young Staffray had found himself a real beauty, and if in the restaurants, at race meetings and theatres, ladies passed them with averted eyes, his fellow officers buzzed around Viola like bees round a honey pot. She was the toast of the town, always surrounded by an entourage of smart young soldiers, and her nickname, Duchess, was on everyone's lips, bandied in club, mess-room and drawing-room with shocked disgust or wild admiration.

James showered gifts on her. He delighted in spoiling her. He was proud of her unerring natural taste, and to see her in beautiful clothes. He loved to show her off. He had a young, proud man's pleasure in knowing that every other man who saw her envied him. He hired horses and took her riding in the Row, delighting in her quickness to learn, the strength of her long slim wrists, adoring her in her skin-fitting habit, the little hard hat veiled over her fiery hair.

Sometimes they did not get up until midday, lying in each other's arms in the blue brocade room, then they would go out to lunch at the Cecil or the Savoy, a bonny couple, beautifully dressed. In the afternoons they would drive out to a race meeting, or take a punt to Cookham and laze and laugh the summer hours away.

Through the little pubs round Belgrave Square where the grooms and footmen went, the scandal slid from mouth to mouth, out into the country to the great houses, so that in smoking-rooms men guffawed, and in the drawing-rooms ladies whispered together in hushed tones, clamping into warning silence if any unmarried girl were present.

'What a terrible thing,' they murmured. 'Poor Lady Louderdown! His poor *dear* mama!'

Herbert Netherby heard the news from one of his favourite young gentlemen in the haberdashery. He told his sister. There had been many other occasions when Arthur Netherby had noticed an attractive assistant in his emporium, but Herbert had never felt that they were a danger—until Viola came.

He saw the scandal as his chance of a kill. This would finish off any chance that impertinent bitch had with his father. One evening, when Arthur sat silent and preoccupied at the head of the dining table, Herbert told him what had happened. Arthur regarded his son coldly. His protuberant eyes were filled with dislike. To him Herbert was not only a nelly but a whining sneak as well.

'*And* living with Lord Staffray openly at Staffray House,' he faltered before his father's frozen stare. 'A *common* shop-girl! What his lady mother would say if she knew, I *can't* think! Everyone in the shop is talking about it now. Why, she had the impudence to send a maid in for gloves and handkerchiefs on Friday. To be charged to his lordship. I think it would be as well, sir, to dismiss that little friend of hers, a stupid little thing anyway, *all* thumbs—and then so far as we are concerned, the whole thing will be over and done with . . .'

'It is disgraceful,' exclaimed Emily. 'It will give the store a bad name if it was known you ever employed such a woman!'

Arthur Netherby slammed his hand down on the polished table. He glared at his offspring. He remembered Viola's fresh young beauty, now, it seemed, lost to him for ever, and they appeared to him more dessicated, more like their dreary martyr of a mother than ever before. Carping, life-hating. When he spoke they both shrank at the tone of his voice.

'I do not wish to hear anything about this matter. And as for you, Herbert, perhaps you would keep your mind on your work at the emporium, and not go round gossiping and mincing like a girl apprentice. It is for me to decide whom I shall dismiss.'

He rose, threw down his table napkin and strode out of the room.

'Well!' exclaimed Herbert. 'The old brute! I was only trying to help!'

'What is the matter with him?' wailed Emily. 'He's drinking so much. He's out every night after dinner. He never goes to church now. Huggins says that in the kitchen they say he's *in love* with this awful woman. Herbert . . . *supposing* this young lord gets tired of her, and Father brings her back here?'

'Don't let your imagination run away with you,' said Herbert crossly. The boy assistants he drank with in the local pubs were talking along these lines. 'Not that this Staffray *won't* get tired of her. All men get tired of *that* sort of woman. I mean, what do they have? But Father has too much sense to bring such a woman home . . . but, I tell you, Em, I wouldn't like it even if he set her up somewhere . . . she's the kind that might really rook him . . .'

If he had followed his father out of the house that night he would have been even more alarmed.

Arthur Netherby went to Belgrave Square and stood outside Staffray House, looking up at the tall façade from the far side of the road. The great plane trees in the square cast heavy shadows between the gas lamps and his dark-clad figure could hardly be seen. He knew the store was buzzing with gossip about Viola, but pride had not allowed him to question anyone about her, least of all Herbert. But now, at least, he knew where she was.

It was nearly nine o'clock when a carriage drew up and the door opened, sending a brilliant shaft of light under the columned portico and across the steps. He saw the golden boy and girl, hand in hand, come out of the house. James, so tall and fine and handsome in his evening clothes, the tall hat tipped back on his crisp brown hair, Viola with pearls round her long white throat, and a greenish orchid in her red hair, matching the colour of her chiffon gown. It was so hot that the long opera cloak of flame-coloured taffeta banded with Valenciennes lace was thrown back, displaying her low cut décolletage, her beautiful shoulders and bosom rising from a froth of frills. Even her shoes were green, the buckles glittering as she ran down the steps.

Both of them were completely unaware of the world around them. They had eyes only for each other. They were consuming time, drawing every sensation from every hour of every day, every vibrant touch, look, every burning caress, every abandoned moment, into themselves, storing memories against their coming parting.

Arthur hailed a hansom and followed them to a restaurant in the West End. He hung about outside, jostled by the crowds, the target of every street-walker, standing like a beggar, waiting for her to come out. He followed them to a music-hall, and sat in the stalls watching Viola sitting in the front of a box, the stage lights illuminating her beauty as she leaned towards the stage, watched the shadow envelop her as from time to time she whispered to James, and kissed him softly behind her fan. She seemed to have a new beauty, radiant and almost unearthly.

Arthur Netherby watched and burned with a monstrous jealousy, her remoteness from him, her intimacy with her young lover, destroying his sanity.

It was their last night in London together. In the morning they would travel up to Yorkshire so that James could go to Louderdown and say good-bye to his father before he joined his regiment. They would stay in an hotel, because they could not be parted even for one night. James had sent Jevons ahead to Aldershot to rent a villa for them, discreetly outside the town, where they could be together until the regiment embarked. On this, their last night in London, James took Viola to the opera and they sat together in his mother's box.

He did not quite know why he had done this—a defiant gesture in the face of society. A proclaiming of his passion for her—the feeling of finality —'we who are about to die'. The last night of their wildly beautiful fling before he joined his regiment.

Afterwards Viola went back to Belgrave Square in a trance. Everything in her, every drop of Italian blood had pulsed to the music. The orchestra, the splendid soaring voices, the beautiful melodies; it was an experience beyond her dreams.

As they went into the Empress's room she said to him, 'It was like when you and I are making love, James . . . that music. I could feel it like I feel you . . . taking me up and out of the world.' She put her arms about him, lifted her mouth to his seeking lips. 'I don't care what happens. Ever. This has been so grand . . . nothing could be better if we lived to be a hundred.'

The blue Dresden lamps with gilded rams' heads had been lit and the room was warm with the soft yellow light. James went into the dressing-room and Viola to the window to draw back the heavy brocade curtains, and fold the shutters. She pushed up the window to let in the cool night air, and looked out at the stars above the trees. Glancing along the square, she saw a man move into a pool of yellow lamplight, his heavily moustached face raised towards her. She knew it was Netherby, and drew back at once, closing the shutters. Revulsion and a terrible pity swept over her. Poor devil. Poor, silly old devil! Standing out there in the dark! What for? What on earth had she ever done that he should feel like this about her? What good did it do him?

James came out of the dressing-room, clean, smelling of lavender water, wrapped in his gown of thin white Indian silk.

'You look as though you've seen a ghost,' he said.

'Something like that . . .' She shivered. 'There's a cool breeze blowing.' She did not tell him about Arthur Netherby. What was there to tell?

They travelled up to Yorkshire in the style in which James was accustomed, a reserved first-class carriage. It was not so long ago, he told Viola, that the Staffrays had their own coach kept on the sidings at Louderdown, to be coupled to any express they wished to take.

They lunched romantically on the train, recalling their first meeting, ordering the same menu, entranced and sentimental, laughing at what Viola called their 'soppiness'.

In Leeds, at the best hotel, James took a suite, and if the booking clerk had any doubt about the respectability of the beautiful young woman accompanying him, he kept it to himself. It was none of his business.

The next morning she kissed him good-bye. He was going to see his father. 'Don't be afraid, my lord. I won't ask to see Louderdown.'

'If you want to, you shall,' he said, and meant it.

When he had gone she went to the window and looked out at Leeds, the city she had known so well, and where she had worked all her life until she and Betsy had gone down to London. Only four months ago! It seemed a lifetime. She did not seem the same girl who had bidden Sam Hardcastle good-bye.

It was the first time since that extraordinary first night together in Staffray House that she had been alone. The first time that waking, sleeping, eating, James had not been by her side. She shivered, thinking of the parting ahead and the long grey days without him. Perhaps for ever. But—

if he came back, it would be quite different. He would come back on the other side of danger. To his parents, to a great estate and fortune. He would not just be a young soldier going to war, but the heir to the Earl of Louderdown. The passion would cool and the pressure ease. What would she mean to him then?

'I thought I'd go to London with Betsy to seek my fortune and make something of my life,' she thought soberly. 'I never thought of anything like this.' She could not imagine living without him now.

She looked at her reflections in the triple oval mirrors. She was pale, with blue shadows beneath her eyes. From too much loving?

'There's no such thing,' she said aloud, rising sharply to her feet. 'Not with a lad like my James. No woman living could get enough of his loving.'

Suddenly she wanted to get away from the loving and the luxury, to be alone. She wanted to go out into this grey North-Country city and talk to someone with their feet on the ground, and immediately thought of Sam Hardcastle. Of course. She would go and see him.

She dressed carefully. Sam was always particular, had given her good advice about clothes. She put on her hat, took up her gloves and parasol. It was curious how quickly one became used to taste and luxury. She wore what she had come to think of as a simple summer town outfit. But when she swayed through the entrance of Hardcastle's in her beautifully cut tussore dress, and her little golden straw hat trimmed with silk marigolds, the chief floor-walker came sailing obsequiously towards her, and it was only when he had bowed, asking Madam how he could help, that he recognized her. His jaw dropped in astonishment.

He went red and then pale, and gasped, 'By God! Vi Corbett!'

'Aye,' she said, dropping into the old vernacular. 'It's me, Mr Shaw. Viola Corbett. I'm in Leeds for a day, so I thought I'd drop in and see the old shop—see Mr Hardcastle too, if he's about.'

'Mr Hardcastle is not here. He is very ill. He had a stroke a week ago, and is not expected to recover.'

Viola went white, and reached for the counter behind her. All her adult years Sam Hardcastle had been there. The man who had let the fatherless child play in his garden. Who had given her mother extra money. Who, later, had found a place for her in his firm, who had her taught her job and protected her, spoiled and loved her in a simple and undemanding way. The man whom she had always gone to for advice, affection and help —Sam, half-father half-admirer, whom she had known since childhood.

'Where is he?' she asked.

'At his home,' the man answered. 'There's been a specialist and a nurse in attendance.'

'When did it happen?'

'As I said, a week ago. In the office here. He's been very tired, not himself for some time. Like the life had gone out of him.' He did not say 'since you left' but she knew he was thinking that.

She turned towards the door, and he trotted after her, nervously twisting his waxed moustache.

'I understand he can see no visitors . . .'

She smiled, but her eyes were full of tears.

'Happen he'll see me,' she said.

She took a train to Guiseley, and from there hired a carriage to drive her out to the big square house on the moorland road, standing among its prim orderly gardens and broad paddocks.

It was still the same. The white lace curtains, which once her mother had washed in the outhouse at the back, slaving over the steaming copper. The greenhouses. The rigid beds of geraniums and dahlias. The hothouse where Sam had grown his grapes and peaches and carried her on his shoulder to reach the highest fruit, giving her a weekly sixpence when she went home with her mother on Saturdays.

'Wait for me,' she said to the driver. 'I'll likely not be long.'

She went up the whitened steps which her mother had scrubbed and hearth-stoned, and rang the polished brass bell. A plain elderly maid came to the door, a woman she did not know, who looked questioningly at the beautiful, exquisitely dressed young woman on the step.

'Is Mrs Hardcastle in?'

'Well, yes, miss, but she's seeing no visitors—the master being so ill. She's none so well herself.'

'She'll see me. Tell her Vi Corbett.'

The maid left, and in a few minutes, glancing at her curiously, asked her to come in.

Mrs Hardcastle had risen from the sofa, her face red with indignation. She was a plain woman, whose adopted illnesses had been a screen for her entrenched frigidity.

She had not seen Viola for some years, although of course she had heard the scandalous whispers about her and Sam which had made her demand her dismissal. She had expected a pert, common little shop-girl, whom she could browbeat. She was taken aback at the vision in cream and orange, perfect from her kid gloves to her lace and fringed silk parasol.

'I've just heard Mr Hardcastle is very ill,' Viola said without preliminaries. 'I'm in Leeds for a day. I hoped I could see him.'

The woman opened her mouth, but the indignant protest died beneath the calm, sad eyes of the girl before her. Sam had scarcely moved for a week—until yesterday. The doctor said he was dying, and the only words he had said were about this girl.

'Vi,' he had muttered. 'Where's she gone? Where's my little lass, then?'

Mrs Hardcastle swallowed, hesitated, patted her iron grey hair.

'Well,' she said, 'you'd best see him. The only word he's spoken since it happened was your name. It's more shame to the pair of you that he should think of you, his fancy woman, and not of his lawful wedded wife.'

'It was not like that, Mrs Hardcastle.'

The woman bristled. 'Are you trying to tell me he worn't daft about you?'

'He was very fond of me—and I of him. How could I help it? He was so good and kind to me, but it wasn't like you think. Nothing to be ashamed about.'

'Well, it makes no difference now.' Mrs Hardcastle looked at Viola resentfully but could not help admiring her. 'You're bonny enough to set any man off. The doctor says he's dying. Tha'd better come up.'

Viola followed her up the stairs to the first floor and into the darkened room smelling of illness and medicine. She could see the square, motionless, grey head, the tired face, yellow against the white pillow. She dropped her handbag and parasol and went swiftly across the room to him, lifting his head on to her arm, laying her warm, smooth young cheek against his.

'Sam,' she said. 'Sam, love! I've come to see you.'

His eyes opened, looked round blindly, a helpless hand wavered in an effort to take hers.

'It's Vi, isn't it?' he said hoarsely and his face lit with joy. 'It's my little lass. Vi.' And turning his face into her sweet, warm breast he gave a long, shuddering sigh, and died like a child who had fallen asleep.

Viola knelt beside Sam without moving, until the doctor came, then she rose, picked up her handbag and parasol, and went down to the waiting carriage, the tears streaming down her cheeks.

James had lunch with his father, and afterwards they strolled through the great house together, along the marble-tiled corridors beneath the ceilings of carved golden oak, and across the gardens to the paddocks where his father's valuable brood mares and their foals cropped the grass.

James had not mentioned Viola. If the scandal of Belgrave Square had reached his father, he did not speak of it.

'Don't get yourself killed, James,' he said gruffly. 'Someone has to inherit this place. Apart from the fact that it would be the death of your mother.'

'I'll do my best, sir.'

They talked about racing stock, the prospects of the jumping season and the autumn shooting as though James would still be there, and then walked to where the high-wheeled dog-cart was waiting to take him to the station.

'Write to your mother as soon as you know you're going. Very wise not to tell her before. She would only have made a damned fuss. We've got to stop these Boers. Teach them a lesson.'

They shook hands and exchanged the ceremonial family embrace. James climbed into the dog-cart, took the reins and drove to Louderdown Station.

Back in the hotel room in Leeds he found Viola in tears. He had never seen her cry. She burrowed into his arms as though seeking consolation from his strong, living body and told him about Sam Hardcastle.

'I put my arm round him, and he just smiled and died. He was so good to me when I was a child and my mother worked for them. He gave me pennies and peaches, and sometimes a ride in his carriage. And he gave me a job in his shop, bought me pretty clothes, and gave me a good time—just as if I were his daughter. Nothing cheap or nasty. He really did love me. And I loved him. He was so kind.'

'Don't cry,' he said. 'You were there—that must have made him happy.'

He thought of the troopship waiting for him somewhere, and the coming war. Where would she be if death came to him, this spoiled child of love? Who would care for her and comfort her then? He embraced her with an aching tenderness.

'It's not that he's gone,' she wept. 'He was old, and ill, and we all have to go . . . it was the waste of him, his goodness and kindness. He had so much love to give, and no one but me to give it to, and I didn't deserve it. Not really. His wife was a cold woman—and he had no children . . . I don't think love should be wasted. It's too precious. A chap like Sam should have had a whole brood of kids and a real woman to love.' She raised her tear-wet face to his in a sort of desperation. 'We won't waste a minute of our time of loving, Jim . . . not a minute, so long as we're still together.'

When they returned to London a telegram was waiting, ordering him to Aldershot at once, and they packed up and left immediately for the small villa Jevons had been able to rent for them.

Every day James spent at Headquarters with the regiment, and only in the evenings could he be with her. The hours were numbered now, but still their love burned with a bright, consuming flame. Viola sometimes wondered if it were possible to die of love, and if so, she wished it could happen to her if ever she heard that James was lost. She clung desperately to the now hopeless hope that war still would not be declared.

CHAPTER SIX

James and Viola had a month together in Aldershot before his regiment sailed for South Africa, and the reckless pace of their honeymoon in Belgrave Square was over. In London he had been Lord Staffray, the rich, smart young man about town, and she had been his beautiful, scandalous young mistress, Duchess. In Aldershot he was a captain of his regiment. The brilliantly uniformed toy soldier, caparisoned for parades and ceremonial attendance on Royalty, vanished overnight. He was a real soldier now; preoccupied, working long hours, responsible for the equipment and embarkation of his men.

Nominally he was in barracks, but almost every evening at some hour he managed to go to Viola. It was a strange new James who came to her, often tired, clad in khaki service uniform, his hair clipped close for active service—'like a convict' she said, running her hands over the crisp stubble.

Now she was alone a great deal, running his home, making certain, in the brief hours that he could be with her, that everything was done for his comfort and relaxation. She was not lonely—she lived only for his arrival. In London she had been an outrageously attractive figure, courted by his mess mates. In Aldershot she had no place. She knew she would not be accepted by the ladies of the regiment. The husbands who would kiss her hand gallantly at Epsom would look the other way in their wives' presence. She stayed in the villa, waited, damming down her fears of the future without her lover.

They employed a maid of all work as well as Jevons, so that he had very little to do. As the days passed she was again aware of familiarity in his attitude towards her, something sly and suggestive in his bold yet evasive eyes. Although she was wary of him, it did not occur to her that he would dare to step out of line while James was still in England.

She lay in a hammock in the garden one hot day in August. She had abandoned her corsets for comfort, and was wearing a Japanese kimono of embroidered azure silk. She heard the french doors open and raised her head. Jevons came out of the house towards her and she sat up eagerly, yet with dread in her heart, thinking it might be a message from James—and every message these days might mean farewell.

'Mrs Smythe-Brown, the owner of the house, has called, madam, to enquire whether his lordship found everything satisfactory.'

She swung her feet down from the hammock.

'Is she—is Mrs Smythe-Brown here?'

'She is waiting outside in her trap, madam. She sent the groom to enquire.' Jevons dropped his professional manner, showing his teeth like a randy tom-cat. 'Strike me, Duchess, you've brass enough for anything, but you can't invite *her* into the house. She's a colonel's widow. She don't know about you. You'll have all the memsahibs in Aldershot in an uproar if she finds out about you and his lordship.'

'Tell Mrs Smythe-Brown that Lord Staffray thanks her, and everything is in excellent order. And Jevons . . .'

He turned insolently, and she said, 'When she has gone, will you come back here. I wish to speak to you.'

He made a mocking little bow. 'Anything you say, Duchess.'

She kept a tight rein upon her temper and wished she were wearing something more formal. One of those high, imposing collars which at least gave an air of authority. She was not afraid of a cheap joker like Jevons, but she lacked the weapons to put him in his place.

There was the sound of a pony-trap trotting away, and Jevons came back into the garden. The very way he walked was different, lounging, natural, the stiff-shouldered stance and precisely bent arms of the manservant abandoned.

'What arrangements has his lordship made for you—when he goes abroad with the regiment?' she asked him.

'He's accepted my notice. The rooms in Half Moon Street will be closed. He did offer to find me a place at Louderdown but I'm one for town life. He'll give me a reference and a decent present—always open-handed, is my Lord Jim. But then, the likes of him can afford to be. Look after you, too, I expect. You ought to get a real shake-down, Duchess. A fine girl like you.'

He leaned his hand upon the lime tree above her head, and stood looking down at her soft red mouth and the triangle of skin showing between the folds of her kimono from which her long throat emerged like the stem of a tall white flower.

'Come off it, Duchess,' he said. 'Come down to earth. He may never come back, and if he does, it's evens he'll have different ideas. I've got ideas, too, Duchess. I've got savings. A nice little house somewhere near Piccadilly, and a few tables running: roulette, baccarat, and a girl like you to bring the custom in.' He touched her shoulder with his thin dry finger. 'How's about it? Not a word until m'lord's gone, though. Don't want to spoil his last few days at home . . . just between the two of us, eh?'

She walked away from him, hoping he could not see she was trembling. He called after her but she did not turn round. She felt a little sick and frightened, realizing how James's presence, position and money had protected her. When he came home that evening she told him exactly what had happened, and for the first time saw his anger. He dismissed Jevons immediately without a reference. The man was still impeccably polite before his master although his sly eyes glinted dangerously as he passed Viola. When he had gone the dull little house with its Benares trays and pampas grass seemed free of a baleful presence. Viola had not realized until then how much she disliked him.

The regiment entrained for the docks one morning in early September, and Viola travelled alone to London by train, and on to Tilbury, booking a room there in an hotel. It was almost midnight when James came to her, grey-faced with fatigue, hoarse from shouting orders. He would have to leave before dawn. At first they neither slept nor made love, but just lay quietly, her arm about him, his head on her breast. It was their last night together. For many months. Perhaps for ever.

It was dark in the bedroom, and out upon the estuary they heard the plaintive sounds of sirens as the shipping nosed its way up river on the tide. It was a mournful, haunting sound, and James's Irish blood was stirred as at a banshee wail of premonition. This last dawn left them with nothing more certain than the next few hours. The parting would be like a real wound, a tearing apart. He had the regiment. His men. Perhaps war, the excitement, a man's life, with the demands of his profession. But what had Viola?

'What will you do, Duchess, when I am gone?'

He had given her money, and would arrange for more. She would find a flat, she said, get her little friend Betsy from the shop to live with her, and wait for his return. He would write to her at Half Moon Street. The porter there would give her his letters. He would leave instructions.

He saw his splendid girl, caged like a young tiger, and said despairingly, 'What will you *do?*'

She spoke softly into his shoulder. 'Don't worry about me. I've always managed. You're not to worry about me, only of taking care of yourself. I'll wait—until you come back. Never fear!'

'If—I should not come, Duchess?' He moved his head restlessly upon the pillow, like one of his own thoroughbreds struggling to free itself.

She calmed him as she would have done an animal or a child.

'Hush, my love, my Jim. Hush. Don't talk like that.'

'But . . . it might happen.'

'If you don't come back, Jim, I'll die. Oh, I'll be walking about—and happen there'll be other men. I'm not pretending I'm the kind to live my life out like a nun. But there'll never be another man I shall love. Not like it's been between us. That's been something for poets to sing about. But you'll come back to me.'

Something for poets to sing about. He buried his face into her hair taking in the smell of her, the smell and feel of clean silken hair, the smell of young sweet flesh, the scent of gardenias that hung about her. They had never talked much before. They had laughed, and touched and caressed, and loved, and now there was no time to say all the things that should be said.

'I've been thinking of what you said, Duchess, about that shopkeeper fellow up in the north, who loved you, and who died, and how just knowing you was all he ever had from life. Well, I've really had you. If I die, Viola, and I might—a soldier has always to accept that—it doesn't really matter now.' He felt her sudden movement of protest, the impassioned tightening of her arms, and held her closer. 'Ah, yes, I know . . . it will be you who will be left behind. But remember, dearest, that life cannot give me anything better than these weeks with you. Out there I want to do my duty, and have courage, and command well, and look after my chaps . . . but there'll be lots of fellows who'll be thinking of what they might have had from life. Not me. I've had you, Duchess, the very best.'

'Ah, Jimmy,' she said, 'what a long speech, my darling, my love, my dearest one . . .' She raised herself on her elbow, and bent over him, her falling hair about him, her lovely breasts naked above his face, and they took each other in a long farewell before the dawn, so that she cried aloud in rapture even while the salt tears, hidden by the darkness, ran slowly down her cheeks.

She stood on the dock next day a little apart from the other families, watching until the ship moved away from its moorings on the tide, and into the grey, misty September afternoon. James had once or twice come to the rail to wave, and she had gazed at him intensely, as though trying to photograph that beloved face into her soul. The crisp brown hair, now cut so short, the sweet laughing mouth with the beautiful teeth that had kissed all her exigent young body, the deep blue Irish eyes. Momentarily she saw him, broad shoulders clad in khaki, snatching a second from duty, coming to the rail to look at her, to raise a hand, and then a final salute, as the pilot went aboard, and the dripping mooring ropes were released, glittering in the sunlight. She stretched her arms out to him, as though she could fly across the intervening water to his embrace. Then the regimental band played the *National Anthem,* and as the big steamer moved out into midstream behind the tugs, growing fainter as the ship slid slowly into the sunrise, '*Will Ye No' Come Back Again?*'

Her hands dropped to her sides. The ecstasy subsided, like sand running from an hour glass, leaving her completely empty.

The ship faded from sight. The other women ceased to wave and turned away from the dockside. Presently she was alone—except for the stevedores winding ropes, and the watermen with their wherries. Another big steamer began to edge towards the dock, and a sergeant asked her to move away. More men were arriving to be shipped away to South Africa. Viola returned to the hotel to pick up her case before starting on her journey back to Aldershot.

James had paid the rent of the villa until the end of September and had given her £1,000 in cash which she was to bank and draw upon. If he was away for a long time he would instruct his lawyers to make further provision for her. Neither of them had thought about the future, and Viola had asked for nothing. It was only in the last few days that he had begun to worry about her, and, belatedly, drew out this large sum of money for her immediate needs.

The train wound along the Thames valley, passing riverside stations, with glimpses of house-boats and rippling water. The summer was passing and with it part of her life. As she travelled she seemed to come out of a dream, and slowly her real, self-reliant North-Country self began to reassert itself. She had lived during these past weeks entirely for and with someone else. It was time to come down to earth again.

At the villa in Aldershot she found the little maid-servant in tears. She had locked up and gone home for the night, being 'feared' to stay alone in the house, and there had been a burglary. The police had been and gone. The desk had been broken into, but nothing else touched. The money which James had left her had been locked into one of the drawers; it was, of course, gone. She was wearing the pearls he had given her, and the small brooch, Erhmann's gift, was in her handbag. She counted her worldly assets. Her two pieces of jewellery: about £10 in cash in her handbag: and in the bank about £20 more, the remains of the present Sam Hardcastle had given her when she left Leeds—most of which had gone on pretty clothes to please James. But she still had all the beautiful clothes James had given her in London.

She should have had more sense than to leave the money in the villa. She might have expected Jevons to take his sneak-thief's revenge.

There was also a letter from the landlady, Mrs Smythe-Brown. Having learned of the irregular situation existing between her tenants, she requested Miss Corbett to vacate the premises as soon as possible. Her solicitors would be returning a month's rent to Lord Staffray's solicitors. Legally Viola could insist on staying, but she did not want a scandal buzzing among the army wives. It did not matter to her, but it would matter to James's family—and perhaps, one day, to him.

She packed the few clothes she had brought with her to Aldershot, and wrote a note to Mrs Smythe-Brown saying she was leaving immediately.

It would be different when James came back. She must start to face up to that now. He could not give his whole life to a woman his family and his world would never acknowledge—they, the regiment and society, would all be against her. When he came back it would no longer be a time of wine and roses, a few weeks of snatched passionate bliss. It would be all their lives . . . and what would it hold for her? Would she be content to become an anonymous woman waiting in humiliating obscurity for the brief moments he could spare for her? She who loved life, pleasure and admiration.

The thought haunted her all the way back to London and she thrust it angrily away. She had to think about the present—what she would do *now*. She must be sensible and practical. She felt Sam Hardcastle's loss acutely. If he had still been alive she would have gone straight up to Yorkshire to seek his help and advice, and the comfort and kindness which he had never denied her. But it was no use thinking about that.

She booked a room in a small private hotel for the night and the next morning she took a cab to Staffray House to collect the rest of her clothes. All her lovely evening dresses, her wraps trimmed with fur and ostrich fronds, her elegant day dresses and pretty hats and shoes were there. It was a relief to find the house still closed and shuttered—otherwise she might not have dared climb the imposing steps.

The young footman opened the door and his jaw dropped at her request to collect and pack her things.

He went red to his ears, rolling down his shirt sleeves for he was not in uniform. He was a country boy not used to handling the sophisticated difficulties of his betters.

'Why, madam, Miss Corbett,' he said, terrified, 'I thought you had them. That Jevons, his lordship's man, came yesterday and said he had orders to collect anything you might have left here. Said it was more tactful like, in case my lady came rushing home once she heard his lordship had joined his regiment overseas.' He looked sheepish, for he had lost his heart to his master's beautiful young mistress and would not have offended her for the world.

'Well, it was tactful all right,' said Viola. She could well guess what Jevons had done with her wardrobe; sold it to a dealer. There was nothing to be done. She gave the scared boy a smile and a tip. 'Don't worry, Simp-

son. You did the right thing,' she said, then went down the steps, paid off
her hansom and walked thoughtfully back to her hotel near Victoria.

A job—and a place to live. But first of all she must go to see Betsy.

She waited until just after eight o'clock, because she did not want to
cause comment or get Betsy into trouble by seeking her out in the shop.
When she reached the hostel in Eastcastle Street and rang the tinny bell
she felt a little shiver pass over her. It was so shabby, the whole house run
to take advantage of the helpless poverty of Mr Netherby's employees. It
was everything she hated, everything she had left behind. Sal Perkins
came shuffling along to open the door and gaped when she saw Viola.

'Hallo, Sal. I've come to see Miss Holder. Has she finished her supper
yet?'

'Yes, I expect she's in the bedroom . . . that's where she usually is.
Keeps to 'erself since you left. Sits up there alone.'

'Right, I'll go up.'

'I don't know, Duchess, whether I orter let you . . . not without letting
Mrs 'Arding know, she's that perticlar . . .'

There was a little flash of anger in Viola's eyes as she swept past into
the drab hall and up the stairs. The late summer evening sun made the
house look grubbier than ever. She opened the bedroom door.

Betsy was sitting by herself at the window, gazing down on the street.
Her little figure with its tightly clenched hands looked so alone, so utterly
bereft, that Viola was stricken with self-reproach. In the wild abandon of
her love affair, she had forgotten Betsy. Forgotten her timidity and loneli-
ness, forgotten how much she needed protection from spite and teasing,
from the bullying of her superiors or the criticism of customers. She
looked like a little prisoner in a cell waiting hopelessly for release.

'Betsy!'

Betsy turned her head and at the sight of the tall, red-haired girl standing in the evening sunlight, she leapt to her feet, and stretched out her
arms, and Viola was hugging her, incoherent with tears.

Betsy gabbled the whole story. It had been so awful. The girls had
teased and tormented her about the Duchess and her 'fancy chap'. Miss
Heath and Mr Herbert had found fault all the time. She kept making
mistakes, and Mr Herbert wanted to sack her, Mrs Harding had kept on
calling Viola awful names, and then Mr Lyttelton had had to stop seeing
her.

'But why on earth?'

'They said he'd have to leave,' wailed Betsy. 'The Vicar and Mrs
Everard—because of me. And he can't, because of his mother. Oh Vi, I
just hadn't anyone . . . no one . . . and I've been so miserable . . .'

Viola rocked her little friend like a mother.

'Stop crying, Betsy love. It's going to be all right. I've got a little money. I'll get somewhere to live for both of us, away from this pig sty. I'll get a job, and I'll look after us both . . . and then, perhaps, when my lord comes back, you can stay with me as my little companion. There now, Bet, it will be all right. I swear you won't be here more than another week . . . I promise you.'

Mrs Harding appeared at the doorway, baleful with indignation.

'It is only through Mr Netherby's mistaken kindness that she is here at all. I'd thank you, Corbett, to leave at once. I will not have your sort here. This is a decent house and we all know what you are . . .'

Why, Viola wondered, should Arthur Netherby protect Betsy? She had known him dismiss other assistants instantly for trifling inefficiencies. She bade Betsy good-bye, promising to see her soon, and without speaking a word to the fuming Mrs Harding, she left.

She spent the next week looking for work and somewhere to live. Work she found in an expensive French glovers in Piccadilly. She had hesitated about the reference she must supply. There was no point in writing to Hardcastle's now Sam was dead, and she did not want to apply to Arthur Netherby: she did not want to be beholden to him. She remembered the waiting figure outside Staffray House with a touch of dread. What had he been waiting for? For her to come within his power again? Was that why he had been so lenient with Betsy? In a way he both embarrassed and frightened her, but she needed work urgently, so she wrote to him and was relieved and a little taken aback when he immediately sent an excellent reference to her new employers. Her heart warmed a little towards him. Perhaps he was not so bad; perhaps he had forgiven her for her brash, unthinking actions. She had lived a lifetime during the past weeks and now knew what heartache could be, weeping through the long nights with empty arms and the fear of war.

To find a place to live was more difficult. Clean, comfortable rooms with good food were expensive, and even with her new job and commission, she would not have money to burn. And they were inclined to be hedged about by rigidly moral landladies, with rules, regulations and prohibitions about visitors, about keys and what time one was allowed to stay out. The free and easy places, on the other hand, were raffish and dubious, and she could not possibly take Betsy into that kind of place.

She went further out into the suburbs, and one afternoon found a cottage to let in Clapham Old Town: one of a small row, two rooms up and two down, a cold pump over the sink, an outside privy at the end of the garden. But dry, with a good oven, and tiny gardens back and front. It was not cheap for what it was, £30 a year, but with the horse-drawn tramways and local trains coming out rents in the suburbs were rising.

They would have fares, and would have to buy furniture, but she paid a quarter's rent in advance, and with a few secondhand bits of furniture, they moved in. By herself she could have lived more comfortably—but the sacrifice was worth it to see Betsy's beaming face when she first saw this shabby little home.

On October 18 there was a fever of excitement in the air. The streets were raucous with the shouts of the newspaper-sellers running through the streets with flaring poster headlines. Knots of men gathered, talking excitedly together. Sometimes flushed and a little unsteady they broke into cheers and songs. A rash of red, white and blue erupted over the whole city. War had been declared.

The staff of Dwyer & Netherby's hurried with the clearing-up and dust-sheeting that night. Even the sour-faced Miss Heath was too excited with the news to quibble, and to Herbert Netherby's petulant irritation the young men employees gathered together, whispered about 'going for a soldier', and even looked at him with a challenging defiance as they thought of being heroes and getting away from the hated 'crib'. 'What about it?' they seemed to ask. 'What about the boss's son? Would he stay in safety, working in the store, or would he be a man, answer the call and volunteer?' The very thought of army life made Herbert blench, and he avoided his cronies and their patriotic talk.

Betsy was one of the first out of the store. Since she had been living in Clapham with Viola she looked quite different. She loved the cottage so much she would have been completely happy to live there for ever, if only she could have seen Matthew occasionally. Even the long journey by horse tramway, which was so tiring after a day's work, did not seem to matter. She and Viola were up at dawn every day and not home until nearly nine o'clock. Betsy cooked and cleaned with West Riding enthusiasm, relieved that Viola seemed so good, quiet and subdued and uncharacteristically content with this simple, hardworking life.

Viola had received a letter from James, written immediately he arrived at the Cape. Like her, he was a poor correspondent and it had been written in great haste. They would be going up the line at once, he said and there was a lot of work involved in getting organized. *The line takes everything, men and ammunition, plus the stores up to the front, and it's loaded to capacity. Some of the chaps I knew brought all sorts of kit, champagne, tennis racquets, polo gear . . . posh tents. All of it has had to be dumped. Don't expect many letters. The post is all right here in Cape Town, and I have your first dear letter, here in my wallet, with your picture which we had taken. But once we move, it will be different. I think of you every night, my darling. Think of me and the time when we will be together again.'*

Viola put the letter with her pearls and brooch, another treasure valued above all else. She went on writing to James every week. She did not tell him about Jevons and the robbery. He had enough on his mind, and must not be worried by her foolish carelessness.

It was a fine, chill October evening, and the nights were just beginning to draw in. Betsy buttoned her coat up to her chin, put on her hat and gloves and started off down Regent Street to meet Viola.

La Rue's, situated in Piccadilly, was a luxury shop, selling handkerchiefs and exquisite artificial flowers as well as gloves. Everything they sold was expensive and beautifully fashioned, a large part of the stock imported from Paris, Vienna or Milan. They did bespoke orders too. A lady could bring in a pattern of silk, velvet or chiffon and within a week La Rue's could supply a pair of gloves toning, or exactly matching, embroidered to perfection.

The glove-makers were mostly French and lived in Soho, working in attics and basements for the French company who employed them. They made gloves for a few coppers a pair. Pale perky boys brought the gloves round wrapped in tissue, packed in shell-pink boxes lettered in silver. Gentlemen bought them for presents, and already many were aware of the beauty of the new assistant. As at Dwyer & Netherby, Viola's success as a saleswoman was obvious from the start.

Betsy walked quickly, not glancing round her, not looking in the attractive shop windows. Once the shops closed no respectable woman walked alone in the streets. It did not concern working girls, respectability being considered an essentially middle-class prerogative. The town teemed with women, strolling in the gaslight, painted and extravagantly dressed in great feathered hats and furs, for The Dilly was the promenade of the more expensive street-walkers. Round and about them, eyeing them from beneath the brims of their tilted top hats, the men cruised, sometimes singling a girl out, bearing alongside, whispering an assignation, making their sordid bargains.

Working girls on their way home were used to being accosted, so that Betsy, a little peg-top doll, walked very stiffly, staring straight ahead through her spectacles, her old green umbrella clutched in her hand like a defensive weapon.

She made Viola laugh. 'What? You with your little pink innocent face? No chap's going to bother you, love, you've got innocence written over you like an electric advertisement.'

Nevertheless it was with relief that she saw Viola coming along to meet her, wearing the brown costume she had worn when she had left Leeds and the valiant little hat with the bright yellow buttercups, her shoulders wrapped in her old cream Shetland shawl, with all the air and confidence of a woman wearing expensive sables.

She walked proudly through the crowds, and if the sauntering men came alongside or spoke she gave them one cold hostile look, and they backed away, apologizing.

But as she drew near, Betsy saw that Viola was white-faced, her eyes big and brilliant. She took Betsy's arm, and they turned together towards Piccadilly Circus, where they could take an omnibus down the Haymarket to the tramways terminus on the Embankment.

Regent Street was crowded tonight, full of cheering groups wearing Union Jacks. Uniformed soldiers were surrounded, their shoulders thumped until they ached, dragged into public houses and bought drinks, so that the bewildered boys in their red jackets and pill box hats drifted about, bemused, already heroes in a war they had not yet seen.

'Well, it's happened,' said Viola. 'It's war. It's started. It says here that the Expeditionary Force is entraining to go up the line, and it mentions James's regiment.'

'What does—up the line mean?'

'If you look at the map you'll see a railway line that goes up from Cape Town—miles and miles to Mafeking and beyond and that's what they mean by going up the line. They've not been fighting yet—only preparing in case it happens.'

'And now it has?'

'Yes. Yes.' Viola drew a long, deep breath. 'Yes. But he'll come back. I know he will.'

They walked along, arms linked, lost in their own thoughts, and became aware, suddenly, that a man was walking just behind them. Viola, expecting the usual casual masher, stopped abruptly, so the follower nearly ran into them. It was Arthur Netherby.

It was more than two months since she had seen him. He looked just as immaculate as ever, but older, the protuberant eyes bloodshot, as though through sleeplessness, or deep anxiety.

He looked at Viola with a painfully placating smile, which she found embarrassing and incomprehensible. Why should he want to please her? Why should he be so kind to her? She was grateful and she wanted him to know it, but she could see no reason for his devotion. It gave her an uneasy sense of foreboding, as though in some way he was threatening her instead of trying to be her friend.

She was a little taller than he. She stood, holding her petrified little friend's arm within hers, waiting for him to speak. He raised his hat, exposing the strands of dyed hair carefully brushed across his balding head, and the red sweat line his hard hat made across his forehead.

'Mr Netherby,' Viola said suddenly, 'I want to thank you for giving me a reference. It was kind of you.'

He appeared relieved as though he had expected her to be angry because he had followed her.

'I am always glad to help you. I am happy to hear you have found such a good place. Are they treating you well?'

'Yes, thank you.' She made a move to pass on, and he said hurriedly, 'Don't go. I want to speak to you.'

'You were following us?'

'Er, yes. I am sorry. I did not wish to alarm you or Miss Holder in any way. May I walk a short way with you? Or perhaps we could go in somewhere—here, for instance?' They were standing outside the Café Royal. 'If I could offer you some refreshment? Please—just while we talk?'

Viola looked at the gilt and marble entrance with interest. She had never been inside the famous Bohemian restaurant, the meeting place of the London art and literary world, but she had heard about it. Life had been dull of late—any harmless distraction was welcome. She felt Betsy tugging frantically on her arm.

'No, Vi! We can't go in there!'

'All right,' Viola said to Netherby. 'A few minutes, then. Oh, give over, Betsy,' she said impatiently. 'No one's going to eat you!'

He led them to a table on the balcony and ordered a bottle of hock and a plate of smoked salmon sandwiches. The wine was served in an ice bucket, chilled and delicious. Betsy did not touch hers. Viola drank greedily, and bit into the delicate little sandwiches. She looked down at the packed restaurant crowded with the city's Bohemia. Marble-topped tables, red velvet benches, huge mirrors duplicating the room. Journalists, writers, artists, men-about-town, their women, wives, mistresses, artists' models. All talking, laughing, arguing.

Viola's cheeks brightened, and she leaned forward eagerly. She had not been to the West End since James had left for South Africa. It was no use pretending that she had not missed it. The Café Royal had not been one of their haunts, since James liked the exclusive, more expensive places. But still, it was a taste of the old life. If she was not afraid of hard work, it was no use pretending she *liked* respectable poverty. She never would. The little cottage did not mean to her what it meant to Betsy. When she left work at night and saw the carriages taking other women, bejewelled and in evening dress, accompanied by their menfolk, to the theatre and fashionable restaurants, she ached with nostalgia for those delirious weeks with James.

'I've always wanted to come here,' she said. 'It wasn't Jim's sort of place. But it's interesting. Look, Betsy . . . that man over there, he's a famous comic. And look, over there—the pretty girl with the fair hair, she's on the stage . . .'

'Miss Corbett,' interrupted Netherby insistently. She had forgotten him in her eager interest in her surroundings.

'I'm sorry,' she said. 'It is such fun to be in this sort of place again.'

'You miss it?'

She shrugged, smiling frankly. 'Of course. I'm not one for a quiet life like Betsy. What was it you wanted to say, Mr Netherby?'

'Miss Corbett—' Netherby coughed, tactfully—'I understand your—protector has left for South Africa with the army.'

'Yes.' Viola stiffened.

'Then if you will forgive me, I must assume, as you have had to take this new position—in a shop—that he has made no provision for you?'

'You assume quite wrongly,' she flashed. 'It's true I'm working. Lord Staffray made very good provision for me. Through my own carelessness, I was robbed. I am certainly not going to worry him about money while he is away—fighting for his country. I am able to work, so I am working. You need not worry about me.'

'Viola,' Netherby burst out desperately, 'face up to your position. He won't come back to you. Even if he comes through this campaign, it is impossible. A young man like that has family duties—he is heir to a great name.'

'Then I'll just have to wait and see,' she said. She wished he would not sit there, with his clean pink hands folded across his waistcoat, and tell her these frightening truths.

'Viola,' he said, 'in spite of what has happened, the offer I made you still holds. You have only to say the word—just say it, and you need never worry again as long as you live.'

She rose, and for the first time her hands were trembling just a little. For the first time the offer of his name and protection was tempting. To be spoiled, sheltered and waited on again . . . not to have to think of money, the next quarter's rent, the weekly bills. To be taken to exciting places and bought pretty things, the life that was natural to her and which she loved.

She shook her head. 'Thank you, Mr Netherby. But I shall manage. Good night . . . and thank you again. Come on, Betsy.'

They went out into the clear, chill evening. Over the glow of the Circus where the flower girls called their wares, 'Vi-lets, luvly vi-lets . . .'

where the restaurant and theatre signs blazed, where Gilbert's silvery boy-god shot his invisible arrow, and the crowds had grown. There was dancing and singing. 'We don't want to fight but by jingo if we do.' Drunken voices; above them the dark bowl of the sky brilliant with stars. The voices of the newsboys were shouting, 'Boers attack. First Battles in Natal!'

The omnibus came round the long curve of Regent Street and at Viola's signal the driver drew in his horses at the kerb.

'Let's go upstairs,' said Viola, 'then we will be able to look down on the crowds.'

As they looked down on the shouting, flag-waving mob, Viola thought of James going with his men towards the enemy lines and shivered.

'I don't see why they're all so happy,' she said. 'People will be killed.' She drew close to Betsy, as though cold. 'I wish Mr Netherby would leave me alone.'

'He seems to be trying to be kind.'

'He scares me more when he's kind than when he's bullying. Betsy . . .' She put her head down on Betsy's shoulder. 'Bet, I've something to tell you. I'm going to have a baby.'

Betsy gave a gasp of horror and Viola was surprised. She herself had felt elated, because at least she would have something of James, whatever the future held. He would look after them, of course, as soon as he knew. She had experienced a swelling pride at the thought. The Italian side of her nature, like the women in the small food shops in Soho with their spoiled brown babies, looked upon motherhood with pride. The idea that James's baby could be a disaster for her had never crossed her mind.

She laughed at Betsy's stricken face and kissed her.

'What are you bothered for, love? It's not your worry. I shall manage, and as soon as James knows, he'll be thrilled, I know.'

'But supposing he *never* knows? What will you do?' wailed Betsy. 'You're not married. What will people say?' It seemed to her that Viola was discarding the last claim to respectability. How could she say to others that she was 'a good girl'? Now everyone would know. She thought of the sly comments of the shop girls. She thought how shocked Matthew would be. But Viola only smiled.

'People will say that the Duchess has had an earl's grandson. And whatever my lord does about it, he'll be the gradliest lad in the whole world.' Her words were defiant but behind that defiance was a creeping fear.

'How will you manage?' demanded Betsy. Her big myopic eyes were full of anxious tears. 'You'll have to give up work for some time and my wages won't keep both of us. And afterwards who will look after the baby while you work? You can't put a baby with one of those dreadful baby farmers who starve and murder babies . . . you read about in the papers . . .'

'Hold up,' said Viola, teasing her. 'Don't go on like that. I'll write and tell James. I wouldn't have bothered him, not just for me, but this is different. He has a right to know about it.'

'But Mr Netherby said he'll never marry you. Not a great swell like him.'

'But he will look after us. I know he will. I'll write again tonight and, with luck, in a month he'll have the letter. I'll tell him about the baby, and about Jevons taking my money and clothes, and everything. He'll telegraph to his solicitors to look after me. You'll see.'

So after they had supper she sat in the tiny kitchen, with the oil lamp on the table, writing in her big bold hand, occasionally reaching for the dictionary, occasionally smiling to herself, the glow of yellow light illuminating her like a picture, and Betsy sat watching her, wondering wistfully how she could seem so confident and happy.

Viola looked up suddenly. 'Don't you ever see Matthew Lyttelton now?' she asked.

Betsy coloured. 'Sometimes. I go to the church and stand right at the back, and listen to him, then I go away quickly before the service is over. I don't let him see me. It's safer that way.'

Viola smiled wryly into the earnest little face. 'Safer from temptation. Oh, my Betsy. At least your intentions—and Matthew's—are honourable.'

'You may laugh,' said Betsy stubbornly, 'but it wasn't easy. Just because we're not mad-heads like you—and—and his lordship, it doesn't mean it's easy. Sometimes—' and in spite of herself, the sobs shook her—'sometimes I think I'll never see him again.'

'Ah, *don't*, love! You were both good, sensible and wise. You'll see him again. Look at me. *What* a position! No husband, no money, baby on the way.' But she smiled as she spoke, and her long white hands ran over her breasts, beginning to swell a little, and the long line of her waist free from the constriction of corsets. From a girl's point of view, and a *poor* girl's, *everything* was wrong, yet Viola smiled with slow contentment, as though the world was safe and wonderful. She licked the flap of her envelope and addressed it to Company Headquarters H.Q. Cape Town, and stamped it. 'Will you post this for me, Betsy? Jim should get it within the month, and then we shan't have to worry any more.'

When Betsy had gone out with the letter, she stirred the fire, and put her work-box on the table, spreading out lawn, very fine flannel, and edging silk. Now Betsy knew she could begin to sew. She hoped James would write soon. She did not want to work, to get up before dawn in the chill autumn days, sometimes wet, the rain slanting across the common, and take the interminable ride on the horse-tram through Stockwell and Kennington to Westminster. She wanted to be safe, warm, a little lazy and well-fed, protected, waiting for her baby to be born, and her man to return.

CHAPTER SEVEN

The Christmas trade had started and the shops were displaying the yearly splendour of gifts and glitter, with a strong emphasis on patriotism—handy little gifts for serving men, and a proliferation of red, white and blue. In South Africa men struggled up the line in overloaded trains, heavy equipment chafing their shoulders under the merciless heat. As their letters began to trickle home a shocked realization of the fighting conditions began to dawn, together with the gloomy news of early defeats, of towns cut off and besieged by sharp-shooting, fast-riding Transvaalers. The newspapers said that when General Buller and the main expeditionary force went into action, there would be a change of tune—but the newspapers, like the General Staff, were whistling in the dark.

Lady Louderdown, distraught that her beloved son was in danger, was pestering everyone in office to extract him from active service, without result. She had forgiven him for his wild indiscretion with Viola, which of course had been retailed to her by every gossip in London, but she had not forgiven him for not sharing his last days in England with her. He should have wired to her in Rome, and she would have returned at once. It was unforgivable that he should have spent them with a common, wicked, worthless girl.

Viola wrote regularly to her lover, but had had no letters since the beginning of December when James's regiment had left on the long hot trail up country towards the Modder River. No reply to her letter telling him about her baby. Like his mother, anxiety and dread gnawed at her, but unlike Lady Louderdown there was a tough resiliency within her that would not give way to panic or despair. Besides there was nothing she could do. Like women all over Britain in those first months of war, she could only wait and hope.

One night in late December, as Betsy turned into Regent Street, she was startled to see Matthew Lyttelton waiting for her at the corner. The colour rose to her cheeks and her heart began to race. His thin, boyish figure was huddled up in his shabby coat against the wind, and when he saw her he came forward. She felt her breast constrict and the colour flood her face.

They gazed at each other with hungry longing. To Matthew she looked just the same as when he had last seen her. The word adorable occurred to him. The round pink and white face, the clear grey eyes shining through her spectacles, her little hands in the worn grey gloves clutching her old green umbrella. To Betsy he was simply—wonderful. She felt no anger because he had tried to break their relationship. It seemed to her in her humble meekness 'only right and proper'. To her no other man could hold a candle to this round-shouldered young curate. And his voice, when he spoke, the melodious, cultured voice speaking her name, and the way he took off his hat so politely made her hold her head high with pride and love.

'Mr Lyttelton.'

'My name is Matthew.'

'Matthew, then . . .'

'May I walk with you a little?'

She nodded like a porcelain mandarin, and he gravely offered her his arm. She noticed the frayed sleeve of his coat and her heart ached with the longing to mend it. If she had the right to serve and care for him he would never be shabby. They walked down Oxford Street together.

'I heard you were living with Viola Corbett.'

'Yes. Out in Clapham. It's a long way—but very nice.'

'Do you think you should,' he asked solemnly, the clergyman suddenly emerging, 'after what happened between her and Lord Staffray? I would not like to think you were in any moral danger, Elizabeth.' He saw the little pink face darken stubbornly, and hastened on: 'I know she is not a bad girl at heart, but she did create a great scandal—she might lead you into temptation.'

Betsy looked up at his earnest face like a robin, her head tipped to one side, and her anger melted into surprised delight. He was anxious about her. The idea that he considered her attractive enough to worry about made her deliriously happy. She gave his arm a reassuring squeeze.

'You don't have to worry, love,' she began, and then was covered with confusion at her own boldness. 'I mean, I wouldn't . . . well, I couldn't, could I? Not while . . . not while I think all the world of you, the way I do.'

'Ah, Elizabeth!' His thin face lit with delight. It was like falling in love all over again, but better.

'And Viola's changed. She doesn't go out at all. She's got a nice job in La Rue's in Piccadilly, first sales, gloves. She's very quiet. Waiting, you might say. She—' She looked into Matthew's earnest eyes—'She's going to have Lord Staffray's baby, Matthew.'

'Oh, God!' said Matthew. 'The poor, unfortunate girl!'

'She doesn't think so,' said Betsy, 'although she's not heard a word from him lately. You'd think she was the first woman ever to have a baby, she's that proud. I don't know how she'll manage. But she's still glad about it. She's not ashamed. Most girls would be going mad, trying not to have it. But she wants it more than anything in the world.'

'God,' said Matthew, 'moves in a mysterious way.'

'Yes,' agreed Betsy. 'She thinks Lord Staffray hasn't had some of her letters, so doesn't know where she is.'

'No one has heard from him,' said Matthew. 'At the moment letters are not coming through from the front. His mother heard only that he was sent straight up the line to Kimberley and that, with these terrible setbacks and retreats, everything is in confusion. Many families have had no word.'

'But nothing shakes Viola's belief in him. She is quite sure he will come back to her.'

'Oh, Elizabeth,' said Matthew, 'what weak sinners we all are. It's very worrying—Viola does everything wrong, and yet she has a faith of her own.'

She asked shyly, 'Why did you come to meet me tonight?'

'I heard you walked alone down Regent Street every night after work. It's not right for a girl like you.'

'Oh, and what could happen to a plain Jane like me?' asked Betsy, blithely honest. 'Nobody takes any heed of me. I'm not tall and pretty like Vi. And when she's with me she soon sends the chaps off with a flea in their ears! It's all right, honest it is.'

'It's not right that you should walk alone,' he said tenderly. 'But I think we are safe here. There is little chance of anyone from St Botolph's seeing us, because no one walks here at this hour.'

For the first time he was astonished to see a flash of anger ruffle the surface of her humility. Her cheeks were very pink, the challenging look in her grey eyes reminded him of Viola.

'Oh, no!' she said angrily. 'There's no one of importance about now. No ladies. Only—only these street women, and shop girls and workers, like me, who don't count, I reckon.'

'Elizabeth!' he cried, deeply wounded. 'I did not mean it like that at all.'

'But it is like that!' she said fiercely. 'I wish you hadn't come. I was getting used to being without you. I know very well what it means to you if we're seen together. You were quite right to end it. It's best we don't meet. We're not my Lord Staffray—and we're not daft-brave like Vi. We can't afford to be different.'

He stopped, holding her by the arm, his mild brown eyes burning.

'Stop it, Elizabeth,' he said. 'If we're seen together, I don't care. Not any more. I've been wretched without you. It's been like years instead of weeks. If I have to leave St Botolph's then I'll have to. I'll sweep the streets—anything—but no one is going to tell me I must not love you.'

'Matthew!' she breathed, her eyes shining. 'You are *brave!*'

They stood on the busy corner and kissed each other, trapped by poverty and love, and quite unreasonably, wildly happy.

A newsboy ran past, shouting above his blaring caption.

BATTLE ON THE MODDER. HEAVY CASUALTIES. EARL'S SON WOUNDED. A BLACK WEEK FOR BRITAIN.

Matthew bought a paper, and they opened it, the wind tugging at the sheets, telling themselves as they struggled that James Staffray was not the only 'son of a belted earl' fighting before Kimberley. But it was James. Very seriously wounded, it said. There were grave fears for his life.

It was only a small paragraph. The main space was given to the disastrous defeat along the Tugela River. Matthew stood, dazed, thinking of his young friend, so handsome, gay and generous. The boy who had protected him at school. He could still hear the gently amused voice. 'I say, young Lyttelton, you'd better stick with me or the bully boys will eat you alive.'

His friend, protector and benefactor.

Betsy could only think of Viola. She set off hurriedly towards Piccadilly and Matthew ran after her. Across Regent Steet, darting through the traffic, past the dark little cul de sac of Vine Street where the blue lamp shone above the police station and where, at night, the whores, pickpockets, and the drunken young swells who climbed up the Eros fountain, were hauled. Down into Piccadilly. She was nearly at La Rue's when she saw Viola walking towards her, a newspaper clutched in her hand, white with a deathly whiteness, staring blindly before her, reeling like a drunken woman as she walked.

Betsy stopped her, put her arms about her.

'Vi. Vi, it's me.'

Viola stared down at her, then at Matthew. She was not crying. She was numb with shock. She stared at them resentfully, refusing to accept disaster.

'It doesn't say he is dead,' she said fiercely. 'He's still alive. That's all that matters.'

Suddenly she dropped and Matthew caught her, thinking she was going to faint. Her head rolled against his shoulder, and she whispered, as though to herself, 'What shall I do? James . . . my love . . . my lord . . . what *shall* I do?'

Viola clung desperately to her belief that James would come back to her. She did not care how, or on what terms. He was still alive, while other men were dead. They had a chance. They had loved each other beyond belief. He *would* come back to her, but still there were no letters.

She read in a newspaper that Lady Louderdown planned to bring her son home. She read reports of the lack of medical aid in the line, of men dying of gangrene and infections rather than wounds. She read that James had been decorated for bravery under fire, but that his injuries were grave. It was feared that he had lost an arm. She read that in the tram going home and she had to put her hands over her mouth to prevent herself crying out loud, remembering the fine, flawless man's body, and the strong arms that had held her so often.

In January she lost her job. La Rue's told her that they had been informed of the scandal in which she had been involved. Theirs was a good class business. Her work was good but they could not afford to affront ladies of quality. Madame La Rue's shrewd French eyes moved over Viola's growing waistline and the triangular shadows on her pale cheeks. To be *enceinte*, she said, in their sort of smart establishment was not *comme il faut*.

Viola got work as a barmaid in a large public house at the crossroads near the cottage. It was hard work, ill-paid, with late hours. Her back ached from standing and her long, lovely hands became rough from washing glasses in cold water, harsh with soda. But, behind the high mahogany bar, her condition was screened to some extent. She hated the work. She hated the obvious, boring, repetitive advances of the men who came to the bar. Her cool glance kept them at a distance, but did not make her popular. Her splendid vitality thinned down to a finely drawn beauty of angled cheekbones and shadowed eyes. A strange distinction.

'When my lord comes back, what's he going to think of this skinny scarecrow?' she asked Betsy in disgust.

'I don't know,' said Betsy thoughtfully. 'You look like a real duchess now. Distinguished, like. But it's not much use being a duchess without brass.'

They ate on Betsy's meagre wages. Viola's just about paid the rent, fuel and Betsy's fares to work. The cold early days of the new year dragged by and the news from Africa began to be more reassuring; Ladysmith was relieved and there was great rejoicing. Viola searched the newspapers for some word about James. At last she read he was being brought home by his mother who had been given permission to travel with him on a hospital ship. His condition, the newspaper said regretfully, was still very grave. The Queen had sent her personal good wishes to Lord and Lady Louderdown.

The day the liner docked Viola did not go in to work, she was at Charing Cross waiting for the ambulance train to arrive.

The station was crowded with families from all walks of life, all waiting for a glimpse of, or a word with, their dear ones. The police guarded the barrier to the platform; only the medical people, apart from a privileged few, were to be allowed through. Lord Louderdown, and two distinguished men, one in uniform, passed through, and a small group of well-dressed ladies and gentlemen. The working women around Viola began to press forward, shouting protests, but Viola was only intent on keeping her place near the front of the crowd.

There was a rush forward when the train was announced and she was pressed right up to the gate. When the train hissed to a stop, the wounded officers were taken off first, and as they limped past, on crutches or some still stretcher cases, a strange sighing groan went up from the crowd, class resentment forgotten in their pity for these maimed young men.

Lady Louderdown descended, to be greeted by her husband and the waiting gentlemen; the ambulance men gently eased a stretcher out of the hospital carriage. The gentlemen went forward after speaking with James's parents, and looked down with embarrassed pity at the broken young man on the stretcher, then the small procession moved towards the barrier, the police clearing a way through the crowd.

Viola was so close that her skirt brushed the scarlet blanket. She looked down at the white, emaciated face on the pillow and could not restrain her tears. James had come back, broken and sick, but not to her. Her arms would not be allowed to comfort him, her voice to soothe him. A long red scar seared one side of his face, threading from his chin up into his bonny hair. On his right side the blanket was tucked closely round, and there was nothing where the outline of his left arm should be. His eyes were closed, the thick dark lashes making him seem young and pitiably vulnerable.

Her arms stretched towards him, and a cry rose to her lips.

'Jim, oh, Jimmy, my love . . . Jimmy, look at me . . . it's Viola . . . it's your Duchess . . .'

For a moment his eyes opened, and he looked round with a wild, unseeing start, then there was a waft of scent and a rustle of silk and Viola was looking into Lady Louderdown's pretty, faded face and very cold blue eyes.

'Oh, your ladyship,' she cried. 'Please . . . please . . . tell me how he is . . . tell me he's going to be well . . .'

'Constable,' said Lady Louderdown, 'please get this woman out of the way. She is hysterical. My son must not be upset.'

A burly blue arm pushed Viola back into the crowd. A tawdry girl looked at her and said with rough sympathy, 'Your fancy lad, is 'e? Looks a proper wreck, poor young gent. I come to see if I could see my bloke . . . 'alf a chance, I don't fink, with all the gentry 'ere . . .'

The little procession, stretcher men, nurses, Lord and Lady Louderdown, the local Member of Parliament from Staffray, the uniformed emissary from the Palace all threaded their way through the crowd to where a private, electrically driven ambulance awaited James. Viola, running through the outskirts of the crowd, was in time to see it drive away. She stood, breathless, wide-eyed, and beneath her clasped hands, she felt the baby stir for the first time.

When Viola arrived at work that night the landlady gave her notice. She was getting too big, she said, customers noticed. It wasn't nice. She went back to the cottage, walking past the tall handsome houses built round the common.

In these houses lived rich tradesmen and city business men. The curtains were only just being drawn against the cold twilight. In warmly-lit interiors firelight flickered on the walls; warmly-clad children, rosy-cheeked from their walks, were being divested of their fur-trimmed coats and bonnets, well-dressed women were talking and laughing over tea.

Viola looked up into one such window, feeling the weight of her child within her. The child she wanted to protect, and to love, to whom she wanted to give all the good things of life. Unless she had help from someone, how would she manage? What was she going to do? Scrub floors like her mother had done? Ruin her health and looks slaving for a pittance? And afterwards, after the baby was born, would she stand behind a bar or shop counter while her baby was cared for by some inefficient drab of a minder? For the first time despair crept nearer, nibbling its rat-bites into her confidence.

She let herself into the cottage. The fire was not lit—they always left it to the last possible moment in order to save fuel. At weekends she and Betsy collected wood blown from the trees across the Common. Their meal tonight would be bread and broth, and some cold meat left from the night before. Suddenly she longed with a passionate greed for all the things she had so briefly known. The warmth, the feel of silk, the smell of scent, the delicate food, the enfolding comforts of luxury. She hated this mean poverty, and the bleak little house seemed to close down on her like a lid, shutting her life away.

When Betsy came in, frozen from the slow bus journey, Viola told her that her job at the public house had finished and saw the small face tighten.

'What are you going to do?' she asked in alarm. 'Have you heard from his lordship? I saw in the newspaper today that he had come home.'

'I went,' said Viola. 'I went to the station to meet him. But there were lots of nobs there—and his parents. He did open his eyes for a minute. But he didn't see me. Happen he's forgotten. Or he's never had my letters.'

'You must write again,' Betsy insisted. 'He ought to be told about the baby. It's only right.'

Viola sighed. Yes, he ought to know. But she hated writing like a suppliant. She wanted him to come storming back to claim her with pride and love. But, poor love, he was sick and weak, and surrounded by people whom she could guess would be her enemies.

But she made herself write again. Had he received any of her letters? She could not bear to ask him for help, although she needed it desperately. If he still loved her, of course he would help. She went on scribbling.

'*Happen you've not had my letters since you were wounded and therefore don't know about our baby. I don't want to worry you when you are so ill, my darling, but things are a bit hard with me . . .*' She stopped writing, filled with self-disgust. 'As though I were a beggar,' she thought furiously, half-minded to tear it up. But—she needed help desperately. She concluded hurriedly, '*I love you, my darling, and always shall.*' Then, so furiously it was almost illegible, '*Please help me.*' She signed it '*Duchess*'.

She waited. A week passed. She walked the cold paths of the Common, too cold that week for even the most be-furred and warm-gloved children. She watched the postman passing. Then one day, at last, he turned in at the gate.

It was a letter from a firm of solicitors, Sattherwaite and Sattherwaite. Her letter had been passed on to them by Lord Staffray, who had no recollection of ever knowing such a person as Viola Corbett. If she continued the attempts at impudent blackmail, appropriate action would be taken.

It was early that morning, about two o'clock when Betsy woke with a start, to find Viola standing by her bed, a tall figure in her white nightdress. She was shaking with cold.

'Can I come in, Bet?'

Betsy hurriedly moved over and pulled down the covers. Viola slid inside; they lay close together, Viola's head on Betsy's thin little shoulder. She was crying; not noisily, silently, the tears coursing down her face.

'I couldn't sleep,' she said, 'worrying about things. I've dragged you in too, Betsy. I mean you only came to London because of me.'

'Don't go on, love,' said Betsy. 'We'll manage.'

'Yes, but I've got to think how. I keep thinking, Betsy, of that first night with James. At his big house—in the Empress's bed. We were crazy—like two children on a mad party, but not children . . . by no means . . . it was a sort of fever of pleasure. I keep thinking how kind he was, and how gentle . . . how fierce. It always ought to be like that the first time. I was lucky there.' She gave a long shiver of remembered pleasure, and Betsy lay stiffly, shocked, blinking in the dark. 'You see, Bet, because he was so different from anyone I'd ever met or known, it was special to me, and I just thought it was for him too. But he'd had lots of women, and I was just another girl. When I saw him, so thin and broken and with those empty eyes, it was awful. Then, when that letter came today, it was as though he'd hit me. I felt angry at first, then I remembered what he had been through, and thought, well, poor love, he was too ill to read. And they wouldn't show anything that might trouble him. Well, it wouldn't be right. I'm not going to make more trouble—not with her—his mother. I won't. She's black with pride, that one. But I'm proud too. I won't write again.'

'But he's rich, Vi. He could let you have a little money . . .'

'Yes. But I'll not pester him. Those that are near to him don't want him troubled, and I don't either. It's no use hankering after what's gone. And he's gone for me. I've got to stop hoping, pretending, dreaming . . . I'm on my own again and I've got to help myself. And I've got to look after this baby because there's no one else in the world that will. I've got to think of a way.'

Betsy was filled with apprehension. After the lost, loving, wild months, here was Vi Corbett again. Not beaten. Weeping, but not with remorse, only for the loss of her love. She recognized the decisive voice, the mood which had brought them, two inexperienced girls, from Leeds to London to seek their fortunes. The Duchess mood, brave and reckless, risking trouble, taking chances.

'I'm on my own again. I'm *not* going down, Bet. *And* I'm not standing behind a counter or a bar for the rest of my life . . . and I'm not scrubbing for my baby like my poor mother did for me. I'm getting something better out of life for both of us. I've had a taste of the best. I know what it's worth!'

'What were you thinking of doing, Vi? I mean you weren't thinking of doing anything awful?'

There was an odd sound, half laugh, half stifled sob. Viola had not laughed for a long while.

Suddenly she hugged Betsy close. 'A woman always comes back to men, Betsy. At least my sort does.'

'What men?'

'Well, I can write to my friend, the Count. He gave me an address and said I was to if I needed anything. He meant it too, I think. I hope. I just need help until the baby comes, and for a bit after. Then I can get started again. If he doesn't come up trumps there's always . . .' She drew in a long breath and said slowly, 'There's always Mr Arthur Netherby.'

'Oh, *Vi!*' breathed Betsy. 'You are an awful girl. An awful wicked lass. You wouldn't dare ask Mr Netherby for help?'

'Why not? He asked me to marry him once. I'm not asking a lot. I only want enough to tide me over, until I'm brought to bed, and for about a month afterwards . . . so that I can find someone really good to look after the bairn, and get a good job.'

So next morning she wrote to Count Eugene Erhmann. To the address he had given her in London, to his English broker, Grant Eckersley. The letter was sent on with a courier's bag to Vienna, but Eugene was in South Africa, travelling about that war-ridden country. So the letter remained in Austria awaiting his return.

Meantime in London the weeks went by. Betsy's meagre wages barely paid for their food, and Viola, big with child now, was hungry all the time. She had pawned the diamond amethyst and emerald brooch and her pearls, her last lovely souvenir of James. She hated to part with them for a bunch of grubby notes and a yellow ticket, but the rent had to be paid and fuel bought. She felt she was parting with the last of her gay and glittering youth, and she knew that she was given poor value for them. The baby was due in May and, as the date approached, she became restless and nervous, a young mother cat searching for security, warmth, peace and the safety of her young. Never once did it enter her mind that her baby would be an encumbrance or not wanted. Not once did she think of it as a shameful disaster. She longed to see it, to hold it, to love it with her whole being. But her money was nearly gone. She wavered indecisively— how long should she wait to hear from Eugene? Another week? Another day? She could not wait, and in a mood of desperation she wrote to Arthur Netherby.

It was spring again. Round the Common the lilacs were out in the gardens, the little rich children had shed their furs and brought out their kites and hoops. Viola had walked for an hour, and when she came in sight of the cottage she saw the closed carriage standing at the gate and recognized it instantly. She had often seen the Netherby family driving in it in the park on Sunday mornings. She went slowly forward, watchful and suspicious, a prowling cat, unsure of its welcome. Arthur Netherby got down from the carriage and stood waiting for her.

'You look well, Duchess,' he said grudgingly.

'I am, thank you, sir. It was good of you to come. Won't you come in?'

He gave the man instructions to return for him within the hour, and followed her into the little house. She took off her shawl and hat and put a match to the fire. He noticed with his finicky love of cleanliness that the cottage was spotless—and Viola too. The almond-shaped nails still polished, her blouse fresh, her magnificent hair a soft and shining mass, the colour of autumn leaves. She had fought the grubbiness of poverty like an enemy.

'It will be warm in a minute.' She drew out a chair. 'Would you care for some tea?'

He shook his head, sat down and waited. He remembered the shameful catastrophic evening when Erhmann had rescued her from him, and her flaunting affair with Staffray. She sat opposite him, the rising flames lighting her bright hair, the long line of her white throat, the curve of her full breasts. He realized it was not going to be easy.

'Well, I had your letter.' He extracted it from his wallet with his thick, clean fingers. 'What can I do for you, Duchess?'

She looked at him ingenuously, her smile frank and appealing. 'I know I had a nerve to write to you, sir. But that's my way. And you have been kind to me. You can see I'm pregnant. And I'm broke. It's no use beating about the bush. I want to borrow some money. If old Sam Hardcastle was still alive I wouldn't have to ask you.' His eyes shifted beneath her grave look. 'Will you lend me, say, one hundred pounds? It isn't a great deal.'

'Most girls in your position would consider it so,' he said shortly.

Her eyes did not waver. 'Yes. But then I'm not like most girls. I don't want to part with my baby.'

'This child, is it Staffray's? Why doesn't he look after you?'

Her cheeks flamed, and her eyes filled with unshed tears. Her pain gave him his first *frisson* of pleasure.

'I don't *know* why. He went to fight for his country. He was badly wounded and now he is very ill. Perhaps he has not received my letters. Perhaps things are just too much for him. I can't press him. I won't. He meant too much to me.'

Suddenly his calm broke. She saw the veins stand out on his forehead and his heavy jowls darken with chagrin.

'Meant too much to you—and he has deserted you. You went to that boy and treated me like dirt, and now he's left you without a penny like a common pick-up. So now you condescend to come to me! I would have done anything for you—I asked you to be my wife. What makes you think I would help you now?'

She rose and paced the little room with the swaying, lovely walk which even the heaviness of the child could not detract from, and he was aware of the perfume that always hung about her, which seemed to shake from the folds of her garments as she moved. To the people of Tewkesbury Square—people like Herbert and Emily—she was a common girl, a fallen woman, disgraced, and deserved to sink into the gutter. But to him she was more beautiful than ever, and he still longed to own her, and with an even more terrifying desire, to bring her to her knees.

'I know I hurt you, Mr Netherby. I was young and foolish. I am sorry for that, though not for anything else I did. I am not bargaining. I am asking you because you cared about me once. I need help. I need money to tide me over. I swear I'll pay you back—with interest if you wish, after the baby comes; *if* you could give me a reference? So that I can get a good crib and pay you back, and look after the bairn. It's not much to ask. You're a rich man. Just give me a chance to get through the next few months.' She smiled, a touch of mischief lighting her pale face. 'It will cost you a lot less than if I'd married you.'

He gave a stifled exclamation, pulling out a silk handkerchief and wiping his forehead and his pale thick lips. His hands were trembling when he spoke, like a man who stakes his all on the turn of a wheel.

'No. I won't lend you any money, Viola!'

'Ah!' Her shoulders dropped with disappointment. 'I'm sorry I bothered you.'

'It would bring you no nearer to me. When you are over your trouble you would be off again.' His eyes were fixed on her with an intensity that frightened her. 'I know what kind of woman you are. You are what they call a *femme fatale*. You are very young, there will be other men who will want you—that damned Austrian, for instance. I will not lend you money, but I will still marry you, as I offered once before.' He looked at her with desperate pleading. 'I promise you would never want again.'

She stopped her pacing, came back to where he sat, and with a swift lithe movement, knelt beside him, peering into his face.

'Are you sincere? Do you mean it?'

'I would not offer if I did not.'

'You're very generous.' She sat back on her heels. 'Not many men would be so. Forgive me if I thought badly of you. But why should you do this?'

'I—I have ambitions,' he said with difficulty. 'I set my mind on things. I set my mind on being rich, on the success of the emporium. I've set my mind on you. I've always wanted a woman to be proud of, to turn every head, like when a queen passes. My first wife was—was *not* like this. So I want you.'

'You—don't love me?' Her beautiful face was near to his, but he made no attempt to touch her. He could not have touched her.

'Love!' he burst out. 'What do I know of love? You say you loved Staffray? What good did it do you? I only know that from the day you came to the store I have wanted you, and still do. And if marriage will bring you to me, then I will marry you—if you wish.'

She gave a little sigh, and stood up. If he had offered her a word of tenderness then it would have brought them closer. She folded her arms in the ancient protective gesture over her full womb. 'But would you look after the baby as well as me? Would you see he has all a child should have? Home, care, a good education?'

'I would be prepared to make provision for the child—that I promise you.'

'You would do that for me?'

'I have said so. I would like to know your answer soon. There will be many arrangements to be made.'

She still hesitated, doubtful, puzzled. 'Mr Netherby, are you sure of what you are doing? There's your son and daughter to think of—they will not welcome me.'

'It is not their affair. I do not make offers lightly.'

'When—when would you want it to happen? You will not want me—yet?'

'Indeed not!' he said distastefully. 'You would stay here until after the birth—I will see you have every care and comfort. After a month we would marry, and I will announce it in the newspapers. We would go abroad immediately for a protracted tour, and afterwards I will take you back to Tewkesbury Square as my wife. I should not want anything known until after our marriage—a *fait accompli*.'

'But the baby?' she asked frantically. 'The baby while we are away. I could not leave my baby.'

'We will employ an excellent nurse to care for it. You shall see. Everything will be arranged with discretion. I will make myself responsible for you, and for the child's well-being. You will have no material anxieties—that I swear.'

He rose and held out his hand compellingly, and after a moment she slowly put hers into it. It was the first time she had, voluntarily, touched him, and his fingers closed over hers. The touch of flesh on flesh, formal as it was, sent her senses panicking away from him. She pulled away her hand.

'I don't think I could do it,' she said and her eyes were wide and frightened. 'I don't think it would be right—not for either of us. And I must not think of myself. I must think of my baby. Mr Netherby, it would be better my way. Better for you too. Just lend me the money to help me over the next months, and I swear I'll repay you. I can promise that. I cannot promise to make you happy.'

'Happiness,' he said, 'is for fools and children.' He took out his wallet and extracted a ten-pound note. 'I shall not press you. Think it over. In the meanwhile, there must be things you need. Would you accept this?' He put the note down on the table and picked up his hat. 'If you decide to accept my offer, write to me at the shop. Mark it confidential. I will come at once. I will hope to hear from you. Good night, Duchess.'

He went out of the cottage, leaving her alone.

There had been a desperate dignity about him which she had found touching. She wondered if, when he was alone at night, he lay awake wanting her as she sometimes wanted James? Poor devil, if he did. The note lay on the table. There was a heel of a loaf in the cupboard until Betsy came home with her wages, and Viola was gnawingly hungry.

When Betsy came in after eight o'clock, tired from her long journey from the West End, the fire was crackling, the table laid, and the house smelled fragrantly of baking meat and potatoes.

'Why,' she gasped, 'what's happened, Vi? Have we come into a fortune?'

Viola straightened up, turning from the oven, her cheeks flushed from the heat, her eyes tragic and reckless, unable to meet Betsy's enquiring glance.

'Well, you might say that, love,' she said. 'I've decided to marry Mr Netherby.'

'Oh, *Duchess!* You *never* have!' cried Betsy, and they clung together and both burst into tears, but whether with relief or despair Betsy could not say.

Netherby leaned back in his carriage as it jogged smoothly home to Tewkesbury Square. He felt as exhausted as though he had been through some physical ordeal. Courage she might have and a brash honesty, but she was a woman born for riches and luxury and she had felt the real pinch of poverty. The hollows beneath the beautiful eyes and her expression when she looked at the money he had given her had told him that. It was what he had bargained for. This time, he was sure, she would come to him.

In May of that year Mafeking was relieved and the news was greeted with joy, fireworks, rioting and dancing in the streets, and James Carlo Corbett was born with the minimum of trouble, a fine, strong, fair child. Viola called him James for his father and Carlo for her unknown Italian father. He was born in a small but scrupulously clean nursing home run by a Mrs Brasher, a midwife who also cared for very young children when their parents were away abroad. She had, she told Viola, looked after some very aristocratic by-blows.

A month later Viola and Arthur Netherby were married at the local church, privately. Arthur would have preferred no friends or guests, but Viola was still weak from her confinement, so Betsy was allowed to attend.

Netherby waited in the empty church for them. Viola came in the silvery grey dress which he had had sent from the emporium, and a hat trimmed with roses and silver leaves. Betsy, following behind, despite her new dress and hat, looked like a little lady's maid following her tall, graceful mistress.

Netherby saw Viola hesitate, saw her sudden wild backward glance, like a mare about to bolt, and went forward and took her hand, his clean pink fingers closing about her wrist with a surprising strength.

'I've kept my promise, Duchess,' he whispered. 'Now you must keep yours.'

After the ceremony Netherby drove back to Oxford Street. He had many things to arrange before they left by the night boat for France.

He had never left the store for so long before—they would be away for eight weeks travelling in France. He had put Herbert in sole charge and there were many last-minute instructions. He did not trust Herbert, or enjoy allowing him any responsibility, but he worked on the assumption that your own were less likely to rob you than strangers.

Herbert was overwhelmed—the thought of being *Mr* Netherby, in charge of the whole big store, filled him with pride. He could not quite understand why his father should take this step; he always behaved as though the emporium would collapse without him. Rather more sophisticated than his sister, Herbert was quite aware of the dubious properties his father owned and visited in St Giles. He knew that, even before his mother's death, his father had led a furtive sexual life unknown to her—and to Tewkesbury Square. He knew that his father had pursued pretty girl employees, favourites for a while, then inexplicably dismissed. There had been one or two attempts at blackmail. He suspected that his father's interest in a trip to Paris was not purely in the line of business. But that was not his affair. His father's absence meant he would have the opportunity of running the store. He was surprised that Arthur had such confidence in him. He was soon disillusioned.

'I am sure I will be able to manage, sir. I shall look forward to taking a position of responsibility.'

'Yes, I can see you do,' said Arthur witheringly. Herbert gazing at him ingratiatingly through his pince-nez reminded him of a fawning spaniel.

'And if you must drink port and lemon with the juniors and clerks, don't do it in your lunch hour or near the store.'

Poor Herbert's cheeks flamed. Sweet drinks and the company of young men were his two weaknesses, although he had neither the courage nor the will to approach anything that could be termed a vice.

Arthur continued, the booming voice heavy with sarcasm: 'Up to now you have shown no initiative whatsoever, so I have arranged that there will be no need for you to exert any during my absence. Consult the department heads and my secretary who will know where to get in touch with me.'

Arthur had not told Herbert and Emily about his marriage. He did not want scenes of jealousy and accusation at Tewkesbury Square, although he could imagine their chagrin and dismay when they learned what had happened. They would read the announcement in the newspapers and he would post a letter to them from Victoria when he and Viola caught the boat train. Whether they would continue to make their home with him at Tewkesbury Square was a matter of indifference to him, but if they thought he would provide them with another home, they were mistaken.

The heavy luggage had been sent ahead, and it was arranged that a hired carriage should call for Viola and take her to Victoria to meet him at the boat train. He had engaged a first class compartment and a cabin on the steamer.

In the few hours before she left, Viola walked across the Common to Mrs Brasher's. She would not see James Carlo for eight weeks, and she was trying to control herself as Arthur wished. If luxury was her natural element, motherhood was too. The pains and the slithering rush of birth neither shocked nor scared her—her arms went out for her son, wet and bloody as he was, before the cord had been separated. Mrs Brasher had been quite shocked. 'Unnatural,' she had said. 'Foreign blood, I shouldn't wonder!'

Viola rang the bell of the large, airy, semi-detached house overlooking the Common on the north side.

Mrs Brasher's house was, as usual, immaculately clean, scrubbed, and smelling of antiseptic polish. James was tucked firmly into his cot, asleep. He had, Mrs Brasher said, been as good as gold.

'Better not disturb him, ma'am,' she said. 'He's having a nice nap. He's too young to know anyway.'

'Do you think so? Some people say they know from the start, before they're born, if they're really wanted. '

'Some people,' said Mrs Brasher with a sniff of disdain, 'know nothing about babies.'

There was another child in the gleamingly clean room, a boy of about a year, with a curly golden head, very pretty, also asleep.

'He's only just come,' explained Mrs Brasher. 'I said I'd have him for six months. His folk have gone to Africa—the gentleman's an engineer or something.'

'He looks so pale,' said Viola, 'and not well. Is he all right?'

'Oh, yes, ma'am. Tired out. Well, he cried his head off yesterday, when they left. The mother too. Never had such a scene. Doesn't help the child or the mother, or me, I says. If these decisions have to be made, they have to face up to it.'

'Poor baby.' Viola suddenly lifted James Carlo, and held him in her arms, kissing the round knob of a head where a floss of reddish blond hair was appearing. He yawned and stretched, and bobbed his lips wetly against her neck, searching instinctively for a nipple as babies will. Viola felt torn apart. 'Oh, my darling, my darling,' she said, 'this is the only time. I won't leave you again.'

'Now, ma'am, please.'

'When I come home I shall be here to see you every day,' she promised him. 'And I shall take you out for walks, and give you your meals, and you'll really know me.'

Mrs Brasher took him from her reprovingly, and tucked him firmly back into the cot. He gave a few complaining little noises, and closed his eyes again.

'Mr Netherby, no doubt, will have something to say about that,' said Mrs Brasher primly. Neither the marriage nor James's illegitimacy could have been kept from her. 'You're a very lucky young woman, Mrs Netherby. There's not many young women in your position has a fine man like Mr Netherby to marry her and make her a rich respectable lady. He won't want you popping across here every minute. You've your duties as a wife now, you know. And it isn't as though you need to worry. He'll be looked after like a little lord.'

Her words faltered, meeting Viola's eyes.

'He had better be for that's what he is,' said Viola coldly. 'Mr Netherby is paying a great deal for you to care for him, but I shall expect you to answer to me. I have given you the addresses where we shall be staying abroad, and I expect a report every week.'

'Yes, ma'am,' said Mrs Brasher stiffly.

'And, Mrs Brasher, I'd be glad if you'd keep your advice to yourself. Your business is only to care for James Carlo, not to criticize me. Good day.'

'Good day, ma'am,' said Mrs Brasher closing the door indignantly. She stood in the hall, cooling her temper. 'That *one!* I knew she'd be a trouble.

Jumped-up little whore.' One of the children upstairs, the older child, gave out a plaintive whimper. 'Oh, shut up, you little perisher,' said the immaculate Mrs Brasher. She went down into her not so immaculate kitchen, and took a nip of gin to sustain her against the unreasonable demands of inexperienced young mothers.

Viola walked back over the Common towards the cottage. A glance at her watch told her she still had half an hour before the carriage came to take her away to her honeymoon, and her wedding night, but for the moment everything was forgotten except the anguish at leaving her baby. She would go. She would try to be the beautiful and admired wife Netherby so blatantly desired, but every day and minute she was away she would be thinking of James Carlo. She neither liked nor trusted Mrs Brasher, although she had been an efficient midwife.

Viola still wore the dress she had been married in, with a less elaborate hat of plain straw. There was a May breeze stirring the dust, blowing her silken skirts back against her graceful body, making her bend her head and hold her hat.

A man stopped immediately in front of her, and as her head came up she found herself looking into Erhmann's silver grey eyes. She went white with shock and her great eyes filled with tears.

'Duchess! I would have recognized that walk anywhere.' He looked at her with concern. 'What is it? Has something upset you?'

She shrugged. 'The baby—I have to leave it for a while. He is very small, and new, and dear to me.'

He had whipped off his fawn Homburg and the afternoon sun gleamed on his fair hair and beard.

'Ah,' he said. 'The baby. I am so sorry, *mein liebchen*, but I was away— in South Africa. I was travelling about, and only business cables were sent on to me. I arrived back in Vienna five days ago and found your letter awaiting me. I came at once. I have been to the cottage and saw your little friend, who told me you were out walking. So—' he offered his arm and she put her hand into it, and they walked slowly together back towards the Old Town—'he deserted you—the handsome young lover?'

'No, I don't believe so. I had this.' She opened her handbag and gave him the solicitor's letter from the Louderdowns. He read it, shaking his head.

'He was very badly wounded. I saw him once. He did not see me . . . or seemed not to.'

'So the wounded hero returns, and the family pull up the drawbridge! Your letter was desperate. You said you were without money, but you look like a queen—a sad queen, but a queen. You have survived—dare I ask how?'

'I married Mr Netherby this morning.'

In his astounded silence she saw all the arrogance of pride and breeding, and irony touched her smile.

'My friend the Count is shocked?'

'I am outraged! *You*, Duchess! *You* have married that vulgar haberdasher. That fat, drunken, lecherous, clumsy oaf? It is impossible?'

'It is a fact,' she said, and her temper flashed. 'Should I have starved and asked Betsy to starve with me? Living on *her* wages? Should I have gone scrubbing like my mother? Should I have gone on the streets and been a whore? I had nothing and a baby coming. Netherby offered to marry me and take care of us. It was a generous offer—or so most people would think.'

She was astounded to see his hard mouth trembling.

'Ah, *liebchen*, I would have done all this for you.'

'You—a great rich important man—you would have married me?' She searched his face and realized with a shock that he was quite sincere. She put out her hand, touched his, turned away, confused. If only she had known! She had thought him a friend. She had not known he cared for her. 'Signor Count,' she said, 'thank you. But the time came when I could not wait, and now it is too late. Only by a few hours . . . but it might just as well be a lifetime.'

CHAPTER EIGHT

A carriage had drawn up outside the cottage, and Viola said, 'There is the cab for me. I am meeting Mr Netherby . . .' She drew in a sharp breath as the enormity of the step she had taken swept over her. 'I am meeting my husband at Victoria. We are going abroad—to Paris. And then to Biarritz.'

'For your honeymoon?'

She did not reply.

'No, not a honeymoon. Impossible, with that creature! Faugh!' He made a small, spitting expletive. 'When I think of him having any rights over you. *Touching* you! That night at Franconeri's you were in a panic at the mere idea of such a thing.'

Her ironic smile deepened. 'You and he have something in common for all your pride, Count. You both look upon me as a possession. You think I am wasted on Mr Netherby. He thinks he has bought something he has wanted for a long time. Ah, yes, it's true.' She shook her head when he would have denied it. 'I am a very nice possession. You both value me, but want to own me. James was different. He thought, if he thought of it at all—for God help us, neither of us thought of anything but the other—he thought that I was a common girl, far beneath him, but for all that I was his first true love.' Her lovely eyes glowed. 'I was his true, dear love for that short while.'

Poignantly touched, Erhmann took her hands. 'And you would be mine too. Listen, *liebchen*.' The words poured from him. He implored her to come away with him. 'Now. Do not go to the station, Duchess. My apartment is near Victoria. Come there with me. He will not find you. Tomorrow we will be in Paris, the next evening in Vienna. He will never get you back.'

'And James Carlo, my little son?'

'We will take him with us. He shall have every advantage that money and position can give him. I cannot offer you marriage, now, Duchess, because you have taken this so foolhardy step. This—haberdasher stands in our way. But should he ever let you go—divorce you, then I would ask you to be my wife.'

'It is too late, Signor Count.'

'That we are not married will make no difference. You shall have every respect. I will protect you and the child. You shall live in my house in Vienna, or my little castle in the mountains. You shall travel with me, do what you like, live where you like, have whatever you want. But do not give yourself to this man. Listen, *liebchen*—you have only to put your hand in mine and walk across the grass with me, and we will take your cab and go away together. I will care for you and love you, and you and your boy will always be safe.'

She stood, her head bent, listening to his passionate plea, drawing letters in the fine gravel by the side of the path with the ferrule of her parasol. J.C.C. James Carlo Corbett. Her son's initials. Now he was the first thing in her life.

'No,' she said stubbornly. It was the forthright side of her that suddenly flashed out, four-square, North-Country and determined. 'A bargain is a bargain. I've given my word and I'll keep it so long as Mr Netherby keeps his. I was not forced to marry him.'

'You were forced by circumstance.'

She gave a little sigh, like a child after a bout of crying. 'No, I was not brave enough. I was too soft and spoiled. I was afraid of real poverty.'

'If your wild hopes became reality, Duchess, and young Staffray returned to claim you, what would you do then?'

Her colour flamed, and her glance flashed up at him.

'How can I tell? I will try as hard as I can to keep my marriage vows and be straight with my husband. But I will always love James, and if he really came for me, perhaps even a promise before God could not keep me then. But—he does not want me. I know that. If there had been—the breath of a chance—I would never have made this marriage, desperate though I was.'

'And so—there is nothing I can do?'

'Yes.' She opened her bag again, and took out two yellow tickets. 'Pawn tickets. When things were at their worst I pawned your lovely brooch and James's pearls. I think they cheated me. I got very little but it kept Betsy and me for a time. Would you redeem them for me? And then sell them for the best price possible? I hate to part with them. Yours was the first jewel I ever possessed—and the necklace is the only thing I have that James gave me. Everything was stolen . . . But I am worried about Betsy. I swore to her she would never have to go back to living in at the shop hostel. I would like her to be safe. Mr Netherby would not do this for me. He will buy me clothes, furs, lovely things, but not this. With the money you could pay the rent of the cottage for a whole year and more, and I would know she was safe.'

He took the tickets, and put them carefully away. 'I will do that, of course.'

'And—if you could make enquiries about my baby.' She pointed across the Common to the row of tall red-brick villas. 'It is the second of those houses. From time to time. I—I don't like the woman who runs it. It is clean, and the children seemed cared for . . . but . . . I don't know . . .'

He smiled. 'A mother's instinct? You have all the right fundamental instincts, Duchess. You take happiness as it comes. Love, life, passion and babies . . . From the moment I met you, I knew you would demand and deserve the best. Well, then—*auf wiedersehen.*' He kissed her hands with formality and tenderness, and walked to the cab-stand where the main roads met, roused a sleeping cabby with a light tap of his gold-headed cane, sprang into the hansom and drove away.

As he leaned back against the leather seat with his eyes closed, he experienced the drained-out feeling he had known after gambling for heavy stakes. He had lost and that oaf, Netherby, had won. How could such a man keep such a girl? Already her vital youth was marred. She was a woman bracing herself for the ordeals ahead, and to him more beautiful than ever. Somewhere this must end in tragedy. His sense of foreboding was so strong that he almost told the man to drive back to the cottage so that he could plead with her again, but he knew it would be useless. There was another woman, forthright and firm beneath that seductive queen of all silky things. He smiled wryly, remembering the old Arabian tale, and how well the description fitted her. The woman was emerging from the chrysalis of girlhood, a woman of strength and distinction. He shook his head, and sighed, '*Ach, mein* Duchess, what will happen to you now!'

Arthur Netherby's note sent from Victoria Station, announcing his marriage, arrived like a bombshell at Number 40 Tewkesbury Square. Emily and Herbert were even more horrified to find an announcement in the following morning's newspapers.

'Everyone will read it,' said Herbert shakily. 'Everyone in the square. The staff at the emporium. On my first day in charge. They'll be snickering at me behind my back. How could he do such a thing?'

'He can't bring her here!' cried Emily shrilly. 'He won't expect us to share a house with that woman? He wouldn't dare!'

'Oh yes, he would,' said Herbert.

'I will not stay under the same roof as such a person.'

'Can you tell me where else we could live?' he asked bitterly. 'Two of us on my salary? He has not given me a raise since I was out of my apprenticeship—says I don't need it, living here free. No one would think I was the owner's son. Do you fancy living in a couple of rooms in the back streets on what I earn? I don't even earn commission, shop-walking like I do.' He took off his pince-nez, rubbed the two red spots on either side of his nose, and put them on again. 'It's too bad.' His voice rose, almost as shrilly as his sister's. 'I've always known about his women—but to marry her! It's—it's too bad!'

'She's wicked and immoral. She made a terrible scandal when she went off with that young lord and all the square was talking. I shan't be able to face anyone. What will the Reverend Everard say?'

Herbert remembered Arthur's rages and shivered. He knew there was nothing he could do except leave his father's house, and business, and start independently for himself, give up his privileged position and the comfort of Tewkesbury Square.

'She'll be his wife,' he said feverishly. 'She could get everything. They say there's no fool like an old fool. He's always told me I ought to be content with the miserable pittance I get because I'll have the whole lot one day. But he could make a new will. He might leave us penniless.'

Emily went white. The fear that her father would re-marry had always been with her. She would be ousted from her place as mistress of the house. But that her father should choose a woman like this was appalling.

'What will people say? It's a disgrace. He's cruel, he always has been. He hates us because we're refined, like Mother was, and he's never been anything but a counter jumper. And it was our mother's money that started it all—that bought the freehold and built the store.'

Herbert got up, fussing about, his hands behind his back with the bowing, stork-like gait.

'I'll never forgive him, the old thief!'

He went to the window and looked savagely down at the square. Matthew Lyttelton, hurrying from morning service to his lodgings, raised his hat politely as he passed, surprised at Herbert's furious glare.

Emily ignored Matthew, looking down her thin pinched nose. 'He's as bad as Father,' she cried vindictively, 'and *he's* a clergyman. He still meets that girl from the shop—*her* friend. A fine pair. I've seen him; one of the servants told me too. Arm in arm down Oxford Street as bold as brass. Kisses her good night at the omnibus stop. A man in his position—*a gentleman* and a girl from the shop. It's disgraceful!'

'We'll see about that,' said Herbert vindictively. 'We'll see about that. That's one thing we can do something about while I am in charge.'

On the following Friday when the wages came round at Dwyer & Netherby's, Betsy found a slip in hers advising her of her dismissal. No reason was given and her week's wages were enclosed.

She went across to the glove buyer, Miss Heath, and asked her tremulously the reason for her dismissal. Miss Heath said sharply, 'Mr Herbert no doubt has his reasons. Were you expecting special treatment now your friend's gone up in the world?'

The news of Viola's marriage had gone round the shop with every sort of remark from spiteful jealousy to bawdy comments and good-natured well-wishing.

'In my opinion, you never have been efficient, Miss Holder. You are too timid by half. One has to be firm with customers.'

Betsy went back to her place.

'Why don't you go and arsk 'im, H.N.?' said Katy Martin, glancing up the green carpeted stairs. 'Mean little squirt. I'd rather 'ave the old devil himself than sonny-boy.'

Betsy plucked up her courage and went upstairs and was shown into Mr Netherby's office. Herbert was sitting behind his father's large desk. His sharp red nose went up like a ferret nosing its prey, and a little vindictive gleam shone in his eyes.

'I don't have to give any reason for dismissal,' he said in his curious, high-pitched voice, 'but, since you ask, it is a question of behaviour. You know very well what I mean.'

From the depths of her gentle heart Betsy found courage.

'If you mean Mr Lyttelton, sir, we've an agreement. We are going to get married—when we can afford it.'

Herbert shot to his feet in fury. 'I don't believe it. Mr Lyttelton could— and indeed was—paying his respects to my sister . . . how dare you say such an absurd and wicked thing! I shall inform Mr Everard—indeed, I believe my sister has already done so.'

It was a beautiful evening in early June when Betsy left Dwyer & Netherby for the last time. Matthew was waiting for her, not hiding nervously round the corner, but outside the door, for everyone to see. When she came out, he offered her his arm, and returned Miss Heath's caustic glance like a knight errant defending his lady. They proceeded towards the bus stop in Oxford Street.

'I've got the sack,' Betsy said dismally.

'So have I,' he replied.

Their eyes met, and unexpectedly, they both began to laugh.

'Eh, what are we laughing at, love?' she said. 'I've nowt but my week's wages.'

'Nothing, not nowt,' he corrected gently.

'Sorry, love.'

He squeezed her arm. He wanted her to speak correctly, not because he minded, but because he felt impelled to rush to her defence should anyone criticize her.

'I've a few pounds from my last stipend, and a guinea for an article in *The Churchman's World*. I've to leave my lodgings immediately,' he said. 'When she heard about it, my landlady didn't think I could manage the rent. She was, of course, quite right.'

They stared at each other, and to both their astonished young hearts, instead of feeling horror and dismay, they felt a sort of glow of unity.

'I've been thinking, Elizabeth,' he said in his best pulpit manner, 'that for over a year—ever since we met, almost, we, that is I, have been thinking of marriage when I had some security. Well, now we've none at all, I thought, well, I thought we might just as well marry anyway, and if it's going to be awful, at least we'll be together.'

'Oh, Matthew,' said Betsy, 'what a *wonderful* idea!'

'I'll come all the way home with you tonight,' he said.

He did and in the cottage kitchen they made plans, and ate a meagre meal, and when it was time for him to go home, she suggested that, as he had to leave his lodgings, and they would be living in the cottage as long as Viola would let them ('and I'm sure she won't mind,' said Betsy earnestly), he might just as well move in right away. Which he did—and for the next three weeks, until they arranged their wedding, Betsy slept upstairs, and Matthew slept downstairs on two chairs, because both of them considered Viola's room too near for propriety, and even if he fell down on to the floor once or twice during the night, they slept as blissfully at being so near together as though they were locked in a passionate embrace.

'It was the only right and proper thing to do,' said Matthew on their wedding day.

Betsy was in full and worshipping agreement.

'It would have been a terrible temptation to me to have you sleeping so near to me,' he explained.

'But tonight, love, it will be grand to be together,' she said ingenuously.

They were eating poached eggs and drinking coffee at an ABC. Their wedding breakfast. Matthew spilled his coffee and got egg on his lapels trying to hold her hand, full of awe that God had given this loving little creature into his care. She carried a few roses which he had bought her, and wore the new dress Viola had given her before she went away. She was so happy it was almost painful to look at her. He was afraid that something might take a fraction of it away. Nothing ever would if he could help it.

'I wish Vi could have been at my wedding. But she'd have laughed at us, you know, love, sleeping one up and one down these past weeks.'

'If,' said Matthew perceptively, 'she did not cry,' and was sorry at once, seeing a shadow touch Betsy's transcendent happiness.

'When she went off to meet him,' she said, 'Mr Netherby I mean, I cried. She looked like stone. She was always one for showing her feelings, right from the first time I met her, when we were girls in Leeds. Full of life, laughing or cross, talking, enjoying herself, you always knew how she felt. But when she went away she looked beautiful, like a grand lady, but so sad and closed up in herself.' She paused, shaking her head. 'Well, she's Mrs Netherby now, rich and safe . . . let's hope she will be happy as well. Let's hope he will make her happy.'

Matthew, who during his visits to the poor in the districts round St Botolph's, had learned things about Netherby which had shocked him, and which he could never have brought himself to speak about to Betsy, pressed her head against his shoulder so that she should not see the doubt in his eyes.

In Biarritz that summer the talk was all about Mrs Arthur Netherby. The English called her 'the draper's wife' and it was rumoured that the Prince of Wales had noticed her. The French called her *La Belle Tristesse* because of the strangely haunting expression in her eyes, or sometimes *La Prisonnière* because, in spite of the impact her beauty and her clothes had on society, she seemed to have no freedom at all.

She never appeared in public without her husband. In the gaming rooms she sat beside him, beautifully gowned, and he would pass her chips which she would take, and nearly always win, and with an odd, ironic smile, pass the winnings back to him. Although they invariably lunched and dined in public at the hotel or in the best restaurants, although they were seen everywhere, they were always alone together, not talking very much, Mrs Netherby wearing her exquisite Parisian clothes with an *élan* that caught every eye. They knew no one, encouraged no acquaints beyond bowing and casual greetings. Any attempts of friendliness were firmly discouraged by Mr Netherby. The inaccessibility of this desirable newcomer whetted the appetites of the gossips and the rich young idlers, who began to form a group, watchful and opportunist, never far away when the beautiful Mrs Netherby appeared.

Two such gentlemen stood on the terrace of the Hotel Bristol et France, looking down on the sunlit garden where society was taking its pre-luncheon stroll. Beyond the promenade the blue Atlantic breakers crashed on the beach, and behind them the Pyrenees rose, snowy-crested, yellow with gorse, scented with heather, and beyond them to the south was Spain.

The two young men, speaking such correct English together and wearing such perfectly cut English clothes, were in fact a Spanish attaché and a Frenchman. Young Englishmen of their age were still involved with the war in South Africa which, in spite of the rapid northward advances and the relief of the besieged towns, was dragging on towards a belated victory.

'The draper flaunts her like a pimp and guards her like a dragon,' said the young Frenchman speculatively, watching the couple walking below. 'Look, my friends, he says, but *do* not touch. Envy me and desire her, but do not approach. A woman of her quality is bound to deceive him one day. I can see the horns growing on his fat bald head.'

'*Hombre!*' exclaimed the young Spaniard morosely. 'If she does, may I be the lucky fellow! That walk of hers—like a queen! Like a *gitana!* She drives me out of my mind!'

'She has a certain notoriety, you know. She was the mistress of the son of the Earl of Louderdown. I have been told they made a great scandal in London before he went to the ridiculous war in South Africa and stopped a Boer bullet.'

A man sitting near them at a terrace table turned his head sharply as though he overheard their words. He was a gaunt man, his light brown hair flecked with grey, the left sleeve of his beautifully cut coat empty, the cuff tucked into his side pocket. The beauty of his eyes, bright blue be-tween their thick, dark lashes, was emphasized by the hollow, shadowy sockets on either side of the handsome, arrogant, broken nose. A scar ran down one of his cheeks. His glance was both painful and commanding as he rose stiffly to his feet, and walked towards the two gossips, pausing then to look down at the promenaders in the sunlit garden below. He walked with a slight limp, supporting himself with a strong malacca cane.

The couple who had drawn comment and attention were a corpulent man in his late fifties, almost too well dressed. While the majority of men, following the new fashion of the English court, wore suits of light tweed and felt Homburgs, he was dressed in a black, full-skirted frock coat, a large gold chain across his pearl grey waistcoat, and a shining black top hat on his head, as though for the church parade in Hyde Park on Sun-day.

The woman was wearing a dress of lavender-coloured linen, very simple and of a magnificent cut which branded the name of Worth all over it.

Her thick red hair waved beneath a big leghorn straw hat, trimmed with lilac blossom. Her white gloved hand rested on her husband's arm and she matched her steps to his, neither glancing to left or right, the beautiful face expressionless and wary. Only once she smiled, when a nurse allowed a toddling baby to run up to her. Then her face was suddenly irradiated. She bent and would have lifted the child, but her husband spoke sharply, and she twitched into obedience like a puppet, and walked forward with him again. Neither of them looked up. The man on the terrace took off his hat, and rubbed the long bullet scar that furrowed his thin cheek. He stood watching as the couple walked away and were lost to sight behind a group of trees.

He put on his hat and turned to the two elegant gossips.

'Forgive me if I overheard your conversation,' he said. 'I did not intend to.'

'Milord?' said the young French diplomat tactfully.

'Did I hear you say her name was—Netherby? The lady in lilac—walking in the gardens below?'

'Yes, milord, her name is Netherby, and she is married to a Mr Arthur Netherby, who I am told is the proprietor of a large store in London for the purveying of ladies' clothes.'

'And she is staying here—in the Bristol et France?'

'They have the royal suite.'

The man who lacked an arm looked at him with the burning, blue glance, nodded abruptly. 'I'm obliged to you sir,' he said, and walked away.

'And what was that about, *hombre?*' asked his friend.

'That's Staffray,' said the Frenchman slowly. 'Convalescing from his wounds. And that—' as a tall distinguished lady in the flowing train and looped-back skirts of some ten years previously came out of the hotel to meet James—'that is his mama. A very adoring one, too, I am told. She has nursed him back from the brink of death and cannot bear him out of her sight.'

There was to be a subscription ball at the Hotel Bristol et France that night, given for a charity, which all the smartest visitors and all the richest and best local families would attend. Arthur had obtained tickets. He had engaged an exclusive hairdresser to arrange Viola's hair, and ordered her to wear the most beautiful of her new evening dresses, a white chiffon, embroidered with crystals, draped over ice blue satin, the fullness gathered to the back, so that her tall slender figure was delectably accentuated, and the décolletage cut daringly low over her breasts, to display the diamond necklace Arthur had bought for her in Paris.

She had always adored pretty clothes. Both the cheap ones she had bought for herself, the lovely ones James had given her and which Jevons had stolen, but there was no pleasure in being dressed by Arthur Netherby. She had no choice; he had very good taste. He supervised the purchase of every garment and chose every outfit. It was as though she were one of his window dummies in the store in Oxford Street.

He came into the bedroom with a diamanté rose in his hand from which a few delicate ostrich fronds of the same ice blue sprayed like fragile tendrils. A foolish charming ornament from Paris. He put it against her hair and stood back, his head on one side, consulting the hairdresser as though Viola was not there.

'The hair piled high, I think, Antoine,' he said authoritatively, 'and the ornament centred above the forehead. The width of Madam's brow permits us to do something a little *outré*.'

Antoine bowed, looking down at the strange, beautiful girl, so motionless, no expression stirring the long, heavily-lashed green-gold eyes. She wore a wrap of eau-de-nil silk over her chemise and rustling white taffeta petticoat.

'It is rumoured that a Russian Grand Duke may be present. Isn't that so, Antoine?'

'I believe so, sir. I dressed the Archduchess's hair earlier.'

'She is not as beautiful as Mrs Netherby?'

'No, sir, indeed.'

Arthur rubbed his hands together, his eyes travelling over his wife with slow and deliberate pleasure. The hairdresser wondered cynically if that was the limit of the man's pleasure—a *voyeur* if ever he saw one.

'You had better dress,' said Viola, 'if we are not to be late.'

'Yes. I'm going now. The white fan, my dear, and white rose perfume.'

He went from the room, and when the door shut behind him, she relaxed like a puppet whose string is cut. She leaned forward, took a stick of rouge and painted the tip of her nose red, and shook with laughter at the clown face in the mirror.

'Shall I go to the ball like this, Antoine? Do you think I should outshine the Russian Archduchess?'

'*Madame s'amuse*,' he said depreciatingly and handed her a clean napkin to wipe the rouge away. The big eyes gazed at him in the mirror above the white cotton square. 'Suppose it won't come off?' She rubbed her nose, and he, with a little gesture asking her permission, dabbed it with cold cream. She was still laughing, but there was desperation in her laughter. 'My husband would *not* be amused if I looked like a clown.' She rubbed again and the tip of the small strong nose was clean. 'There. Reprieved. Don't look so worried, Antoine. I will be good.'

He took away the napkin, and as he did so slipped a note into her hand before commencing to comb the cascade of her burnished hair up and away from her face. She put the note on the dressing table indifferently. 'I do not accept notes, Antoine.'

'The gentleman is English. A great gentleman. He has one arm.'

'*Ah!*' The little exclamation was forced from her. Her hand went out for the envelope. She ripped it open. It was James Staffray's card and written across it the words: 'I am here in the hotel. I must see you.'

'Thank you,' Arthur said from the door. He had taken off his frock coat and donned a dressing jacket of quilted red silk. He came forward and took the card from her hand, read it, and a sadistic anticipation lit his eyes. He remembered standing by the railings in Belgrave Square last summer, watching them together, hand in hand, always laughing, two crazy, careless children, so much in love.

'Ah, it will be interesting to see how he behaves. My wife is greatly admired, Antoine. Many young men will give you messages for her if they learn you are her hairdresser . . . always bring them. It amuses me. But give them to me, not to her.' He tore up the card, and dropped it in a waste basket. His hand fell on Viola's shoulder, pushed back the pale green silk until the upper arm was bare, took a piece of white flesh between his strong, clean finger and thumb and twisted it until she winced. Then he let go. A flaming mark showed on the soft arm. The horrified hairdresser saw that her upper arm bore several such marks, dark purple or fading to yellow.

Arthur bent, touched the corner of her mouth, twitched her face round and kissed her full on the lips.

'That's my good little girl,' he said. 'Get dressed.' He turned on the appalled man and shouted, 'Get on with it, you bloody frog! I don't want you in here all night. There's enough rubbish chasing her bitch's tail without hairdressers entering the race!'

He went into his own room and banged the door.

The little hairdresser was trembling with fury.

Viola pulled up the shoulder of her wrap, covering the bruise, and smiled up at him.

'It won't show. My gown conceals it. But please do my hair nicely, won't you?'

The appeal in her eyes was unmistakable . . . she must look beautiful—she dare not be otherwise. He finished his work in silence, his lips folded tightly. If he saw the English milord he would tell him of this scene. Even as he thought this he met her eyes in the mirror. She gave a small shake of the head.

'Don't tell Lord Staffray—or anyone. It does no good.'

The ball began at 8.30 and at nine o'clock Mr and Mrs Netherby entered the ballroom. If Netherby had planned a triumph for his wife he had certainly achieved it. There was not another woman in the place who could hold a candle to her.

Arthur Netherby had made certain that a conspicuous seat had been reserved for them. He sat beside Viola, nodding to acquaintances, beaming above his large expanse of crackling white evening shirt, delighted when the young men approached and bowed. He would shake his head and say insolently, 'My wife does not dance, sir,' and then watch them retire, discomfited. Puppies, he thought, with their tails between their legs.

Viola sat beside him like a statue. He knew perfectly well that every nerve in her young lovely body must yearn to swing in time to the waltz music. He could see the tip of her satin shoe tapping to the rhythm.

From the surrounding balcony James Staffray watched them—watched her hungrily. His mother was in the card room with some friends playing bridge. He had slowly recovered from his terrible wounds, and as he recovered had tried to get news about Viola—his mother had been disapproving but sympathetic. Had declared that, in spite of all the solicitor's enquiries, no trace of the girl could be found. His mother had insisted on him travelling abroad with her for a change of air, and that morning, in the gardens, he had seen Viola again, and heard of her marriage for the first time. He longed to go down and take her into his arms, as she sat there in the frosty glory of her blue and silver, her sparkling diamonds, and the jewelled flower in her flaming hair. Still, smiling, expressionless, a queen of ice.

She belonged to him and not to this fat, crude man, and knowing her to be so near, passion returned, flowing through his shattered body, bringing back the surge of youth and desire, of love. He had no thought for Netherby. He did not know what desperate need had driven her to marry the man and he did not care. He only knew she was there, and he wanted and needed her as he had never done before.

It was the supper waltz. Netherby had raised the gold-rimmed spectacles, held by a ribbon about his neck, and was consulting a large menu, a waiter hovering solicitously beside him. Suddenly James went along the balcony and down the steps to the ballroom.

All the guests watched his progress, the tall, gaunt young man in his elegant evening clothes, limping slightly, one sleeve empty, fastened across his chest. He went slowly and steadily across the centre of the floor until he stood opposite Viola. Netherby lifted his eyes from the menu and the difficult decision between *saumon pôché* and *homard à l'Américaine*. His mouth dropped open. James neither glanced at him nor spoke. He merely held out his one hand to Viola.

She flushed into life like a statue touched with dawn light. She rose in a second from despair into joy, stretching out her hand. James led her into the centre of the floor. No one else was dancing. Everyone was watching. She saw his haggard face grow young again. He dropped her hand and put his arm about her; she swept up her glittering train and they were off, swinging together to the lilting music, their faces entranced with joy, like people in a dream.

There was a murmur of laughter and comment. Netherby's face was suffused with crimson and his eyes murderous as he watched them. They circled the floor twice, not speaking, James's good arm lightly about her, and then other dancers joined them on the floor and he could no longer see them through the waltzing figures.

The music ceased, and James and Viola stopped by the open french windows leading out on to the hotel terrace. They were quite unconscious of the many curious eyes watching them and Arthur Netherby, like an audience at a melodrama. They turned and went together out of the ballroom.

It was a brilliant night, a full moon silvering the sea and mountains, a breeze lifting the laces and chiffons of the ladies' evening dresses. James and Viola walked across the terrace and down into the gardens, he very erect and soldierly as she swayed along beside him, her gown glittering frostily in lights festooned between the trees. They walked without speaking until they were hidden from the hotel in the shadows and then they were in each other's arms, kissing hungrily, obliterating the starved months of separation.

'Viola, why didn't you come to me?'

'I wrote to you.' She told him of the letter she had received from his family solicitors, and he gave a groan of anger and despair.

'They have conspired to protect me—what my mother calls protecting me—anything which she thought might cause me anxiety was kept away from me. I saw no letters after I was wounded, and the ones you sent me before I never saw again. I could not remember the address. Medical help was terrible at the front. The line had to be kept clear to get the men and ammunition and supplies up to us and there was no room for medical supplies. By the time they got me back to the Cape my wounds were infected—that was why they had to amputate. It was my arm or my life, and sometimes, except for memories of you, I wished it had been my life.'

'My darling, my poor Jimmy.'

'With this bullet wound in my skull I was delirious half the time. I remember calling your name. When my mother came she took over and she was wonderful, but I was still very ill when I got back to England. They still feared for my life. For a long while my memory failed completely. Then slowly it returned. When I was convalescent I asked them to find you, but they said you had disappeared.'

'I was at the station the day they brought you home. I called your name and you opened your eyes, but you did not see me.'

'I thought it was a dream. Since I have been well I have looked for you everywhere. I had no address. No one knew where you were. That place behind the shop where you used to live—the housekeeper did not know—or would not tell me.'

'She knew where I was. She knew Betsy and I were living together,' Viola said bitterly. 'But I could not make trouble for you. Or ask your people for money. I would have been ashamed. But the baby was coming and I could not go on living on my friend—she earned little enough. If you did not need me, then at least the baby did . . .'

'A baby? We have a child?' he asked incredulously.

She spread out her arms, folding them across her breast in a small cradling movement. 'A beautiful boy. He is nearly two months old. He is in London with a nurse. I am longing to see him again. That is why everything happened—for his sake. That is why I married Mr Netherby. I was a fool. I should have waited, but I dare not. I had to have help. I couldn't work and I was afraid.' Her eyes pleaded with him for understanding, and he held her against him quickly. 'I was so afraid of being poor, Jim. On my own, I would have been all right. But with a baby, unable to work, I know how hard it can be. I've seen other girls leaving their babies in filthy wretched homes or in orphanages. Perhaps I was a coward, but there it was. I didn't think I would see you again, and Mr Netherby offered me marriage and to care for the baby and educate him . . . it was generous. Don't look at me like that. You've never known in all your life what it is to be poor . . .'

'But I left you provided for, and would have sent more.'

'It was stolen from me. Jevons took everything, my clothes, all my money.'

'This man Netherby—your husband. Has he possessed you? Made love to you?'

'Oh, men!' she thought savagely. 'Men with their rights and ownerships!' But this one she loved. She shook her head in denial, and said, ashamed and sorry for Arthur, as she had been since their disastrous wedding night, 'He—cannot. It is not possible.'

'He is good to you?'

'He has kept his word,' she said stubbornly.

'But you must leave him now.'

'I cannot. I have given my word.'

'How can he prevent you?' said James arrogantly. 'I need you. You can come now tonight . . .'

They all thought it was so easy, these men of power, breeding and wealth. James and Erhmann. A man's word of honour was respected, but a woman's, particularly a woman like herself, was expected to be false. To break her contract without a thought.

'I cannot,' she said painfully. 'I have married him. He is not a nice man, nor a kind one . . .'

'He is cruel to you?'

'He does not beat me, if that's what you mean. But there are other ways of hurting.' She repressed a little shiver. 'But in his way he loves me, and he has kept his word to look after me, to provide for my child. I cannot leave him without a word. Don't look like that, James . . .'

'I cannot understand you.'

She suddenly began to weep.

'Viola,' he said in agony, 'you must come back to me . . . When I lost my arm, I did not want to live. The army was my life, but if you come back to me, I will have something to live for . . . Viola, I implore you . . .'

His arm went round her, and once more with a hungry little cry she lifted her lips to his. Footsteps were heard along the path, and on the moonlit gravel they could see Netherby's bulky silhouette approaching, and they fell apart.

He rounded the corner of the wall where a great bougainvillia sprayed purple blossom, saw the gleam and glitter of Viola's gown in the shadows. In his silence and despair he had a terrible and fatuous dignity. He was cruel with the cruelty of the unloved and unlovable. In spite of her revulsion Viola was filled with pity for him. If she could have made him happy, she would. She went to his side and put her hand through his arm. 'It's all *right*, Arthur,' she said.

His hot dull eyes did not change, did not light with relief or love. He was hating her.

'My wife,' he said stiffly, 'will not dance again. We are leaving now.'

Impetuously, as though he neither heard nor saw Netherby, James cried, 'Viola . . . I must see you again.'

She shook her head with a swift, tragic glance, 'No, James. There is nothing to be done. It would have been better if we'd not met tonight.' She turned to Netherby. 'Please, Arthur, take me to our rooms.'

They walked in silence through the gardens, across the terrace, through the crowded rooms, the glances following them, the hum of comment rising as they passed. They entered the great ornate gilded lift. 'A bird in a gilded cage as the song has it,' a wag murmured maliciously as they rose out of sight.

Lady Louderdown came into the great salon, looking for her son. She saw him through the open windows, sitting alone on the terrace. She draped her lace mantilla over her white hair, and went out to him.

'Am I late, my darling boy? The game went on so. Did you look in at the ball? Were there any pretty girls there? Some of these little French bourgeois girls are very charming, and I am sure would be flattered to dance with you if your poor leg would only allow it.'

His head jerked up to face her and she shrank at the angry accusation that blazed in his eyes.

'I asked you to try and trace that girl I knew. Viola Corbett. Did you ever *really* try? Or did you tell me a lot of evasions and lies?'

'Oh, James darling, are you still dwelling on that foolish affair? I told you everything was done. Your father instructed Sattherwaites to try and find her, but they had no success. What more could we do?'

'Well, I have found her. She is here. I saw her tonight. Your solicitors wrote to her insultingly as though she were a whore trying to blackmail me, so she believed I did not want or care for her. I presume these were your instructions?'

'I told Sattherwaite to—discourage her,' she admitted.

'He succeeded admirably. Because she was alone, without work or money she married a man old enough to be her father to protect and care for her child! My child!'

Lady Louderdown breathed a sigh of relief. The girl was married. Perhaps it was not going to be difficult after all.

'An admirable and wise thing for her to do. So many of these poor girls go to the bad, although it is the fault of their own stupid weakness and immorality. I warned you, my darling, that you were making too much of the whole thing. That kind of girl is not to be taken seriously.'

His single hand slammed down on the table.

'She wrote to me. Did you hold back the letter? Did you steal the letters I had before I was wounded? I had them here—' he put his hand over his heart '—in my wallet with her picture. Did you destroy them? Ah, I can see you did. She has had my child.'

'How do you know,' she said icily, 'that it is yours? How can such a girl tell?'

The deep-set blue eyes, so like her own, blazed.

'How dare you say that? You do not know her. Viola would not lie. I would answer for her honesty with my life. I have to see her again.'

'James . . .' She was white, an implacable pride showed. 'Have you forgotten your position?'

'I have to see her again.'

'James, I have gone through a great deal—I nearly lost you. You are our
only son and you have a great position in the world. You promised me
there would be no more wildness, no more scandals . . .'

The burning eyes silenced her.

'It is easy to promise when one has nothing to live for. I had lost the
army.' He moved his hand to his empty sleeve. 'And my girl. I thought
there was nothing.'

'But we talked, my darling, while you were so ill. There would be so
much for you, Louderdown, taking your father's place—and one day his
title. We would travel together, you and I—this is the first of our travels,
and one day there will be another girl, one of your own kind and class, to
be a wife you can be proud of.'

He had not heard. 'She is so beautiful.' He bit restlessly at the thumb of
his right hand, feeling the nail tremble against his lips. 'Tomorrow I'll
speak with her again whatever that damned haberdasher says.'

But when he sent up his name in the morning he was told that Mr and
Mrs Netherby had already left for London.

The journey through France seemed interminable. Viola lay in her berth,
her face and jaw aching where Arthur had struck her. He had never
struck her face before—he had been too careful of her beauty. But that
night his anger seemed to have released an almost homicidal storm.

In the eight weeks of their marriage he had alternately petted and humiliated her, alternatively insulted and praised, tormented and then
pleaded for her affection. He wanted to reduce her to a doll woman, to kill
her spirit and her pride. Once she had laughed at him and the memory
had rankled deeply. Part of his wish to marry her had been a morbid longing to have her in his power so that he could punish her for that
indifference and mockery. He loved to cause her pain, because pain was
the only sensation his exhausted body could give to her. She had pleaded,
she had argued, she had even tried to charm, please and tease him into
some kind of normal affection. But it served no purpose. A doll beauty for
everyone to admire in public; in private a frightened suppliant begging for
his mercy. She could be the first but she could not be the latter. Every
inch of her stubborn North-Country spirit rebelled.

His impotence had been manifest from their first night together in
Paris, and she had learned he took tablets in an endeavour to stimulate
himself. She managed to hide her pity and disgust. She told herself many

married women suffered and concealed such treatment, and she was now his wife. But the sickening alternatives he wanted, the kind of services he told her could be bought at the houses he frequented in St Giles, left her frozen with horror. She was a whore, he ranted, and a poor one at that.

After the ball he had ripped the exquisite white and blue dress from her, the glittering beads spitting round the room like hail-stones.

At last he had left her alone, telling her to get the *femme de chambre* to help her pack, as they would catch the early train to Le Havre.

During the journey he watched her ceaselessly. She wore a thick veil to hide the bruises along her brow and cheekbone. She was apparently calm. She did not cry. She should cry—all women did. His first wife always had. Emily cried when he was angry with her, and he often reduced the women who worked for him to tears. He had even reduced Herbert to snivelling pleas. But Viola did not cry. When he had taunted her with the fact that he would never permit her to see Staffray again she had quietly agreed it would be better for them all.

He hated the dignity with which she bore his treatment. She reminded him of the grand, rich women customers who came to his store, who patronized him with a vague graciousness and whom he would like to see grovelling for mercy.

They arrived at Tewkesbury Square on a hot August afternoon. The coachman had brought the carriage to meet them. The big leather, brass-fitted trunks and the long dress boxes from Paris would follow later by the railway goods cart.

The footman jumped down, opened the carriage door and lowered the steps. Arthur handed Viola down. He was relaxing; here at home he had her safe and she was certainly something to be proud of in her travelling suit of light amber-coloured silk and her small veiled hat of gold-tipped leaves.

Behind their starched curtains of Nottingham lace the eyes of Tewkesbury Square watched them cross the pavement and enter the house. Mr Netherby had really brought *that woman* home. Poor Mr Herbert. Poor Miss Netherby.

Viola followed Arthur into the hall. It was gracefully proportioned, although the expensive furniture was undistinguished. There was a lot of dark red as to flock wallpapers, velvet curtains and Turkey carpets, and several large art pots containing green indoor plants, but no flowers. There was a great display of silver. She wondered if the urns, trays, rose bowls, salvers, punchbowls and épergnes that gleamed against dark mahogany were ever used. There were large oil paintings which Arthur had told her he had bought direct from the Royal Academy at great expense, of Highland scenes, both snowy and heathery, with woolly cattle; others of children, carrying baskets of flowers, petting dewy-eyed dogs, kittens and ponies beneath the indulgent gaze of smiling adults. It was all very rich.

Arthur led the way into the drawing-room. The summer loose covers were dark maroon, as much sunlight as possible was excluded by thick white lace curtains and heavy, rich-looking red drapes, half drawn. Again there was the sense of a weighty opulence with a prevalent gloomy crimson. Arthur's taste, so excellent where women's clothes were concerned, had a lurid oppressiveness in his home. Like the contrast between his private and public lives.

Herbert and Emily were sitting before the empty fireplace, screened and packed with red paper for the summer. They rose apprehensively, obviously dreading the meeting. Viola too was nervous. She knew she could not possibly be welcome.

Herbert had not changed since she had last seen him in the emporium. His thin, lank hair was perhaps a little thinner. His stammer, as he greeted his father, rather more pronounced. His Adam's apple agitated up and down in the triangular opening of his high starched collar. He shot his cuffs, removed his pince-nez, and put them on again.

'Glad to see you, Papa.' He shot a baleful yet timid glance at Viola, and looked away again.

Emily did not speak. Viola's tall grace and beautiful clothes were salt rubbed into her wounds. Her father had never bought her nice things, had never disguised the fact that he considered her dull and plain. At Viola's tentative smile she averted her eyes as though she had seen something unmentionable.

Arthur regarded his children with smiling distaste, relishing their position. He turned sharply to his son.

'And what, may I ask, sir, are you doing here at five o'clock in the afternoon when you should be at the store? Have you ever seen me here at this time on a weekday? Am I to presume you have been slacking here every day since my departure?'

Herbert coloured and paled, stepped back, panic-stricken as though he would have bolted if he could. He had been free of his father's intimidating presence for two months, but all his authority and would-be defiance crumbled in an instant, and he lost every rag of dignity he possessed. Viola felt sorry for him.

'I came home especially to welcome you, sir,' he protested shrilly, 'and to have tea with my sister.'

'When I left you in charge, sir, I *meant* in charge. Has anything gone amiss then? Heh? Heh? Are you running away again?'

'No, sir, indeed not, everything is quite smooth. The takings are a little down . . . well, August; and the war . . . ladies are, er, pulling in their belts, so to speak . . .' He ventured a laugh, which died in his throat.

'The takings in August do go down,' said Arthur menacingly, 'but if they are below last year's I shall want a reason. Greet your stepmother,' he barked. 'She will be living here with us now!'

Herbert took off his pince-nez, put them back, and jabbed towards Viola's hand. She shook it firmly, bowed her head, said nothing. They had been so obviously nerving themselves for some protest and their purpose had dissolved in their habitual fear of their father. Emily still appeared defiant. She folded her hands and looked determinedly at the floor.

Arthur waited ominously, stripping his gloves from his clean pink hands. Emily's sallow face flushed a patchy red.

'I'm *waiting!*' he said menacingly.

'Arthur,' Viola said quickly, 'it doesn't matter. We have not had time to know each other. You cannot expect . . .'

'Do not presume to tell me what I can expect?' he roared. 'I expect my daughter to behave like a lady. I expect her to greet me and my wife with affectionate respect. So long as she lives in my house she will do so, or answer to me. I will not have female jealousies and wranglings.' He looked balefully at his daughter. 'Do as I say, Emily.'

Emily thrust her hand towards Viola, who once again gravely and silently responded. Unhappiness closed down on her as though the overpowering, gloomy red house was a prison. They would all be prisoners here. These two unhappy people and herself.

'Now, get back to your work,' ordered Arthur peremptorily. 'I shall follow you there as soon as I have taken tea. Do not tell any of the staff I am coming . . . I prefer to surprise them. Let us hope that I find things in reasonable order and no mincing jackanapes of a junior promoted because of his pretty backside!'

Herbert in agonized embarrassment almost ran out of the door. Emily, white and affronted, followed him, her handkerchief pressed to her lips.

Arthur smiled, rubbed his hands, and said to Viola, 'No doubt, Viola, you will want to rest after our journey?'

'No. I'm not tired. I would like to go out for a couple of hours.'

'Where are you going?' he asked suspiciously.

'I want to go to Clapham to see little James.'

His jaw dropped in astounded disbelief. 'Are you out of your mind?'

'But, Arthur, it was arranged that Mrs Brasher should report to me on his progress. She's not done so. I must know how he is.'

'She has reported to me.' He avoided her startled glance. 'One of the rules I insist upon in this house is that *all* letters—I repeat *all* letters—are brought to me and I open them. It was so with my late wife, and it is so with my children. There should be no secrets from the head of the house-hold. It is the only way to keep a united family.'

'But . . .'

'Mrs Brasher's reports came with my letters. She writes that the child is well and happy and there is no need for anxiety.'

'Then why didn't you tell me?'

He fidgeted, pulling out his gold watch, and looking at it, shooting his cuffs, picking up the newspapers, putting them down.

'Arthur?'

His colour rose angrily.

'I will not be questioned, Viola. The truth is that it is painful to me that this child exists. I have no wish to speak about it with you, or anyone, un-less it is absolutely necessary.'

'But, Arthur! *Necessary?* What d'you mean? He's my baby. I've said I am sorry for what happened in Biarritz. Haven't you punished me enough? I swear I did not know Lord James was there. How could I? I was taken by surprise or I would never have danced with him. But I must see my baby.'

'That is quite enough. Go to your room and change, then come down here and pour tea for me.'

'But I have not seen my baby for two months. He will be quite big. I shall be there and back before dinner, I promise . . .'

'Do you want to flaunt your shame for everyone to know? You are aware I have not told my family of this child's existence? I do not want it known. How can your past be forgotten otherwise? You cannot go rushing off to Clapham at all hours—people will become curious.'

'But before we married, you promised to take care of him. You never said I could not see him. For God's sake, Arthur, it was for the baby's sake I married you. I am his mother. I *must* see him.'

'Of course you shall see him. But you will have many duties here and your first one is to me. I want to have a social life befitting my position. Gradually the scandal of your past will be forgotten. We will entertain, I shall accept invitations. There is the house to run, many things to organ-ize. Once a month I shall drop a note to Nurse Brasher and make an ap-pointment for you and you will travel out to Clapham to see the child. That will be quite enough. Better for you, and better for the child, to get you ready for the final parting.'

'*Parting?*' she repeated, aghast.

'You cannot expect this situation to continue for ever. Children grow. You cannot bring him here. He will have to be provided for. A boarding school, perhaps. One of those military places where they take orphans and bastards . . .'

'And this is what you meant when you said you would care for him and educate him?'

'I consider I am being generous. Do as I tell you. I will ring for Baines, and tell him to bring tea.'

She hesitated, then moved towards the door. As she passed Arthur he took her face between his hands, and she winced as his fingers pressed into her bruised cheek. He pressed his mouth down on hers, his tongue searching her lips. She stood quite still, knowing what any sign of revulsion would bring.

'We must learn to obey, mustn't we?' He gave her cheek a little slap, just enough to raise a faint red mark and set the bruised nerves in her forehead singing. 'Now, no naughty defiance, Viola! Off you go. Put on one of your pretty teagowns—the new blue chiffon, and hurry down. I want to leave for the store as soon as possible.'

She went into the hall. She had travelled all day. It was hot and she was very tired. Her cheek stung where he had slapped it and her head throbbed beneath her bruised forehead. She was possessed with a black despair.

There was a heavy rat-tat on the door and the late post splattered through on to the mat. Automatically she picked up the letters and riffled through them. To her astonishment two were addressed to her. She heard Baines's footsteps coming up the basement stairs and thrust them into her bag. Baines came round the corner, a heavy, waxen-faced, watchful man. She dropped the rest of the letters on to the hall-stand.

'The post has come, Baines,' she said, and went towards the stairs. 'I am going to change.'

He collected them into the silver salver. 'Are these all, madam?'

She turned and stared at him and his eyes shifted away.

'All letters delivered to the house go to Mr Netherby first, madam. It is one of his strict rules.' She realized he had seen her through the hall mirror.

'So I understand,' she said mildly. 'Well, take them to him then. But, first, perhaps you can tell me which room I shall occupy.'

'Yes, indeed, madam. On the first floor, the door facing the head of the stairs. Shall I send up one of the maids?'

'No, thank you.'

She went to the bedroom, newly decorated for her at great expense, Arthur had said. Pink and gold, mirrors, crystals—a tart's room for Arthur's living doll. Her trunks, dress and hat boxes were piled ready to unpack.

There was another door on the right of the elaborately draped bed. She opened it and glanced through. It led through to a dressing-room, and presumably to Arthur's bedroom. There were wardrobes, a wash-stand, a medicine rack with rows of bottles and pill-boxes. She tore open the letter. It was from Erhmann. He had instructed his agents to sell the jewellery and the price had been sufficient to buy the small cottage at Clapham outright. He had told his solicitors to go ahead with the purchase as he felt that this would give her friend, Miss Holder, the necessary security of tenure. He had also made enquiries about Mrs Brasher at Clapham Common and had to tell her that all the reports his agents had sent were highly unsatisfactory. Neighbours reported that the woman was a heavy drinker and that she had a dissolute, gambling son, who lived on the premises, and that the children in her care were neglected and recently a child had died there.

She read no further. Panic possessed her. She started towards the door, then remembered she had no money. Arthur never gave her money. He would pay fifty guineas for a dress but, apart from small change for tipping, no cash. He would not permit her to go out without him. After her meeting with James in Biarritz he had been obsessed with jealousy. On the train home he would even stand in the corridor when she went in the toilet in case she spoke to anyone.

She went into the dressing-room, pulled open the drawers of the wardrobe, turning through ties and handkerchiefs and underwear, hoping to find some change. She looked at her hands, at her gold and topaz bracelet, her diamond ring. The pawn shops stayed open in the early evening. The time? What *was* the time? She could pawn something—she had done so before when she and Betsy had been so poor. No. She would first ask Arthur for the money to go to Clapham. He could come with her if he wished: he must see the necessity. He would have to detain her physically to stop her going, and she did not think he would go to that length, although she shivered, remembering the cruel strength of those plump, clean hands.

She was no longer tired. She was filled with the cold energy of sheer terror. She had to go to her child. She heard the bedroom door open and Arthur came in. His eyes had the curious glittering look of anticipation which she had come to dread. It meant baiting and insults as he elaborately contrived a scene to provoke her defiance or helpless silence. ('Come now, we don't want any naughty sulks, do we? I can't allow that, Viola.') He sought an excuse to exercise his cold, infantile cruelty, though as time went on, the need for reason became less. She had learned to remain stonily indifferent and unresponsive, but beneath her calm manner, she had been terribly afraid.

But she was not afraid now. Her long, gold-green eyes met his, like a leopard in a cage, watching the trainer's whip and hot bar.

'Arthur I must have some money. Only a little. I must go to Clapham.'

'I have already forbidden it. Have you, by any chance, received a letter? All letters that come here are opened by myself and passed on, if I think fit, to the person concerned. Give me this letter.'

She handed Erhmann's letter to him. The other she kept, still unopened, in her handbag. He stood reading through the letter, and finally took off his gold-rimmed spectacles and looked at her.

'Now you will understand why I have to go,' she said.

'You will not leave this house,' he said.

CHAPTER NINE

The blood rose in his face, his heavy eyes were furious, his mouth hanging open, incredulity in every line of his face. He shut the door, locked it, put the bunch of keys in the skirt pocket of his frock coat.

'You are not leaving this house,' he repeated. 'How dare you get in touch with this man of all men? An arrogant German swine who insulted me.'

'Arthur, there is nothing in that letter that anyone could not read. Count Ehrmann asked me if he could be of service to me. I asked him to sell my jewellery for me, and to enquire after my baby's well-being. You have read what he says about Mrs Brasher. That she is a drunkard.'

'I never saw her drunk. The place was clean and orderly. The children quiet.'

'But don't you understand? *I have to know!* I must go at once.'

'You will do nothing without my permission. You are not going anywhere. You are my wife and, like my son and daughter, while you live under my roof and I provide for you, you will do exactly as I tell you. I will show you what you can, or cannot do in this house! If you have not learned to obey yet, I am going to teach you.'

He pulled his cravat and collar loose, took off his coat, and threw it over the bed, and then he went into the dressing-room. She heard water being poured into a glass, and the tinkle of a stirring spoon. She lifted the coat on the bed and took the keys out of the pocket and as she withdrew her hand she heard the swish of a whip and cried out as the thong bit into her hand. The keys fell on the bed. Arthur was standing holding a dog-whip. His eyes were bright with the excited anticipation of pain which she had learned to dread.

'We have had our *little* punishments, Viola,' he said. 'But this time it is going to be a real lesson. This time the naughty little girl is going to be really sorry . . .'

She moved quickly towards the door, and he made a lunge towards her. She picked up a heavy, silver-backed hand-mirror and crashed it down on his outstretched hand. He let out a howl of pain, plunged forward and seized her by the neck. She thought he was going to kill her. She screamed with all the force of her lungs. She heard footsteps outside, knockings, voices calling. He put his hand over her mouth, and she bit into it, her strong white teeth closing savagely into his fingers. He let her go.

She was too desperate to be afraid. Defiance glared back at him.

'How can you keep me,' she flashed, 'unless you kill me? If you keep me tonight, I shall go tomorrow. We made a bargain and you have not kept your word. If you had I would not be going. Even though you treated me badly, I would have stuck to you. But not now. You promised to care for my baby and you let him be put in the hands of this drunken woman. You were not going to let me see him. I was grateful to you for offering me marriage, and support. But no one is going to keep me away from my baby and I am going tonight. If you try to stop me I will make the biggest scene this respectable square has ever heard! I will break the windows . . . I will shriek until the police come . . . I warn you.'

He stared at her incredulously, one hand clinging to a chair, the angry red leaving his face until he was a dull, purplish pallor.

'My God, you bitch!' he shouted hoarsely. 'I believe you would kill me if you could.' Outside on the landing Emily's voice called shrilly, 'Papa! Papa, what is happening? Open the door.'

And Baines, absurdly, over the commotion: 'Mr Netherby? Sir? Is there something wrong?'

'Wrong? This damned, murderous slut . . .' He lurched towards her again, and this time the mirror hit his shoulder. He looked at her with such a look of hatred that she shrank away from the staring eyes and clutching fat pink hands. Suddenly he stopped, clutching the brass rails of her bed.

'Arthur—*Arthur*? Are you ill?'

He stared at her, drawing in great, rasping breaths. She dragged a chair across and he sank into it. The sweat stood out on his forehead.

'Water,' he managed to say. 'Get me water . . . this will soon pass . . .'

She ran into the dressing-room; there was a water carafe on the washstand, and two tumblers, one clean, the other containing some white sediment from the medicine he had just taken. She filled the clean glass and ran back to him.

He drank it down in great gulps, watching her all the time, the whip still across his knees. She backed away from him, then took the keys out of his frock coat. As she did so, she saw his wallet in an inner pocket. She pulled it out and opened it. It was full.

Arthur watched her, his face becoming swollen and dark. He made an attempt to rise. 'You . . . you whore's bitch,' he shouted. 'Will you rob me too?'

In her fear and haste she spilled all the money over the bed. She snatched up enough to get her to Clapham. She left the rest strewn over the bed and floor. She had to pass him to get to the door, and his groping hands were stretched to grasp her. With one lithe spring she was across the bed and searching through the keys to open the door.

His attitude abruptly changed. She did not turn as she heard the blustering anger turn to a pleading whine. She had heard it before when his sadism frightened him and he went too far.

'Don't go, Duchess, don't leave me. I swear I won't hurt you. You shall have anything—anything . . . Duchess, don't leave me . . . I'm ill . . . Duchess . . .'

She glanced at him as though he were a dangerous tethered dog. She was terrified that he would recover before she could escape. She struggled with the keys, found the right one, opened the door and threw them back. Emily, Baines and a cluster of wide-eyed maidservants almost fell in on top of her.

She stood back as they rushed in past her; without a word she ran along the landing, down the stairs and into the hall. For a moment the heavy door balked her, then she found the correct latch, pulled it open and was out into the street. The door banged behind her. As she ran down the square she swore she would never go through it again.

Arthur Netherby had stumbled to his feet and as Viola disappeared he fell full length on the carpet at his daughter's feet. Kneeling by his side she heard him mutter, 'Get her back . . . Viola . . . Viola . . . get her back . . . she's killed me!'

Viola ran down the square and plunged down the first side street which led into Oxford Street. Once in the jostling crowds she was safe.

She slowed down, gasping for breath, and stopped the first cab that passed and told the driver to take her to Clapham Common.

She sat panting like a hunted creature, feeling, although she knew it was not true, that she had killed Arthur and they were pursuing her.

She opened the second letter she had picked up and which was still in her bag, unopened. It was from a solicitor in Leeds saying they had been trying to trace her for several months with reference to a legacy that had been left her by the late Samuel Hardcastle, an investment that would bring in the sum of £300 a year. She stared at it incredulously. 'We had no reply to our first letter of July last year and subsequent letters addressed to the hostel in Eastcastle Street . . .'

Last July. Just when she had left the hostel to go to James. Arthur must have known all those months ago. Long before they were married—before James went, before she was pregnant, before she had lost her job. He must have kept the letters from her. He had known that she had no need to ask for money, to ask him or anyone to help her. But he had not told her. He had kept it to himself so that she would marry him.

She leaned back against the seat, bitter tears streaming down her cheeks.

'All my ships come home too late,' she thought unhappily. 'The Count, James . . . and now this from poor Sam.' Arthur had always talked about 'punishment'. Well, now he had really punished her. For being young, for being beautiful and desirable, for wanting the fine, rich, comfortable things of life.

She spoke aloud to herself, falling into the old West Riding vernacular. 'Poor Sam wouldn't have been proud of me. He always said I had pluck. Well, happen I didn't have pluck, or I'd have held on. I was too soft. Afraid of being poor, wanting the nice things and an easy life. Well, all right . . .' She was touched with hysteria, talking to the dead man who had once been so kind to her, talking, perhaps to God. 'Happen I *was* soft. Happen I deserve all this . . . but just let the baby be safe and well. Don't let owt hurt him, and I can take anything else. Anything so long as my little lad's safe.'

The journey to Clapham seemed endless. Viola was tired—but Erhmann's letter had filled her with terrible fears that dragged the weariness from her limbs. She took the letter out of her bag, and re-read it—there was more than she had seen at first. That he would be in London for some days if she wished to communicate with him or needed any help.

'*At the end of the week I return to Vienna, and if I do not hear from you I shall know you have decided to accept this farce of a marriage and all it entails. But, if you should ever need me, you can find me through my City office. I have told them any word from you has to be sent at once wherever I may be. Everything I have ever said still holds. I am, Duchess, quite literally yours to command.*

                                                            Devotedly, Eugene.'

The words meant nothing. Only the lines about Mrs Brasher burned into her brain with abominable clarity. '*The reports on the woman and her establishment are extremely unsatisfactory. Neighbours say that she drinks, and that only recently a young child died.*'

Terrible memories of babies being murdered, and children neglected, starved and beaten raced through her mind. Guilt oppressed her like the spikes of an iron maiden piercing her breast and brain. She must have been mad to leave her baby and to strike that devil's bargain with Netherby. But she had not imagined this. She had thought she was securing a future for her boy, care and comfort, education. He should be brought up a gentleman. She should have known by the way Arthur treated his own children that he was incapable of affection.

Characteristically she did not blame him. He was what he was. She blamed herself for being tempted by luxury and security. 'But I never knew, I never dreamed he would keep me from my baby,' she said aloud in self-defence.

It was hot and the beautiful travelling suit of fitted silk seemed to encase her like iron. She loosened the tiny buttons in the high-necked yoke and stripped off her long cream-coloured gloves. On Clapham Common children were playing, sailing boats and trundling hoops. There was no wind to lift the kites into the sky. Would she sit on the seat one day, watching while James played with other children? As the cab stopped before the tall red brick house on North Side, the panic closed down on her again. For a moment she could not move. Then she said to the man, 'Wait. I don't suppose I shall be long.'

The place looked reassuringly neat and clean, white-painted with crisply laundered lace curtains and highly polished brass plate. Mrs K. Brasher. Maternity and Nursing Home. She ran up the scrubbed stone steps and rang the bell. After an agonizingly long wait a small, undersized maidservant opened the door.

'Mrs Brasher?'

'I'll see. Who shall I say?'

'Mrs Netherby.'

The girl seemed inclined to close the door, but Viola stepped firmly inside. She heard an altercation going on somewhere downstairs in the basement and upstairs a baby was crying persistently, in a long, fretful, weary wail. She began to move towards the stairs, and stopped. The voices downstairs had quietened and a man came up. He was a short, sturdy young man in a loudly-checked, short-cut suit, and plastered-down black hair. The sort of tout she had seen hanging about the race-courses when she had gone with James Staffray last year.

'Mrs Netherby? I'm afraid it ain't convenient to see the nipper today.'

'But I am his mother. I can see him when I want.'

'Well, yes, if it was convenient.' He was moving towards her, getting between her and the stairs, edging nearer as though to drive her towards the front door.

She did not move, and an irritated expression crossed his face. 'She says—' he jerked a thumb towards the stairs—'that Mr Netherby told her he'd allus write before a visit.'

'I have been away for two months and I want to see James Carlo. Will you tell Mrs Brasher to take me to him.' She glanced up the stairs, 'Is that him crying?'

'No, no. He's not a bawler . . . I mean he don't cry, as good as gold, she says.' He stood across the stairway, his broad shoulders squared aggressively under the loud coat, grinning at her with an insolent good humour. 'Now, take my advice, mum, go off home and come back tomorrow. About eleven in the morning. Then she'll 'ave young James all spick and span and brushed be'ind the ears to see 'is luvly mother.'

'Will you tell Mrs Brasher I am here to see my baby and I shall not go until I have done so.'

He began to bluster. 'Now, look, dearie, we don't want no trouble, do we . . . you do as I say, or else . . .'

'What?'

He drew back. He realized this was no young girl to be intimidated. The green-gold eyes were looking at him with blazing anger. 'Now, dearie . . .' he began conciliatingly.

'Tell Mrs Brasher that if she does not take me to my baby I shall go straight from here to the police station and bring a constable back with me.'

He hesitated, blenched. 'All right, all right. Like I ses, we don't want no trouble. Wait a tick, mum. Don't go up. I'll get 'er.'

He scuffled backwards, and then plunged down the basement stairs. Without waiting a second Viola went straight upstairs into the front room where she had last seen James.

The cot which had held the pale child with the golden fuzz of hair was ominously empty. In the other cot was a fair baby, bigger and thinner than the one she had left, but unmistakably James Carlo. He lay curiously still, crying, with a weak, unhappy, persistent wail. She bent over him and he turned his head from side to side desperately mouthing like a baby bird looking for food. He smelled foul.

She let down the side of the cot, just as she heard footsteps stumbling up the stairs. Mrs Brasher, obviously having hurried into a uniform and starched apron, placket gaping, collar unbuttoned, spotless cap awry on her untidy hair, was standing in the doorway.

'Don't you touch him, ma'am,' she cried. Her eyes were bleary and a heavy smell of gin permeated the room. She swayed across and pulled up the side of the cot. 'The child's not so well . . . been like that these past days.'

'Have you had the doctor?'

'No c-call,' said Mrs Brasher, belching heavily, and clutching the post of the cot. 'Tomorrow if there's no improvement. But there's no call for a lady like you troubling yourself, and if it's infectious you don't want to catch it, eh . . .' She leered towards Viola and nearly fell. 'What'd Mr Netherby say to 'is lady wife getting the measles or chicken pox . . .'

'You've made a mistake, Mrs Brasher,' said Viola evenly. She no longer felt tired or frightened. She was filled with a terrible anger. 'I'm no lady!'

She seized the woman's shoulders and with all the power of her slim, strong body wrenched her away from the cot and threw her against the wall. She let down the side of the cot and pulled the covers back. Under the cover the baby was naked except for a heavily soiled napkin. His tiny wrists and ankles were bound with tapes to the springs at the bottom of the cot. He could not move. Viola let out a cry of pain. She began pulling at the ties, but could not loose them and turned on the woman like a tigress. 'Get me some scissors, damn you!'

The man, hearing Mrs Brasher fall, had come pounding up the stairs.

'Scissors!' Viola cried. 'Scissors!'

'Best let her 'ave her way, mum,' he said. 'It's a fair cop.'

He brought out a knife from his back pocket which he flicked open, and slit through the ties, releasing the baby.

'Get me some clothes, a shawl, something clean to wrap him in. Get me some water and a towel.'

The little servant, wide-eyed and fearful, had appeared behind him. He turned his head, and shouted at her. 'You 'eard what the lady said. Get her something to wrap the kid in.'

She went out and hurried back with a clean napkin and a large white towel. 'Where are his clothes?' said Viola, cleaning the child, which, released, struck out with its tiny limbs, and cried harder than ever, a new, fierce, defiant cry. 'He had plenty. All right, my darling, all right. Mother's come for you . . .'

'Lor' love you,' said the youth, 'she sold those weeks ago.' He went over to his mother, still sprawled on the floor, and heaved her to her feet. 'Up-si-daisy, old dear.'

Mrs Brasher was weeping now, snivelling into her apron. 'She's no call to do this . . . I 'ad me arrangements with the gentleman. No fuss, he said. Don't spoil 'im. She won't be coming back. No special treatment. Same as all the rest . . . same as all the other brats . . . she wouldn't bother, he said, after a month or so . . . they never do.'

'Give over, Mam, and shut up,' he warned her.

The cleaned baby was wrapped in the towel. Viola lifted him into her arms and for the first time he stopped crying and opened his eyes wide and looked at her. Deep blue eyes, the silken baby lashes already dark. 'Ah, love,' she breathed. 'Ah, my love . . . I'll never leave you, never again.'

She turned on the little maid. 'Make a bundle of whatever clothes are left and include a feeding bottle. Go and tell the cabman I am coming down.' She looked at Mrs Brasher and her son with cold anger, and said, 'You may be sure that I shall make it my business to see that no child shall ever be left in your care again.'

She went swiftly down the stairs, carrying her baby in her arms, out to the waiting cab.

'Feeding bottle,' shrieked Mrs Brasher after her. 'F-feeding bottle. You never brought one of them with you. That'll be two bob, that will.' She collapsed in maudlin tears and accusations and vomited over the immaculately polished floor of her nursery.

On the way to the cottage Viola held the baby James tightly against her breast. When she had first taken the cottage with Betsy she had hated the poverty of making do, the sparse meals, the tiny shabby rooms they could not afford to decorate and which had been so cold when they came back from work last winter. She had hated the meanness of it, the pump over the stone kitchen sink and the sedate row of privies at the bottom of the garden to which one scurried through the wind and rain.

But now, as it came in sight, the cottage seemed to shine. It was hers now, and no one could take it from her. The old red roof tiles glowed under the afternoon sun, the tiny front garden had been planted with a riot of late summer flowers. Someone, she supposed it was Betsy, had painted the door and window frames white, and the three small square-paned front windows glittered with cleanliness in the westering sunlight. A little fortress where she could keep her baby safe.

She dismissed the cab and ran up the path. The front door was propped open to let in the cool evening air. She ran through into the kitchen. Betsy and Matthew were sitting at the table taking tea, a Yorkshire late tea with sliced ham and bread and butter, a dripping cake and a big black teapot in a knitted cosy.

Their astounded faces turned towards her, and suddenly the long, frightened hours took their toll, and she nearly fell. Matthew ran to her side, and Betsy took the baby from her, hushing it as it began to cry again. Viola sank into Betsy's chair, shaking and crying.

'Hush, now, love,' said Betsy authoritatively. 'Matthew, get a cup and pour her some tea. It's only just made.' She drew a chair close to her friend, one arm about her, listening to the incoherent story that flooded out, exclaiming with shocked horror when Viola opened the towel and showed the little chafed ankles and wrists.

'He couldn't even get his thumb to his mouth. He was tied up and left to cry.'

'Hush-on,' said Betsy gently. 'Now drink your tea, and take a bite to eat, and then you'll go on up and have a good rest.'

Viola, her tears subsiding, became aware of a great change in her small friend. A new, almost motherly authority. She saw the wide gold band on Betsy's left hand; the new maturity in her two timid friends, a different, proud, cared-for look about Matthew, so brushed and smart, his wispy hair neatly cut, his shabby linen sparkling white and crisply ironed, his thin face already fuller, his once anxious eyes clear and bright.

'Betsy!' she exclaimed. 'And Matthew Lyttelton? You're *never* married?'

'We are,' Betsy said, smiling proudly. 'This month past. And Matthew's working for a newspaper. *The Churchman's Gazette.*'

'On the editorial side,' said Matthew. 'Only a small job as yet. But it's an opening.'

'I wrote to you,' Betsy said. 'I wrote to Paris at once.'

'I haven't been getting letters,' said Viola bitterly. 'I didn't hear. Can I stay here with you?'

Betsy made a little gesture. 'It's your house, Vi,' she said. 'When the solicitor wrote to say you'd bought it, and we could stay on rent free, we couldn't believe it. It was like a grand wedding present. But it's your home and it's Matthew and me that's the lodgers . . .'

'Oh, never.' Viola's arms went round her. 'Never, Betsy. It's your home too, and Matthew's, for always if you want,' and she sat back, drying her eyes, their small, perfect happiness tearing at her. They were so right together. She thought suddenly of Arthur Netherby, and a long shudder ran through her. Was he really ill? Would he be recovered now, planning to follow her and bring her home?

'I'm never going back to him. To Arthur. Never. I won't go back. He can't make me.' She looked over her shoulder, and, aware that the front door still stood open to the sweet summer evening air, sprang up, went to it, closed and locked it. Matthew and Betsy exchanged anxious glances. Viola came back, and sat down again, taking off her little gold and brown toque that had been bought in Paris, lifting the cup of hot tea again to her lips. The beautiful, heavy-lidded eyes had the look of a hunted animal. She took the letter from Hardcastle's solicitor from her handbag, and showed them. Matthew read it aloud gravely, his voice incredulous.

'Arthur knew, Betsy,' she said, 'all the time that Sam had left me this money. The letters must have gone to Eastcastle Street and someone, Mrs Harding, I don't doubt, gave them to him.'

'She always did take all the post and give it out to the girls,' said Betsy. 'She could easily have kept it back.'

'I did not want to marry him. I asked him to lend me just enough money to tide me over. But he would not have it that way. He wanted to marry me. He promised to take care of me, and the baby. But all the time, even then, he knew I was independent and needed no favours. And he made me leave James with that wicked woman and tried to stop me seeing him. I would have played straight if he had—I tried. If I was wicked when I went off with my lord . . . well, I've been punished for it. But I'm never going back to Arthur now.'

'But it is an awful thing,' Matthew said timidly, 'for a woman to leave her husband whom she has promised God to serve and cherish.'

'It's an awful thing to be lied to and ill-treated.'

'It's difficult to believe it of Mr Netherby,' Betsy said incredulously. 'In the shop he was always so proper.'

Viola lifted the hair from her forehead disclosing the purple, yellowing bruise. She unhooked her dress and pulled it from her white shoulder slowing them the livid little marks.

'Of course,' Matthew said, hurriedly averting his eyes, 'you must do as you think right, Viola. It is terrible to think he could do such things. You are quite safe here with us.'

She gave him a grateful glance.

'I don't know what I'll do—only that, whatever I do, the baby stays with me.' The baby, as though knowing they were speaking of him, began to cry. 'What's the matter with him?' cried Viola anxiously. 'Is he all right?'

'Happen he's hungry,' said Betsy practically. 'Give him to me. I looked after t'little uns at the orphanage up North. Did you bring a bottle?'

Betsy diluted and heated milk, and filled the bottle, trying the heat professionally on the back of her hand, and gave James Carlo his bottle. 'Eh, he's a grand little lad,' she said, 'a bit on t'thin side, but grand.'

'You're a wise and clever little thing,' Viola said. 'You're very lucky, Matthew.'

'I know.' He put his arm proudly round Betsy, who sat feeding the baby as though he were her own. 'I know. I don't think badly of you, Viola,' he said hurriedly. 'I've been brought up to believe a woman's duty is to her husband and she should try and stay faithful and make him happy.'

'I have been faithful and I did try,' said Viola.

'You did not see . . .' he began awkwardly, but persistent, because he was, after all, a clergyman. 'You have never seen Lord Staffray since your marriage?'

'Once—in Biarritz.'

'And this made Mr Netherby angry?'

'Oh, yes. It made him very angry.' She looked wearily at her good, simple friends. How could she explain the blazing joy of seeing James again and of knowing that he still wanted her? How could they understand Netherby's obsessive passion, his impotence, and his cat-and-mouse cruelties? 'Yes. I saw him. It was for a very short while and I could not avoid it. Perhaps—' the slow lids lifted with defiance—'perhaps I would not have avoided it, even if I could have done so. But I promised I would not see him again and I was going to keep that promise.'

'Well . . .' Matthew hesitated. 'Go and rest. In the morning you must decide what to do. But if you want to go and see Mr Netherby . . . your husband, I would come with you. He would not dare abuse you if I were with you.'

'Thank you, Matthew, that is kind and thoughtful of you.'

She rose, wondering how Matthew would stand up to Arthur's bullying. 'I'm tired. I'll go up.'

Exhaustion suddenly claimed her. She went upstairs and Betsy carried the baby, sleeping now, his thumb in his mouth. She laid him on the bed, helped Viola unhook her beautiful and elaborate dress, and pulled the covers over her.

Viola slept like one stunned, and it was eleven o'clock when she was awakened by the sound of the knocker hammering on the front door. She sat up in bed, snatching the baby up against her, and listened to voices downstairs. Presently Betsy came up, her eyes big with fear. She put the candle down on the mantelpiece and came and sat by Viola.

'Who is it? What is it, Betsy?'

'It's the police, Vi. To ask you some questions, they say.'

Viola shot to her feet, wide awake, her big eyes dark with dread. Had they come to take James away from her?

'Why? What about?'

'He wouldn't say. It's an inspector.'

'Help me dress . . . no, not that . . .' She pushed aside the golden-brown taffeta into a rustling heap. 'Aren't there any of my old clothes in the cupboard. I don't want anything of Netherby's.'

'Yes. They're all there.'

She pulled on the old brown skirt she had come to London in and a crumpled cotton blouse, twisted up her hair and pinned it on top of her head. 'Stay up here with the baby, please, Betsy. Don't let anyone have him.'

'If you say so, love.'

'Yes.' She ran downstairs and opened the parlour door where Matthew stood, silent and anxious, with the uniformed constable and the plain-clothes inspector. The three men turned, startled, as she came in, the tall, magnificent girl, big eyes tragic in her white face.

'It's my baby,' she said fiercely, 'and no one can take him away. I'm his mother. He's registered in my name, and no one has any legal right to him but me.'

'What baby, Mrs Netherby?' asked the inspector mildly. 'This is the first I have heard of any baby.'

'What are you here for then?'

'About your husband, Mrs Netherby. Mr Netherby is dead.'

'Arthur is dead?' she repeated. 'When—how?'

'He died about half an hour after you left the house. How we don't know. So I would be glad if you would answer a few questions.'

He pulled forward a chair, and she sank into it, thinking of Arthur Netherby, his face a strange, livid, purplish pallor, the beads of sweat round his slack mouth, his eyes fixed on her, his fat hands stretched, trying to grasp her as she edged past to freedom.

She began to shake, leaning on the table, burying her face, the tears coming fiercely, hot, running between her fingers. She was not weeping for Arthur Netherby: she was weeping for the waste of her life and her youth. She was filled with overwhelming sadness for this man who had desired her so impotently, and treated her with such sadistic cruelty. She was not sad because he was dead, but because, for the first time, she could not find anywhere in her heart a scrap of pity for him.

James had returned to London immediately on learning that the Netherbys had left Biarritz, and his one thought was to see Viola again.

His mother, for the first time he could remember, was actively displeased with him. Usually when he went against her wishes she employed charm, wheedling and loving flattery or tears to get him to change his mind. All through the long journey through France and across the Channel to England he had remained aloof and morose, barely answering her questions, staring through the windows at the passing country, and at night lying in his berth smoking. The memory of Viola haunted him. His girl; his Duchess. So changed. All the old wild impudence gone, and yet in her silence and subjection, more beautiful than ever. He had no plans— or only wild dreams of carrying her off somewhere away from Netherby. But he was going to London with only one purpose: to find her, to plead with her to return to him.

He would not speak to his parents about it. When he had returned from South Africa he had been nursed back to health in the fresh country air of Louderdown. The loss of his arm, his army career—and his inability to trace Viola—had weighed heavily upon him but now he had found her, and finding her had brought back so vividly the joy and laughter, the passion and tenderness of their brief association.

Lady Louderdown was continually in tears, heavy with silence and reproachful glances. His father made awkward attempts to maintain a hearty man-to-man approach, trying to conceal his underlying horror at the seriousness of James's intentions. The situation was becoming intolerable.

James went into his mother's boudoir to kiss her before going to dine at his club. He could not stand another of those interminably long, impeccably served, silent dinners.

He found his father there with his mother, such an unusual event that he knew something untoward had happened. His mother had been weeping, and his father's expression was one of barely controlled fury.

He had a newspaper in his hand, which he threw across to James.

'I suppose you have seen this, sir?'

James picked it up and read the screaming headlines, announcing Arthur Netherby's death. It also stated that Mrs Netherby had been a close friend of Lord Staffray before her marriage to Mr Netherby, and that it was presumed he was the father of her baby son. It described Netherby's death after a 'violent scene'. Emily Netherby and Baines had given highly coloured descriptions of what had happened. There was no hiding the fact that the Netherbys felt Viola was guilty of causing their father's death. The inquest, the newspapers announced with relish, would be in three days' time.

James's face set like a mask as he read the innuendoes, the morbid suggestions of foul play.

'I must go to her,' he said.

'If you do,' said his father, 'you will confirm all the rumours started by every yapping cur of a reporter in London, and you will do her no good at all. If she is guilty, which she may well be, for she seems an unprincipled fool, it will incriminate you. If she is not guilty, any move on your part will weigh against her.'

'Your father has sent for Mr Sattherwaite,' said his mother, 'and, darling boy, I do implore you to be cautious and to do as he advises.'

He knew they were right. 'But—Viola,' he said. 'Can't we help her? I can arrange for her to be properly represented.'

'And how long do you suppose it will take for Fleet Street to ferret that out? I can think of nothing more fatal than that it should be known you are paying for her defence.'

'I imagine,' said his mother, 'she will be well able to pay for it herself— she will be a very wealthy widow, if what his son and daughter say is true.'

James looked at her with sudden hatred. 'You want her to be guilty, don't you?' he said. 'I feel just like I did when the Boer bullets came,

mowing down my men and I could do nothing to help them. I love her
. . . and I can do nothing to help her.'

Vatel, Count Eugene Erhmann's manservant, walked along the platform
at Victoria Station carrying the London evening newspapers. He saw his
master's light, graceful figure, pacing up and down outside his compartment, smoking a cigar, and his face lit with approval. The Count was certainly a man of taste and discrimination. On this hot August night, when
most of the English gentlemen travelling wore frock coats, their shining
top hats pressing red rims into their sweating foreheads, Eugene was a picture of comfort and elegance, his tall, slim figure in a suit of cream-
coloured linen, wide panama hat of the best quality, set on his handsome
head. He looked comfortable, cool and detached, every inch a European
aristocrat, and Vatel was proud to serve him.

He gave his master the newspapers, holding the carriage door open for
Eugene to step inside. Eugene stood concentratedly reading and, when he
raised his head, Vatel saw an expression in his eyes which he had never
seen before. If ever the Count had experienced emotion, he had never
seen him show it. Something of importance must have happened. A gov-
ernment going into bankruptcy? A disastrous slump on the stock market?

'Excellency?' he enquired solicitously.

'We're not going, Vatel,' Eugene said crisply. 'At least, we are not going
tonight. Come with me.' He began to walk rapidly down the platform.

'I'm sorry, sir,' the guard said. 'Would you get aboard? We're due out.'

'We are not travelling,' said Eugene.

The guard breathed a sigh of relief, and signalled departure.

'Excellency, your luggage is aboard,' Vatel said calmly—he was used to
travelling with Eugene Erhmann.

'Yes. Well, tell the station master to pick it up at Dover and return it.
And get me a cab!'

'Yes, Excellency.'

'Not to the flat in Victoria Street. Book me a suite at the Carlton. Send
my things there.'

'Yes, Excellency.'

'And get the flat ready for guests . . . a young married couple, another
lady, and a child.'

'A child, Excellency?' said Vatel impassively.

'Yes. A very young child . . . you will need a crib, plenty of milk, that
sort of thing . . .' He showed the man the front page of the evening
newspaper. There was a picture of Viola with James, taken over a year
ago at the races, a beautiful girl, wearing a beautiful hat, laughing and

gay, surrounded by good-looking young men. And below a picture of the cottage at Clapham. The flaring headlines told the dramatic story of Arthur Netherby's death just after his young wife's departure from the house.

'I imagine, Vatel, that Mrs Netherby is being besieged by the press. After midnight, when, one assumes, even reporters go home, I want you to take a cab there and bring Mrs Netherby and her baby and friends to my flat where we may be able to secure them some peace and anonymity until this thing blows over. Be sure you are not followed.'

'Yes, Excellency.'

'Get me a cab. Tell him to drive to Mr Eckersley's.'

'Yes, Excellency.'

The cab drew up at the large house in Kensington Gore just as Grant Eckersley was going in to dinner. He came anxiously into the hall. 'Gene? My dear chap, what brings you here? I thought you were leaving for Vienna tonight.'

'I was.' He spread the newspapers on the table before his friend. 'I want you to get in touch with your solicitors at once, and tell them to get the best man in London to hold a watching brief for Mrs Netherby. I don't want my name mentioned.'

'I understand,' said Grant knowingly.

'I don't think you do. There will be enough mud slung before this inquest is over, without my name being brought into it. Not that I care a curse—I don't want anything made difficult for her.'

'I see . . . I remember her. She was at a dinner we had once at Franconeri's. A North-Country girl. A beautiful creature . . . That was before she scandalized London society by her affair with young Staffray. I'll see to it for her.' Curiosity got the better of him. 'What is she to you then, Gene?'

'She is a very great deal.' His eyes met Grant's with a touch of amusement. 'She is the lady I hope one day will consent to be my wife.'

Grant looked at Eugene incredulously. Could it be that Count Erhmann, the rich, the worldly-wise, that superb and epicurean man of the world, was caught at last?

CHAPTER TEN

The inquest on the death of Arthur Netherby, proprietor of the famous department store in Oxford Street, was held in a small church school hall near the Euston Road. The hall was built to accommodate about one hundred pupils but on the day of the inquest a crowd of at least three times that number was milling about the entrance, trying to get in.

Viola's nickname had been discovered and enthusiastically taken up by the press. 'The Duchess Case' was proclaimed across the headlines, with 'Inquest on Mr Arthur Netherby' in less conspicuous type. A brief résumé of Arthur's career from shop-walker to wealthy proprietor was sketched in, but a great deal more space was given to Viola. Her flaunted affair with young Lord Staffray, when the West End of London had dubbed her Duchess. Her rise from shop girl to Arthur Netherby's wife. The stunning impact of her beauty at Biarritz recently—the Prince of Wales himself had noticed her and, it was rumoured, asked to be introduced—and the fact that James Staffray had been at Biarritz at the time was heavily reported. Adultery was rumoured. Scandal in high places hopefully anticipated. The shop girl. The earl's son. The elderly, rich husband. All the ingredients were there.

Outside the red brick pseudo-Gothic building the crowds pushed and shouted. Newsboys called and orange and hokey-pokey vendors did well on the hot summer day. Reporters and photographers, chasing to find advantageous positions for their tripods, bribed and pushed their way to the front, shouting the magic word, 'Press! Make way there, if you please!' Sensation-lovers from all walks of life struggled, swearing and complaining, to get in, and in one or two cases fighting broke out so that police reinforcements were called to regulate the crowd.

Although the proceeding was merely an inquest to discover the cause of death, a great deal of impressive legal talent was present. Sir Charles Manston held a watching brief for Viola on Eugene's instructions, and both Herbert and Emily Netherby and the Louderdowns were represented by counsel. The crowd ghoulishly speculated on the possibility of a murder charge.

Count Eugene Erhmann arrived with Sir Charles Manston and the two men surveyed the milling crowd with dismay as Manston's electric landau edged its way to the door.

Manston, a large, florid man, glossily hatted and tailored, with a luxuriant moustache, said cynically, 'Ha. Good house!'

'They're like vultures over a carcase,' said Eugene disgustedly. 'I'd like to shoot them all.'

'Come, come, my dear sir,' said Manston reprovingly, 'you must allow the press and the great British public to lick their lips. You must admit that the attractive Mrs Netherby has produced classic reasons for it.'

'She had an affair with a wild young man before she married. That is what is exciting their prurient little minds.'

'She had an affair with the son of an earl, dear man, and the aristocracy is always news. He is also a war hero. She also has this picturesque soubriquet—Duchess. And less than three months after her marriage to a rich, middle-aged man he is found dead. It is irresistible.'

'A sadistic and dissolute man.'

'That I shall have to bring out,' agreed Manston, 'if I'm to swing the court in her favour. These coroners can be extremely self-opinionated and narrow-minded. This one, my junior tells me, is both. I can tell you that public moral opinion already considers Mrs Netherby guilty of causing her husband's death—somehow—before any evidence has been heard. The public invariably condemns good-looking people who enjoy life.' He adjusted his monocle and peered out at a carriage which had driven up ahead, the occupants of which were just alighting. He gave a little anxious frown which changed to a smile and a wave of bonhomie as one of them caught his eyes.

'That's the Louderdowns' solicitor, with a learned colleague of mine. Watching brief for the Louderdowns, I should guess. I'm afraid it's going to be a trial by coroner. The Netherbys are represented by silk too.'

'James Staffray is not with them?' asked Eugene in alarm.

'I hope not! What harm it might do him is no business of mine, but it certainly won't do my client any good if he is seen in court.' He looked at the finely carved, distinguished face of the man before him, and said easily, 'My dear fellow, don't be so anxious for her. You mark my words—old Arthur Netherby died of temper or self-indulgence. I had the misfortune to meet him once, a smarmy bootlicker to his betters and a bully to those less fortunate. It was at a public dinner. He got a waiter sacked for spilling a spoonful of port.'

The two men elbowed their way through into the shabby little hall where the court was set up.

Herbert Netherby and his sister Emily were already there, clad in the deepest mourning, together with the butler, Baines, a wide black band round his jacket sleeve, and two of the maidservants from Tewkesbury Square. The press bench was full, and one man was busily sketching various personalities as they came in. As soon as the public were let in an enormous throng pushed in. They were mostly women chattering and crushing into every available place, crowding the hall and small gallery, standing packed along the back. Mrs Harding from the hostel, Miss Heath from gloves, maidservants, great ladies, Mrs Cuthbert Drew, for whom James Staffray had once bought those fateful gloves. The heat was unbearable; as the ladies moved their heads their great hats obscured the view so that those standing behind demanded indignantly that they remove them, as though at a theatre. Their eyes searched the body of the court, and they questioned each other: 'Is she here? Where is she? Have you seen her? What's she like? She's a tart, isn't she? After the old man's money? Where's this girl they call Duchess?'

She came in very quietly with Matthew Lyttelton, and there was a sibilant sound of indrawn breaths. For she was not in mourning. No heavy black. She was wearing the cheap, simple suit of dark brown she had worn when she came from Leeds two years ago, a high-necked cream blouse, and a plain brown hat with a small bunch of buttercups in it like a yellow light above the cloud of chestnut hair. Her face was white and her eyes shadowy and steadfast. She saw Eugene sitting with Sir Charles Manston and a little swift glance of gratitude went to him. James was not there. She had not expected him to be. In fact, Sir Charles, at their interview in his chambers, had told her it would be most damaging to her if he had been.

And *yet*? And yet she *had* wanted him to be there. He had been her love and her god. She had secretly hoped that he would have come to her, openly, unafraid, admitting his love.

She gave a little sigh, put her arm in Matthew's, smiled at him because he was so grave, and trembling just a little as though he, not her, was to be questioned. She went up to the vacant seat reserved for her, head erect, walking with that long, graceful step and slight seductive sway that had earned her her name of Duchess. As she sat down, there was a buzz of talk around the court.

'She's not in mourning,' commented Manston. 'People expect it.'

'She said,' Eugene told him, 'she would never wear a thing Netherby had bought her, nor accept a penny of his money.'

'That's quite a gesture,' the barrister answered cryptically, 'considering he has left her the lot. I heard this morning.'

The coroner tapped sharply on his desk for silence, and the inquest began.

The doctor came first, and described how he had run along the square to Number 40, where he had found the house in an uproar and Mr Netherby in a semi-conscious condition. He understood from Baines that Mrs Netherby had just left the house—no one knew where.

Mr Netherby was then violently sick and immediately relapsed into deep unconsciousness and died within fifteen minutes. He had certified the death as a mild attack of apoplexy preceding total heart failure.

Had Miss Netherby said anything?

'Yes, Miss Netherby had said Mrs Netherby had killed her father. But she was hysterical with shock, and probably did not mean it in that way. She may have meant the altercation had made him lose his temper, thus bringing on the unfortunate attack.'

There was a sound of audible sobbing and indignant protest from beneath Emily's black veil.

Baines described the noise of quarrelling and screaming from within the bedroom, how when the door was finally unlocked Mrs Netherby had slipped past them and out of the house without a word, and Netherby's last stertorous cry, 'Get her back . . . get her back. She's killed me . . . she's killed me . . .'

The Netherbys' counsel asked if a name had not been mentioned.

'The Master called out the name Viola—twice.'

Sir Charles was up again. Had Baines seen or found a dog-whip lying on the floor. Baines had. Sir Charles thanked him and asked if Baines himself was aware that Mr Netherby was dying at that moment?

'Well, not actually, sir, though he looked and sounded bad.'

Sir Charles pointed out that Mrs Netherby might not have known this either.

Herbert Netherby took the stand, stammering, nervous and vindictive. Then his sister, Emily Netherby, hysterical, accusatory, describing the glass of powder or medicine which Mr Netherby had obviously drunk which was found unrinsed. Would, asked Sir Charles, anyone but a perfectly innocent person have left an unrinsed glass? Come, come, he must remind the Coroner that Mrs Netherby was not on trial, that all this court was summoned for was to decide the cause of death and the doctor's evidence had been given.

The Coroner called Viola.

He will pillory her, thought Eugene unhappily. Her beauty was an affront to him; and worse, she was not ashamed—she neither wept nor cringed. She rested her gloved hand on the edge of the box. The heavy-lidded white eyelids lifted with a sweep of thick, long lashes, and the green-gold eyes looked into the Coroner's.

'You are not in mourning, Mrs Netherby?'

'No, sir.'

'Why, may I ask, do you not show this sign of respect to your late husband?'

'The clothes I am wearing I bought for myself before I was married. I did not want to wear anything he gave me.'

Eugene glanced at Manston who did not move, smiling beneath his moustache. 'I'll leave her,' he murmured, 'until she needs help. She'll manage him.'

'Did you not care for your late husband?'

'No.'

A horrified whisper ran round the court, and a woman somewhere called out, 'Shame!'

'Are you aware that he has left you a very wealthy woman?'

Once again the murmurs rose indignantly and the Coroner had to call for order.

'Aye. I was told today. If I accept it, which I won't. I don't want or need the money now.'

She stood quite steadfast, answering bluntly and gravely. Yes, they had quarrelled because he would not let her go to see her child.

'Who was the father of the child?'

'That I cannot say.'

'Is it Lord Staffray?'

She was on oath. 'Yes.' For the first time a touch of colour came into her white cheeks.

Again the loud hammering of the gavel, calling the court to order.

'Is this what you quarrelled about? That you had recently seen this gentleman again?'

'No. Not that day. Arthur would quarrel over anything. He made quarrels so that he could punish me. He was going to whip me. I didn't even care about that. I only cared about going to my baby, to see if he was safe, and I would have pulled the house down to get out if need be. So maybe it *was* my fault he had an attack. He was very angry. I gave him some water as he asked, and got the keys out of his coat; I had no money. He never gave me a penny. I took a pound, that's all. There was a hundred there, but I took only one and went. Thank God!'

'What do you mean?'

'When I found out the sort of place it really was where they had my little boy, I reckon I just got there in time . . .' She looked round the court with great tragic eyes, and held out her arms. 'His little hands and legs, they were tied to the cot so that he couldn't move, and rubbed raw with him trying to kick himself free . . . He was dirty and hungry. That's the sort of woman Arthur had left my child with, when he had promised to provide for him . . .'

The mood of the court suddenly swung from hostility to sympathy. Her voice, her eyes, the slim stretched arms made every woman's nerves move as though they felt a child stir within them. The Coroner abruptly told Viola to stand down.

The only people not touched were the Netherbys—Emily frantically conferred with her brother and her counsel. Their counsel rose. He would like an adjournment. His clients were not satisfied with the medical evidence and were pressing for an autopsy.

Eugene smuggled Viola out of a small side door, and drove her away to the Savoy, where he had reserved a private dining room for lunch. The court had been adjourned for two days awaiting the result of the autopsy.

'Why does Sir Charles Manston keep telling me everything will be all right?' she asked the Count. 'Does *he* think that I poisoned Arthur?'

'A lot of people will think so.'

'I've nothing to be afraid of.'

'Unless he poisoned himself.'

She was startled. 'And they will think I did it?' She shook her head.

'Not Arthur,' she said. 'He only enjoyed hurting other folk. Not himself.' She looked round at the charming room, with the table set with flowers and fruit, coffee cups and small liqueur glasses. The river beyond the trees of the Embankment Gardens. Warm, luxurious, her kind of place. She took a peach in her long fingers, and bit into it with strong, white teeth.

'It's nice here,' she said. 'Thank you for bringing me. Why did you?'

'I thought it was time you had an escape into your own world.'

She glanced at him, swift and questioning. 'My world?'

'Will you really refuse all that money, Duchess?'

'I will.' She gave a little shiver. 'I want nothing of his.'

'And after this is all over, what will you do?'

'You forget I've got the cottage—and three hundred a year.'

Eugene smiled, took a cigar, asking her permission to smoke. She took it from him, lit it skilfully, turning it between her long, white fingers, handed it back, and he rose abruptly, went to the window overlooking the Thames. Every movement she made, graceful and unstudied, made him desire her more.

'Today the Thames is as blue as the Danube under this summer sky,' he said. 'In Vienna everyone will have left for the mountains. I have a little castle, Viola, on a high crag above the river surrounded by vines and orchards, where you can see the snow on the mountains. It would be a lovely place for a small boy to grow up and play in.'

She went to him at the window, took the cigar from him, drew on it, blew a mouthful of smoke, smiling, handed it back to him.

'What are you trying to say, Signor Count?'

'Ah, Viola, a cottage in Clapham and a meagre income are not for you. Fine for little Mr and Mrs Lyttelton. A small cottage in the suburbs. A love nest for that so nice little couple. As happy as doves in a dove cote. But not for you, Duchess. If ever a woman was born to grace the great world, you are . . . and not to be any man's mistress, but to be a wife.'

'To be your wife, Eugene?'

'To be my wife.'

'And my boy?'

'Bring him. He shall have everything my son should have, and if we have sons of our own, he shall have the same as them—always.'

'Except your name?'

'He shall have that too. Count—he cannot have that, when I die. It is not in my power . . . But I will adopt him. He will have everything else, everything you might wish for . . .'

'But—what about you? Would the people in your world accept me? The Viennese may be very gay, but they are also very aristocratic, stiff and snobbish, or so I've been told.'

'If I wish it, people will accept you,' he said harshly. 'I am not an English country gentleman, Viola. I am of the great world, which does what I want. I do not care what it thinks. They dance to my tune. I have what is known as power, Viola. Finance is not just—being rich.'

'That sounds a bit frightening.'

'Oh, I care what you think. What you do. Everything about you.' He took her hand, and kissed it, and she said with a little sigh, 'I believe you!' He not only had power, but charm, when he pleased, and a controlled masculine attraction. 'But not yet. I cannot tell you yet, Eugene. I must wait.'

'You are waiting to know if Staffray will return to you?'

For the first time he glimpsed the depth of suffering behind the calmness of that lovely face. The lovely eyes were dark with agony.

'If he can come to me he will—and I must wait, Eugene.'

The result of the autopsy was a great disappointment to the newspapers. Arthur Netherby had a very severe heart condition, which had been deteriorating for many years. Nothing of any toxic nature had been found in his system. The tablets he had were a very strong and dangerous aphrodisiac which he had been taking increasingly. The dose, taken with his general condition, had probably triggered off the attack from which he had died.

When Viola left the courtroom with Matthew, Sir Charles Manston and Eugene, there were no thrusting black camera boxes and milling reporters, only a few idlers. She looked round, fine eyebrows raised, glancing comically at her companions.

'No one's concerned with me now I'm not a murderess,' she said.

'Did you enjoy the attention?' asked Eugene teasingly.

'I won't deny I like being noticed,' she said candidly, 'but not like that. I like another kind of notice.'

'The sort of notice which is a beautiful woman's right and privilege,' said Eugene.

Herbert and Emily came out of the court, followed by the obsequious Baines. The two Netherbys shot malevolent glances as they passed. They would never believe she had relinquished their father's money until the whole matter was legally settled, and even then they would suspect some kind of trick. It was against human nature to refuse money. It was a gesture they could never have made.

Viola supposed poor Arthur would be buried now. Her skin crawled and sweat broke out on her forehead at the thought of the life she would have had with him at Tewkesbury Square. She gave a quick, searching glance round the street. No tall, one-armed figure waited for her. No word had come, as yet, from James. But he would come, she told herself desperately. She knew he would. He still loved her, and he would come.

Manston bade her farewell and left in his electric brougham, purring off towards the Temple. The hired carriage which Eugene always had when he was in London moved forward at his signal. Matthew stood waiting, looking at her anxiously. The whole thing had been a great strain and embarrassment to him and Betsy, although they had been unquestioningly loyal, and Betsy had cared for the baby as though it were her own.

Eugene opened the door, looked at her questioningly.

'Where to, Duchess?'

She caught the little quizzical note in his voice, and knew what he was thinking. She lifted her chin, and said decisively, 'Home to Clapham. Come, Matthew.'

The morning brought a letter, a brief note asking her to come to Staffray House in Belgrave Square the following day. *'Forgive me for not being with you. I was advised against it. I shall be waiting for you,'* James wrote, signing it *'eternally yours.'*

In an instant she was in a flurry of excitement. Her heart and mind raced between glory and fear. In despair she spread her clothes out on the bed. She did not possess one of the splendid dresses that James or Arthur Netherby had given her. Only her own clothes which she had bought in the days when she and Betsy had been 'living-in' at the emporium. She wanted to look beautiful for James. The days were hot and dry. She chose the white muslin which she had worn that first summer, going out to Maidenhead with Eugene and Sunday afternoons in the park with Matthew and Betsy. The straw hat with the blue flowers. Her magnolia white cheeks were warm with a pink flush of excitement, and her lovely eyes brilliant.

'Am I still as pretty?' she demanded of Betsy, who was standing by her, filled once more with the old love and anxiety.

'You're prettier than ever. More—well, grown-up like.'

'Older?' Viola almost put her nose against the mirror, touching her eyelids anxiously, her lips, examining them closely. She sighed. She was still as lovely, but the reckless girlishness had gone. She was nearly twenty-three. It was not age which had changed her. It was experience, fear, suffering, anxiety, loss . . . and the baby too. The wonderful baby already, even in these few days, looking different, his blue eyes looking up into hers, his toothless gums breaking into a radiant smile. He had stolen a little of her youth.

'I'm different,' she said. 'I'm not simple and saucy. I'm a woman of the world. I'm not forget-me-nots and white muslin any more. Still, it's all I've got to wear now.'

'I'll wash and starch it for you,' said Betsy, gathering up the dress. At the door she stopped, looked back, colouring guiltily, frightened of hurting Viola, but determined.

'Viola, you won't go owt bad, will you, love? Not again. I mean . . . go off with Lord Staffray?' Her voice quivered. 'I don't want you to think we're not grateful for all you've done, letting us live here for no rent. It's been a great help while Matthew's got going. But he is a clergyman. We did hope to have his mother here with us, and . . .' She paused, rushed on . . . 'and really settle. I don't think we could stay here if you were . . . well, I mean, although we'd always be friends, it wouldn't be right, us accepting the cottage from you if you were a, well . . .' She could not bring herself to say it.

'A kept woman?' Viola swept across and kissed her. 'Don't you worry, Bet. Whatever I do won't affect you. You're here in your cosy nest for ever if that's what you want.'

But when her cab drew up outside Staffray House she was seized with a sudden fear. The big tree-grown square in which every house was a mansion represented position, wealth and birth. This was not Tewkesbury

Square with its twitching lace curtains and prurient gossip. This was the great world of England's ruling classes which James had fought to preserve. It was not Eugene's world of international society, finance and cosmopolitan sophistication. In its way it was narrow, however great and powerful, and its one rigid rule was that there should be no scandal; that nothing should ruffle the surface of its smooth and powerful flow. What people *did* was of no importance: it was what they were seen to do. And she and James had thrown decorum to the wind, rioted through a summer's madness, and slept in the Empress's bed.

She was indeed older. Once she would not have given it a thought. She rang the bell and Bradman opened it. His shrewd old eyes regarded the lovely young woman on the step with polite enquiry. If he knew who she was, or saw the sleek tiger beneath the maidenly decorum of fresh white muslin and the simple straw hat trimmed with blue flowers, he did not acknowledge it by so much as a flicker.

'Good afternoon, madam.' He had decided she was not a miss.

'Lord Staffray?' Viola's eyes glinted; she knew exactly what he was thinking. 'I'm Viola Corbett. He is expecting me.' She no longer used Netherby's name.

'Yes, madam. Will you come this way?'

He led her across the big pillared hall to the wide marble staircase, where once she and James, full of champagne and laughter, had raced towards their love-making. On the landing she looked across at a distant door—the Empress's room. Bradman showed her into the great drawing-room which stretched across the front of the house overlooking the square.

'Would you be so good as to wait, madam, and I will inform his lordship.'

'Thank you.'

She watched his disapproving black-clad back depart and looked round the room. Aubusson carpet, flowered summer covers, portraits everywhere, a Winterhalter portrait of the Countess as a young girl, all curls and blue ribbons and lacy crinoline, innumerable photographs in silver frames, great arrangements of superlative summer flowers, James in uniform with his parents, taken at a passing-out parade. This fresh-faced boy soldier was as unlike her lover as the ravaged man with one arm she had seen in Biarritz. Where had the man between gone—the arrogant young hawk with the wicked blue eyes?

She heard the door open, and turned as James came in. He came straight across to her. She looked into his eyes, long and questioningly, and suddenly they were kissing hungrily, greedily, searching for the past rapture, wanting it to be just the same. But it was not the same; the passionate innocence had gone. They stood apart, a little guiltily. It seemed to her, who had once made love so recklessly in this house, that the eyes of portraits and photographs gazed at her accusingly.

'Viola,' he said, 'I've waited so long for this.' His hand grasped her arm, feeling the firm smooth flesh beneath the muslin. 'Just to touch you again. To smell your lovely hair. You are more beautiful than ever.'

He drew her down beside him on to the small, satin-covered sofa, holding her hand, looking down at her eyes and full, sweet mouth. She touched his lips gently, then the grey in the crisp brown hair, then ran her finger along the scar on his cheek.

'Is it really you?'

'What is left of me.'

She laid her cheek against the empty sleeve, wishing for some magic to make him whole and restore his bruised manhood.

'You won't disappear again,' he said.

'Not if you really want me.'

'I do, of course.' He glanced away, although his hand still held hers. 'I wanted to come to court and be with you, but I was advised that it would be most unwise—for your sake as well.'

'Yes, I realize that.'

'It must have been a terrible ordeal for you.'

She gave an indifferent little shrug. 'Not really. It was all spite and jealousy. Poor things. Once I had little James Carlo back safe from that awful woman, I didn't care much.'

'Is he like me?'

'The image of you. Except . . .' She smiled. 'He's not broken his nose—not yet.'

He kissed her again, then said, 'We have all our lives before us. What shall we do, my darling?'

'It's what you want to do, James. If you want me—that's enough for me.'

'Will you marry me?'

She drew back. 'James, are you sure?'

He rose with a distrait, searching look. What was he looking for? Another girl with her face and body? A pure, well-born acceptable girl who had never loved him, never been indiscreet, never been known to the whole of London society as Duchess? Something she could never give him.

'James, love, you don't have to make me offers. You're alive—and we're together, that's enough. I don't need anything now. I'm not saying that I don't love nice clothes and rich things—I always will. But I have the cottage and a small income, and our boy. I can manage. Give me what time you can spare.'

'I want my splendid girl back. I don't want you scrimping in the shadows. I want everyone to accept that I love you. They told me that you had refused Netherby's money. That was wonderful of you . . .' He sat beside her again, his one hand grasping hers so tightly that his fingers sank into her flesh. 'Let us be married very quietly, as soon as all this fuss has died down. Then we can go away!'

'Where?'

'Oh, abroad. To the Riviera—get a villa somewhere by the sea. Take the boy with us. Or we could go to the Colonies. Buy land. They tell me there's a fine life in Africa. Kenya and places like that.'

She gazed at him with big grave eyes, and he said impatiently, 'Don't look like that, Viola. I must be honest. No one will accept you in London —or at Louderdown. We will have to build a new life abroad.'

'Is—this—what you want?' she asked faintly.

'What else have I in life but you? The army is finished—the riding.' He rubbed his shoulder where the empty sleeve hung. His fine blue eyes were haunted. 'My parents will never receive you. My father might. He's stiff-necked, but he's a man and knows a man's needs. But my mother—never! She scarcely speaks to me now.'

'And you would give—all this up—for me?'

'What am I giving up? I told you. I have nothing left but you. You are all my world now.'

She rose suddenly, fearful, unhappy.

'But what is your answer? Viola, come to me . . . I need you . . .' His arm encircled her roughly, and his lips were pressed feverishly against hers. She returned his kiss with a sweet and tender passion, but her eyes were full of tears. He searched her face poignantly.

'You are not just sorry for me?'

'No, James . . .' She smiled. 'It's not you I'm sorry for.'

'And you'll marry me?'

'If you really want it.'

She waited for his pleasure and relief but there was still the restless, feverish, searching look and a sense of doubt obsessed her. He was *telling himself* this was what he wanted. But was it true? He began to make plans.

'Are you free tonight?' She nodded. 'We'll go out. It's so long since we went out to dine together. Not since the old days. We'll go to Scott's, like we used to. And have lobster—go to a music hall. The Empire? Lots of noise and fun, like it used to be. Shall I call for you?'

'Right out to Clapham?'

'I'll send a carriage.' His restless pacing halted, and he took her hand in his, smiling, and for a moment the white smile and the burning blue eyes recaptured the sweet and reckless past. 'I'll be at Scott's, waiting for you. At eight.'

He opened the door and they went together, her arm in his, along the broad corridor towards the head of the stairs. The colour had heightened in his cheeks. He looked young again.

'It will be like old times, Viola.'

At the far end of the corridor, Castle, his mother's lady's maid, was waiting for them.

'Her ladyship would like to speak to the young lady.'

'You mean Mrs Netherby?' he snapped.

'Well, yes, m'lord.'

'What do you say, Viola? Will you see my mother?'

'Yes.'

'Is the Countess in her room?'

'Only the young lady, m'lord. M'lady said so, expressly.'

He said furiously, 'Tell my mother she can see us together or not at all.'

'James, please,' Viola said quickly. 'What harm can it do?'

He looked at her uncertainly and drew back.

'Very well. That will do, Castle. Tell my mother Mrs Netherby will be with her in a minute.'

'Very good, m'lord.' The skinny, rustling black taffeta figure with its incongruously youthful frilly cap and apron went scuttling down the corridor.

'Viola, don't go.'

'Why not?'

'She will insult and hurt you.'

'I'm not afraid.'

'She will try to make you change your mind.'

Viola pushed a stray tendril from her forehead. Suddenly she felt weary—not of the flesh, but of the spirit. The splendid house, the old servants, it all seemed oppressive. A weight on her shoulders.

'She has a right to,' she said gravely. 'She is your mother. I will see you tonight, then?'

He hesitated, kissed her abruptly, and strode away. She went forward into Lady Louderdown's boudoir.

The brocade window curtains were half-drawn. Viola, coming in from the sunlit corridor, was taken by surprise by the darkness. Then objects flickered into sight again, the unnumerable silver-framed photographs, the banks of hothouse flowers, the photographs of James as a child; and then she saw the white-faced figure on the chaise longue in a froth of black lace and violet moiré, as though in mourning. The white hair draped with a small triangle of lace.

She remembered Lady Louderdown at Biarritz. She remembered her aristocratic air, and expensive but old-fashioned gowns; her marvellous jewels and careful maquillage. The still beautiful eyes, heavily mascaraed, were fixed on her with deadly hatred. It was not just the hatred of a possessive mother; it was the hatred of lost beauty for glowing, seductive youth; it was the envy of a woman, afraid of sexual love, for a spendthrift in delight. Viola was not just the woman who had taken her son. She was the quintessence of the type she despised and feared.

'Whatever I do,' thought Viola, 'however much he loves me, I'll always be a whore to her.'

'Leave us, Castle.'

'Yes, m'lady.' Castle bobbed and hurried out. The Countess did not ask Viola to sit down, but if she hoped to disconcert her she was disappointed. Viola stood tall and magnificent, her hands resting on the handle of her parasol, looking at James's mother with her grave, secret, heavy-lashed eyes.

'I would like to know, before you leave the house,' said the Countess, 'if you have decided to ruin my son?'

'You mean—have we decided to marry? He has asked me. I am thinking about it.'

'*You* are thinking? Since when have you ever thought of anything but pleasure, and wantonness and lust? What did you think of when you played the whore here for the whole of society to know? Disgracing our name and house.'

'Aye, yes, I didn't think then,' Viola said wistfully. 'Just didn't think at all.' She went across the big, shrouded room to the window, drew back the curtain a little, so that the sunlight fell fully on her, leaning back her long lovely neck on which her head with its crown of auburn hair always seemed a little too heavy. The sun lit her skin, the tall, slender, voluptuous body in its crisp white dress. 'No, then I did not think. It was all a game . . . two mad children in love . . . but now, it's different. I have to think . . . I think all the time. There's the boy. I have to think of him.'

'He will never be the Earl. Even if you marry. And if you have another boy, what kind of training could *you* give him for such a position?'

'That is another thing I must think about.'

The Countess suddenly cracked. Viola was so unexpected. She had been anticipating a pretty, common girl, out for what she could get. It suddenly seemed to her that this story of Viola refusing Netherby's fortune could be true. This was a woman who could not be intimidated, whose marvellous beauty held an innate confidence.

The Countess covered her painted face with her little jewelled hands and wept as she had always wept to James and to her husband, to get her own way, to weaken opposition.

Viola gave a long, slow, startled glance, but she knew about women's tears.

'How can you do this to us? What kind of wife will you be for him? Who will accept you in society? Or your children? How can you come between us and our only son? Louderdown will be without an heir. Who will take over when we are too old? James says you will live abroad. Certainly you cannot live in England, a notorious woman who has flouted every convention.'

'James,' said Viola softly, 'is unhappy.'

'He thinks because of his arm, and having to leave the regiment there is nothing for him,' said Lady Louderdown. 'The army was his world. So absurd. The wound has healed, but his pride and despair have not . . . but in time he will learn that we need him, that Louderdown needs him and there is a whole life of responsibility and service waiting for him. What would he do with his life abroad—do you imagine you could fill it? A woman he is ashamed of? Do you want him to pay all his life for this mistake?'

'*Mistakes*,' corrected Viola, and there was a smile in the deep, velvety voice. 'We made more than one. No one wants their children to make mistakes, but when you're young, and in love, that's the time to make mistakes. Don't cry, Lady Louderdown, James is alive. We should be glad about that, whatever happens.'

The little Countess looked startled, stretched out her hand, and Viola, anticipating her wishes, picked up a delicate cut-glass bottle of smelling salts and put it into the small, clawlike hand. The Countess felt the warm vibrant touch of her fingers and drew back sharply as though burned.

'The boy,' she said shortly. 'How can we know James is the father?'

Viola laughed, a brief, harsh, hurt laugh. 'No one can know but me.'

'He is like James?'

'Yes. The blue eyes, black lashes. Beautiful. Like yours, my lady—a real Mick.'

'We would, of course, help you financially. We would support the child.'

'If James and I part, I will not accept any help.'

'You are proud.'

'I have a small independence. At least I can afford pride.'

'What will you do if he gives you up?' The Countess could not resist the gibe. 'Find another man to keep you?'

Viola raised her hand, saw a glove button undone, thoughtfully fastened it, long lashes, heavy lids lifting in one of her slow, challenging glances.

'James warned me you would insult me,' she said. 'I can't see why you should. You, after all, are the lady.' The Countess stiffened and coloured beneath her paint. 'The question won't arise—he won't give me up. It would have to come from me.'

'What price are you asking for this?'

'Oh, a high one. *Just to know that he will be happier without me.* If I do, *you* will have to find the answers, Lady Louderdown. James is very unhappy. He feels maimed and lost. You will have to love him, or find someone who will love him at least as much as I do. Now, I must go. We are meeting tonight—I have to go home, see my baby, and change. Good afternoon.'

As she reached the door the Countess spoke her name for the first time. 'Mrs Netherby.'

Viola turned. 'I don't use that name any more.'

'You are a—remarkable girl. I did not mean to insult you.'

Viola bowed her head. 'I think you did. But if you're sorry, it doesn't matter. Don't worry. I have a son myself. I know how you feel. I shall do what James really wants—when I am quite sure what it is.'

She wore the cheap green muslin of peridot green which she had bought from the dress department for that dinner with Arthur Netherby. Careful pressing crisped it. Betsy rushed along to the flower woman who had her basket at the omnibus stop and bought two bunches of Parma violets. One for Viola to wear in her waistband, a few to fasten in her hair.

Betsy still watched her anxiously. Since the inquest Viola seemed to be illuminated from within. The incandescent brilliance of eyes and skin, the slow sweet, sensuous, swaying movements that she remembered so well the week before her friend had run off with James Staffray. She had the same strange, concentrated emotion: the holding back like a dam that must break and inundate everything with passion. As she sat before the mirror, touching her lips with transparent salve, for they needed no red, spraying soft gardenia perfume—remnant from those early days with James—over her hair, she was again a woman in love, single-minded, waiting, longing, for her lover. Only when Betsy brought little James Carlo into the room, did she come out of her dreams. She stretched out her arms and gathered him against her, heedless of dribbles, or the crushing of her muslin, or the little waving starfish hands grasping at her clustered violets.

'My love, my love, my love,' she said, thinking of the little, frigid Dresden china Countess. 'I'd like a dozen like you.'

'A dozen!' cried Betsy disapprovingly.

'Well, six.' She peered at her beautiful reflection in the mirror. 'Beauty —everyone tells me I'm beautiful, Betsy.'

'And so you are, Vi. The gradliest lass I ever saw.'

'It's only the blossom, Bet. Unless it ripens and fruits, it's worth nothing. I saw an old woman today with the remnants of great beauty and nothing else. I'd rather have wrinkles and a mass of grandchildren scrabbling round me when I'm her age. I'm Italian, like my father, at heart.'

Betsy thought that it was an imperishable beauty. Old and wrinkled, it would still be there, like a skeleton leaf is still beautiful when the green flesh has gone. She could not put this into words. But as she stooped to take the baby again, she kissed Viola, and said, 'Good luck, love, and be good, Vi—do be good!'

James was waiting for her when she arrived at Scott's and her heart lifted to see him. The way his eyes lit up as he came to meet her. The superb way in which his evening clothes fitted the wide-shouldered, slender body, the eager way he took her arm, bent to kiss her cheek, and led her into the restaurant.

Although it was out of season there was a fashionable crowd. The moment they sat down they were conscious of a cessation of the chatter and aware that people were glancing towards them. James looked round fiercely, and the curious eyes fell before his challenging glare. The chatter rose high again, the sound like swarming bees.

He looked irritated, flushed with anger.

'Damned gossiping rabble!'

'You forget I'm a notorious woman, James,' she said softly. She leaned her elbow on the table, unbuttoning her long gloves and stripping them off her beautiful, ringless fingers. 'Since the inquest. I ought to be hiding my shame in obscurity, not dining in public. Particularly with you.' She leaned her cheek on her hand and smiled at him. 'The trouble is, James, that I am *not* ashamed. Sorry I've upset people, but not in the least ashamed.'

He looked at her uncomprehendingly, and suddenly, like a cold shaft of steel to her heart, she knew it was over. *He was ashamed.* He could not bear that these people should criticize him or his family. How dared they? He was vulnerable now. In his reckless young infatuation for her he had broken the laws of his class, but now he did care what these rich, established, correct people thought of him. Everything was different—what he could accept for his mistress he would not tolerate for his wife. Nothing was said, but the terrible chasm yawned between them, forcing them apart. They chose their food meticulously: whitebait, lobster Cardinale, Veuve Cliquot. They ate, but there was no chatter, laughter or foolery.

No touching of hands across the table or feet beneath the white starched cloth.

Once they had not been aware that people were watching them. Now James was stiff with resentment and pride. He tried to talk, to laugh, but it was no use. He was a county aristocrat and great gentleman, and he was doing the wrong thing and he knew it and was ashamed.

He had taken a box at the Empire—the big music hall had always been a favourite after-dinner haunt of theirs. They walked along Coventry Street to Leicester Square. They entered the big foyer, with its six double columns and gilded ceiling. James looked round swiftly, and immediately saw someone he knew.

'There's Boy Tallis,' he said eagerly. 'You remember him from the old days? He is in my regiment. He must be on furlough unless he caught a blighty.' He started forward, his hand outstretched to greet his comrade, who, in evening dress, was escorting a middle-aged lady and a young girl. Tallis glanced, coloured, and went past without acknowledging James. Viola knew him well: he had been one of her entourage of wild young officers in her brief reign as the toast of London. James went white and started after him. Viola put a restraining hand on his arm.

'James, please. *Don't!*'

He broke away and stalked furiously after his friend, calling his name imperiously.

'Tallis!'

Tallis turned, his young face scarlet. He excused himself from his companions and came hurrying back.

'How dare you cut me!' demanded James.

People around were beginning to notice and comment.

'Dash it all, Jim. I'm with my mother and sister,' said Tallis ingenuously. He grinned familiarly at Viola. 'Hallo, Duchess, how's tricks? How about a party for the races with some of the old gang?'

James raised his hand and would have struck the boy across the face had not Viola caught his arm.

'Viola and I are to be married,' said James.

The boy looked thunderstruck, stammered, flushed, backed away in confusion.

'Better go back to your family, Boy,' Viola said kindly.

'Duchess,' he stammered, 'it's not that I don't think you're absolutely tophole, but . . .'

'Boy,' she said gently, 'you'll only make it worse. Just go. Please.'

The young lieutenant, so intrepid in war, beat a hasty retreat to where his female relations were waiting for him, ruffling affronted plumage. Viola said, 'I don't think I want to see the show, James.'

'Why not?'

She lifted her head and met his eyes, sad and serious.

'It won't do, will it, my darling?'

He stood before her, miserable, angry that he could not protect her. She took his arm.

'Come,' she said.

They went into the warm London night, walking through the strolling crowds across the Circus where the little silver grey God of Love posed above the fountain and the massed baskets of the flower women. Past Jimmy's noisy, brilliant restaurant where the carriages were beginning to disgorge the more expensive ladies of the town and their escorts, along into the darker, quieter part of the thoroughfare, where the women hung about in the doorways of the closed shops, past La Rue where she had once worked.

'If we go abroad—to France or the Colonies,' he said, 'it won't be like this.'

'It will,' she said. 'You are the future Earl of Louderdown. Wherever you go, people will know who you are. And eventually, they'll know who I am. No use running away, James. Are you prepared to face it out—all the time? Every day?'

'It is my mother,' he said furiously. 'She has persuaded you against me.'

'Not against you. James, you have got your whole life to live. What would you do in the South of France? In a villa, with no occupation? Why should you work as a farmer in Africa, when the whole of Louderdown needs you?'

'I want to care for you . . . and the boy . . .'

She stopped, then went slowly forward, her hand still on his arm.

'Are you offering me compensation, James? I don't want that. I want love. Like it was before, without a thought for the consequences. Enough in itself. I might accept second-best from other men. If poor Arthur had been kind and honest, I would not have left him. But not second-best from you, James. From you it must be everything—or nothing!'

They had stopped before the great edifice of Devonshire House. Above the high wall it was dark, blinds drawn across the window; the season was over.

'What will you do?' he said in distress. 'What will happen to you?'

She felt a pain, sharp and deadly like a physical pain, because his words were of acceptance, not protest. Still somewhere she was the young Viola of last year, who wanted him to blazon his love for her to the whole world. But his words relinquished her. His unhappy eyes told her he was letting her go.

'I told you. I am independent now.'

'There is another man,' he flashed jealously.

'No one,' she said truthfully, 'who could ever take your place.'

'Viola.' He put his one arm around her, drawing her against him. 'What are we saying? Forget it all. What are we doing? Tomorrow we'll go away together, abroad, and get married . . .'

She did not struggle, but she was very still, and presently he let her go.

'No,' she said. 'This was the first taste for you, James. Of what you would have to bear. Of being an exile from your class and kind. There will be a second time, and a third, and fourth and so on—wherever we go. There is Staffray, they will say, with that woman he ruined himself for. Even if we are happy, that is what they will think and say. James—I *don't* care, but you do, and *if* you do in the least, smallest way, it will poison our lives.'

'I will not listen. I will not know them.'

'Then who will you know?' She shook her head, her face shadowed and sad. 'James, my love, my lord, I came from nothing, so people are just people to me. But you have only known one kind—to all the others, you were master. Your mother said of our boy—he will *never* be the Earl. And if we have another boy, what kind of training could we give for such a position? She was right. Living away, in exile, what could we do?'

A cab came clopping along the roadway, and she turned, and threw up her arm, and in reply to the raised white glove, it drew in to the kerb.

She opened the door and got in, and even then was hoping that James would spring in beside her, or draw her back to him.

'I shall see you?' he said.

'No.'

'But where will you go? What will you do?'

She did not answer, and he turned his anguished face away, covering his mouth with his one hand. She knew that he, who had been so valiant in battle, had not the courage to claim her now, and unless he had, any life together would be disaster.

'Good-bye—my lord,' she said softly, and told the cabby to drive to Clapham. In the leather-smelling, straw-smelling darkness she began to weep, and she wept and wept, her heart breaking, hugging her breast as though holding herself together against an inner disintegration, as though mourning, as indeed she was mourning, the death of her youth and hope.

Except for a small oil lamp in a bracket in the tiny hall, the cottage was in darkness when she went in. Everything was tidied and clean, the two cups from which Betsy and Matthew had taken their nightly cup of cocoa rinsed clean on the draining board. *Cocoa!* How Betsy could drink the stuff after living at Netherby's hostel where the weak watery mud-coloured brew had been a staple diet!

She lit a candle and set it on the table. Her breath was still coming in great, shuddering sobs, and she was glad that Betsy and Matthew had gone to bed—she did not want sympathy. She looked round at the poor little room, and it seemed cramped, a cage. She stretched her arms like wings. Eugene knew her very well. Betsy would be ideally happy here. But she wanted a more spacious life. And her boy, the baby upstairs, her son and his father's; inheriting perhaps their recklessness, handsomeness and arrogance. For she was arrogant. She was humble enough to know it now. That was why they had called her Duchess.

She could not live here, and Matthew and Betsy, kind and loyal though they were, would not really want her in their simple lives. She could not subdue herself to their small contents. They wanted to have Matthew's elderly mother to live with them. With Viola and the baby James, there would be no room. Although the cottage was hers, she would be the intruder. They would never complain, but their sort of life was not hers. She needed richness, laughter, spaciousness and love, and if she was honest, admiration. Eugene had said she was born for this, and he was right.

She opened the table drawer and took out notepaper, stamps and envelope, and the pot of ink and a pen from the stand on the dresser where they were kept for Matthew's work. She sat down and wrote a letter to Eugene Erhmann.

When it was finished she stamped and sealed it, put a shawl round her head and ran to the corner to the post box, then walked slowly back to the cottage. It was a beautiful night, cobalt blue sky with many stars and the trees on the Common sighing in a warm breeze. Well, she had always been good at burning her boats. She had done it again. She went in and locked the door and no one saw her cry for her lost love again.

The great trans-continental express was slowing down, snaking through the outer suburbs of Vienna, and Viola and Eugene sat together at a table in his drawing-room compartment. Since leaving London they had travelled like royalty in a private coach, with sleeping compartments, a drawing-room, all like a miniature travelling apartment, upholstered in brocade, filled with flowers, their meals served from the restaurant car. Now they were near their journey's end.

'Ten minutes, *liebchen*,' he said. 'I have a gift for you.'

He took out two jewel cases from his pocket, and put them on the table. 'Open them.'

She glanced up at him, and did so. The little diamond amethyst and emerald brooch, the pearls James had given her.

'You didn't sell them?'

'No—the first thing I gave you—the only thing you had from him. I knew, at least, you valued his gift. I hoped you valued mine.'

He saw a shadow, a threat of tears, and a smile of gratitude flicker across her face. She touched his hand. 'Thank you, Eugene.' She fastened the little brooch into the fine lace on her bosom, and slipped the string of pearls over her head. 'You don't mind—if I wear the pearls?'

He shook his head. 'Life is long and you are very young, Viola. If I cannot make you forget him, at least I can ease the pain.'

'So *you* bought the cottage for me?'

'I confess. Now you have given it to your little Dutch-doll friends I can tell you.'

She smiled, thinking of Betsy and Matthew in their cottage. Blissfully happy, his mother living with them. Matthew was earning good money as a journalist now.

'You are very good to me,' she said simply.

'Why not? I love you and I have everything to give. It is my pleasure.' He rose, a slender, graceful, elegant man, a dandy and, as she had learned through this almost regal progress through Europe, a force to be reckoned with. He looked down at her, the light, silvery, observant eyes teasing her gently. 'One day you will not thank me for anything, *liebchen*. You will take it all as your right.'

The colour rushed up into her smooth white cheeks at his look. As she had always known, he was a man to set her senses alight even if she had left her dreams behind in England. He smiled. 'Put on your hat, *liebchen*, for you are coming into your kingdom.'

He summoned the new maid, engaged in Paris. She came fussing in with the charming creation of curled apricot ostrich fronds and held a glass while Viola carefully pinned it on top of her hair, and drew on her long cream kid gloves, fastening the row of tiny buttons. 'Tell Nanny to bring James,' she said.

The nurse brought the baby, now beginning to look round with his brilliant blue eyes, always with hands outstretched and smiles when he saw this lovely, scented, silken creature who was referred to as Mama. He was rosy, strong, already showing the Staffray temper and will.

The train slid slowly into the Westbahnhof and came to a hissing standstill. A major-domo hurried forward in welcome—there was a bouquet and greetings before he gathered porters, Eugene's man and Viola's maid and began to supervise the luggage, Eugene put on his pale Homburg, and offered Viola his arm.

They made an impressive procession along the platform, Viola swaying along on Eugene's arm, little James in his silks and laces proudly borne by his new young English nanny. The servants and porters, luggage piled high on their trolleys, bringing up the rear. The uniformed station master greeted them and accompanied them out to the carriages.

The young nurse moved towards the second carriage in which the servants would ride, but Viola suddenly held out her arms.

'May I take James with me, Eugene?' And when he nodded, she lifted the baby up on to her lap. 'He must sit up and see this new city where he will grow up and one day be a dashing young man-about-town.'

'You will have him dining at Sacher's before he is breeched,' he said indulgently.

The carriage moved forward as the fine horses set off at a spanking trot through the wide streets, into the Ringstrasse, past the cafés where the afternoon crowds sat or sauntered in the sunshine beneath the chestnut trees.

Eugene watched her—this girl who was his wife. She had changed. Although the mischief, the sparkle, and the love of life were still there beneath the surface, there was a new reserve and dignity about her which he thought made her more beautiful than ever. She sat forward, eagerly scanning this gay and beautiful city which, with his help, she would conquer. People recognized him and bowed, astounded to see him, the city's most sought-after bachelor, riding with a beautiful young woman and a *baby!* A group of exquisite, corseted officers riding past dropped their monocles with astonishment and admiration. One day they would be fighting duels for the privilege of holding her bouquet. No door would be closed against the Countess Erhmann, not even that of the stiff, old-fashioned court, for he had the power and ruthlessness to achieve even this—*if* she wanted it.

What did she want? As he watched her, the baby's small pink hand caught her pearls, and seeing the expression in her face as she looked down, and gently released them, he knew she must be thinking of James Staffray who had given them to her, the father of her son, and a little aching jealousy stirred within him. As though she knew, she met his glance and smiled with a tender gratitude, putting her hand on his, so that to his amazement tears pricked his eyes. Such a thing had not happened since his childhood.

'What were you thinking about—watching me like that, Gene?'

'I was wondering what you would want from Vienna.'

She glanced round, the soft slow sweep of heavy white lids and long, curled lashes, then her eyes met his again, gravely, hopefully.

'I want to be a good wife to you, Eugene, and I want us to be happy.'

He lifted her hand to his lips. He might never be able to make her forget Staffray—but one day he might make her love him too. In a different way, but still as sweet. The carriage drove through ornate wrought-iron gates into the courtyard of a splendid old *palais.* A footman ran down to

B

open the carriage door, to let down the steps, to take the rugs. The young nurse got down from the second carriage and ran forward to take the baby James. Eugene sprang out and handed Viola down, drew her arm through his and led her up the marble steps to the door. Like a fine graceful ship coming safely into harbour, her Excellency Countess Eugene Erhmann had come home.